Letting Go

By: Jennifer Foor

Cover Art by: Wicked Cool Designs

Robin Harper

case of brief quotations embodied in critical articles and reviews.

Check out the other books by Jennifer Foor

Hope's Chance (Contemporary Romance)

The Somnian Series (YA Paranormal)

Book One Ascension

Book Two Absum

Book Three Attero

Book Four Aduro

Book Five Abeo

Coming Soon

Tommy Ford Zombie Chronicles

I would like to thank everyone that continues to support me.

Without you, I would never stay so determined.

Thanks to everyone that helps me with all things book related

Special Thanks to:

Angie Cowgill

Erica Willis

My ARC readers: Shannon Murphy, Jennifer Lafon, Jennifer Harried, and Heather Collins

And everyone who has made this series the success that it is. I am forever grateful.

Thanks to my family and my faith

With them, all things are possible

Prologue

Tyler

I could not believe she had the nerve to break up with me and then cock block me like that. I had every right to be able to bang any girl I wanted to at this party. I was not going to let Savanna Tate dictate what I did. If she thought, I was going to sit around and wait for her to change her mind again, well she was wrong.

Savanna broke my heart. She was the only girl that I had ever loved and that I ever wanted to love. All of our plans for college had been made together, and out of nowhere, she tells me we need to break up. That she needed time.

I got drunk. I cried to her. I begged her to take me back.

When Savanna made her mind up, she did not budge about it. All of my words meant nothing to her. She pretended like I did not matter. She avoided me. I had given her five years of my life and she wanted to throw it all away. Her stupid notion being that we were in college and needed to focus on our education. Who breaks up for that reason?

After staying in my room for over a week, my buddies on the team talked me into going to a few parties. I discovered that booze mixed with the smooth skin of an easy lay, made the pain easier. Problem was...it never made it disappear. .

I pulled my pants back on and started buttoning them, while the blonde chick behind me, who I think was named Heather or Danielle, still remained on the bed. "Sorry Babe, I gotta jet."

I turned around to see her sitting up in only panties. Her perky tits were something I would never forget. Next to her was the empty bottle of Jack that I had finished off myself.

She scrunched up her lips and rolled her eyes. "Whatever!"

I didn't say anymore to her, in fact, there was nothing to say. She was just a meaningless fuck and she knew it. There was only one person I would ever love, and she had just caught me red handed with someone else.

I needed to find her, to tell her it meant nothing. She needed to know the truth before I lost her forever.

I ran down the stairs of the frat house looking for my ex-girlfriend, or my future wife, I hoped.

When I finally got into the main living area, it was so jammed packed with people, that I couldn't find her. I ran into someone I recognized and grabbed them by the arm. "Hey, you seen Van?"

"She ran out of here crying dude," he replied.

"Shit. When?" I asked.

"A few minutes ago."

I ran away from him before even thanking him. I needed to talk to her. I wanted to know what her problem was. If she cared that much, then why did she end things? Why did she shut me out day after day?

I got to the front door. "Where are my keys?" I asked, noticing that my words were slurring.

A bunch of the football players crowded around me. "Let it go Ty. You two will be back to loving each other next week dude," Michael the linebacker, and one of my best friends, stated. He had also attended school with both me and Savanna. He knew of our unconventional relationship. In fact, none of our friends doubted that we would get back together, well except for Brina. She hated me since I started dating Savanna. She had problems sharing since we were kids.

I tried to push past Michael. "I am serious man, give me my damn keys."

Gavin grabbed me by the arm and tried to lead me away from the front door. "Just stay here and sleep it off man. Everything will work out tomorrow. You are too wasted to drive."

I cocked my arm back and punched Gavin in the face. He turned around just as Michael was attempting to grab my arms. "Give me my fucking keys Mike. I need to go find her. I really messed up this time," I admitted.

Another group of peers came rushing toward the front door, all trying to locate the hidden bag of keys. I noticed that Brina was in that group. "Where did she go Sabrina?" I asked.

"I wouldn't tell you even if I knew. I am sure that it's your fault that she left. You should have seen the look on her face. Guess she caught your pathetic ass finally. Way to go asshole!" She said ignorantly.

"Fuck you!" I said as I rolled my eyes and walked past Brina and the gang of other people. When I got outside, I noticed quite a few kids I recognized standing around their cars.

"Hey, you guys seen Van?" I asked.

"She took off dude," some guy said while standing outside of his vehicle.

I rushed over toward him. "Give me your keys," I demanded.

"Hell no man. You reek of alcohol," he stated.

I grabbed him by the neck. "Give me your Goddamn keys. NOW!"

The guy, being much smaller, handed me his keys and I took off in his vehicle. Our college was located off the beaten path forty miles from our small country town. I knew that's where she would go. It's where she ran to every time we got into it.

She needed to understand that it was just sex. I was filling a void that she had left. She needed to know that she was my future.

I knew these roads like the back of my hand, but when I saw something running across the road, I slammed on my breaks. The car swerved off the road and began rolling. Once it stopped, and I was upside down, I closed my eyes and just let go, my last thought being of Savanna.

Chapter 1

Savanna

It's been six months since Tyler had his accident. I still attend school, but barely go to my part-time job anymore. Most of my days are spent in a classroom and then the hospital.

If it weren't for me, he would be okay.

The car was found in a ravine about three miles from the campus. After I left the party, I drove right home and slept in the old barn I had run away to a million times. I turned my phone off and had no idea anything had happened until the next morning. I had a zillion messages from people asking what happened and if Tyler ever found me. I was still so angry with him, so I didn't bother calling.

That night I got a call from his parents. The police found the car lying upside down. Tyler was barely alive and taken by helicopter to a hospital capable of handling his severe injuries. Not only had he broken just about every bone possible, but it was also freezing that night and he had hypothermia. He never regained consciousness, and was finally transferred to a long-term coma ward.

The doctors ran a zillion tests and said that his brain was fully functioning, and that they were optimistic one day he would wake up. It was a forty-minute drive to the hospital, in which I took every single day. Even during the heaviest snowstorm, our town has seen in ten years, I went to sit with him.

I would read to Tyler and talk about all of the good times we had. We were best friends and lovers for so long, but somewhere down the road, something changed for me. Tyler and I had an unconventional relationship. We fought all of the time, because we loved each other so much. No matter what, we were always a couple and neither of us ever doubted that we would not end up together. Things had become strained for me though. I couldn't deal with college life, parties and schoolwork. Ty seemed to soak himself in it. I made the decision to end things, temporarily of course, but he never understood.

His daddy was a farmer, like a full-fledged works the farm himself, farmer. His parents had been together since they were thirteen. We had been together since we were fourteen. So naturally, Ty just always assumed that we would grow up and get married. When we started college, things became intense. Between the schoolwork, the new environment and his pledging with a fraternity, our priorities were not on the same page.

When we entered into our second year at college, I began to really struggle. I figured if we just stopped worrying about "us" for a little while, I could focus on school and get through it, then eventually start our future together. I never broke up with him because I thought it would be forever. Tyler took it the wrong way from day one. His new friends, basically the football team, convinced him I was interested in someone else and that he should move on too.

They were wrong.

My main focus was school. My parents did not have money to pay for my tuition, so through scholarships and grants, I was able to attend college. I was required to maintain a certain grade point average and if it fell, I lost my ride.

On the day I found out about Tyler's accident, my mother insisted on driving me all the way to the hospital. I was in shock. Apparently, he had stolen a car and when they first discovered the accident, they didn't know it was Ty. Finally, they found his wallet at the hospital and the police notified his family. Ty was not recognizable, and it wasn't just from all the tubes and wires that were hooked to his body. His legs and arms were being propped up and they were covered in casts. He had a severe contusion on his head, and they had to shave his hair and operate to remove the swelling around his brain. His face was black and blue and both of his eyes were completely swollen shut, not that he ever opened his eyes.

I refused to leave when my mother left that night. Instead, I slept in a chair. I wasn't supposed to, but the nurse was pretty nice and said that the more time I spent there, the sooner he might wake up. At first, I had this notion that if I stayed long enough he would open his eyes and I could tell him how much I loved him and that I would never leave again.

However, he never woke up.

His mother and father started to only visit on weekends. With him not being able to help and now having the hospital bills, they couldn't afford to hire someone to work the farm while they sat at the hospital. I promised them that I would spend every day there, except when they came, just in hopes of seeing those brown eyes that I loved looking back at me.

My friends tried to get me to go out and get my mind off of things. My best friend Brina had been around for all of mine and Tyler's ups and downs. Our town was tiny and everyone knew everyone. We all even attended the same church when we were younger.

Ty was never Brina's favorite person, but she would never want him to be like that. I refused her offers each and every time. My mother took me to see a shrink, claiming I was giving up on life. She didn't understand that Tyler Mitchell was my life. I couldn't let go, I wouldn't.

The past six months had been hard for me. My professors were very lenient considering what I was going through, and I was the poster child for needing extensions, but I managed to keep up with my grades. I still had a few more weeks left before summer break. One good thing was that the hospital was about ten minutes from the campus. After my classes, I would go straight to the hospital. Some of the nurses had been nice enough to bring a folding table for me to do my class work on.

For hours, day in and day out, I would sit there talking to him. Sometimes I would even study aloud with him. For my literature class, I would read everything aloud. I held his hands, kissed his face and cried against his chest, but he never even moved a finger. He just lay there lifeless, hooked up to machines.

When the accident had first happened, his parents were so kind to me, but as time passed, they began to blame me for everything. To say that I wasn't their favorite person anymore was an understatement. The hardest part of that, for me, was that Tyler had bought me a horse a few years back that I happened to keep on his farm. When I made the drive home, I would always stop and see Daisy, my Morgan Quarter horse mix. She was only about sixteen hands high, but it was plenty enough for me, since I was only five three.

Besides Brina, Daisy was my only friend. People at college even stopped talking to me. It hurt so much and the worst part was that I knew it was my fault. I caused all of this to happen, and every time I looked at him lying there, hooked up to so many machines, it made me want to die myself.

My new shrink had prescribed me some antidepressants when I admitted to her that I had thought up a plan on how I was going to end my life. I had planned it all out so that I would die in Tyler's arms at the hospital. I had even managed to swipe enough pills to do it. My confession did not go over well. I had to spend twenty-four hours in observation for starters, and continue with therapy indefinitely.

When I had suicidal thoughts now, I kept them to myself.

No matter what anyone says to me, I know I caused this. They can use every nice word known to man and candy coat their words, but it doesn't matter. I broke Tyler's heart and after a fight at a party, I ruined his life.

Chapter 2

Savanna

I had set up a makeshift study area at the hospital. Exams were a week away and I needed to get good grades on all of them. The lighting was poor in the hospital room, and I could never get used to the damn beeping of the machines. I was halfway through reviewing my notes when I lay my head down on the desk. My body was over exhausted and I just wanted to take a nap.

I woke to a familiar voice calling my name. When I opened my eyes, I saw Ty trying to pull the wires off his face and body. I got up and ran over to the bed. "Oh my God, you're awake. Ty, I missed you so much. I can't believe you finally woke up. I am so sorry about everything. Please forgive me Ty. I never wanted us to be over."

"Shh, don't cry baby. What happened? What day is it?" He asked while looking around the room.

"It's Friday. God Ty, it's been six months. You were in a coma."

"Stop playing baby," he said as he laughed.

His eyes sparkled and I had forgotten how perfect they were. His dark eyelashes accented them as he blinked. "I'm not kidding. I have to get the doctor," I said as I started to head out of the room.

"Wait! Please just come hug me," he requested.

I rushed back to his side and reached my arms around him. When I placed my lips against his, I could feel the tears rushing down my face. I had missed him so much. Our celebratory kiss intensified and he pulled me up onto the bed with him. I didn't care who walked in, I just wanted to be close to him, to feel him holding me. Our tongues met and mingled together and he reached his hands down the back of my shorts and grabbed my bare ass. He used his hands to grind me against his hardness and I gasped. I had waited so long to feel this again. I reached down and pulled up the hospital gown as he began tearing down my pants. Ty threw the thin white blanket over my back as I positioned myself over his rock hard shaft. He slid inside of me and we both moaned simultaneously at the feel of being together again.

We began moving at a steady pace, when I lay my head on his chest and closed my eyes for a second.

When I heard someone enter the room, figuring that it was just a nurse, I didn't look up. I didn't want anyone to tell me to stop. I didn't even care if they called security. I had waited six months to touch the love of my life, no one could ruin this moment.

After at least four minutes of making mad passionate love in that hospital bed, I heard a man clearing his throat. I jumped up off of the desk and looked around the room. Ty was still hooked up to the machines and everything I had experienced had been a damn dream.

The guy cleared his throat again.

I don't know why I did it, but I just sat there staring at him. He wasn't a stranger; in fact, I had known him since I was around ten years old. The dream was so fresh on my mind that I couldn't let myself speak yet. I wanted to go back to sleep and see Ty. It had felt so real.

"I figured you'd be here," the guy said rudely.

I finally let myself snap out of my fantasy. Seeing yet another rude person from Ty's family was the last thing I needed. "Colton Mitchell, are you really going to be that way to me too?" I asked defensively.

"I aint got nothing to say to you Van. I wasn't here. All I know is what my aunt and uncle tell me," he explained.

I shut the book I had been looking at before I fell asleep. "So what are they saying now?" I asked.

Colt stood in front of me. He had removed his dirty baseball hat and held it in his hands. He was even more handsome than a couple years ago when he last came to visit. When we were kids, he would make fun of me for having a gap between my teeth and a flat chest. He called me the ugliest boy in town. I was a late bloomer, I couldn't help that, but the braces did solve the tooth issue.

Now Colt, well, all the girls liked him. He was older than all of us, at least by three or four years, maybe more. His teeth were always perfect and he had the body of a man by thirteen years old. His shoulders were broader and under that old t-shirt was probably the finest chest this state had ever seen. When we were younger his hair was longer, but now it was only long enough to barely show out of the bottom of his hat. It was messy and I could see the shape of the ball cap still in it.

I didn't know the last time he had seen Tyler, but he would be surprised at how muscular he had gotten before the accident. Being on the college football team caused him to bulk up a bunch and by the first game; he was thirty more pounds of muscle. They shared the same hair color. It was dark in the winter, but from working the crops, got lighter in the summer.

I noticed I was daydreaming about the Tyler I missed, and gave my attention back to Colt.

He shrugged and looked down at his cousin in the bed. "You already know what they are saying Van. Can you blame them?"

Tears filled my eyes. Tyler was lying lifeless, I had lost him, and now I had lost them. The family that I had loved as my own for so many years. "No." I covered my face with my hands. The tears poured out and I could feel my body shaking. "I am so sorry," I said in a muffled voice.

"Ah hell Savanna. I don't know what to say to you. I sure as heck don't feel like hearin ya cry." His southern accent was so strong, but I guess that's what happens when you live in Kentucky.

I stood up and started grabbing my things. "Maybe I should just go then, because all I seem to do is cry and ruin people's lives."

I started walking past Colt. His strong hand grabbed my wrist. "You don't have to leave," he whispered, seeming unsure of his reaction.

I stood close to him and looked up into his eyes. They were still that light green that I always remembered. His brow was creased in a way that made me think he was in pain. He had thick dark eyebrows that made his eyes seem even lighter and accentuated his frustration with this situation.

"If I could take things back, I would. I never wanted this Colt, I swear," I confessed.

He leaned over the bed, looking at Tyler. "Yeah, I reckon it was just bad timing. I know he liked his Jack. His momma and daddy didn't know about that. I don't blame ya, but I would like the whole story. The full one," he replied.

I nodded my head. "Okay, but not here. I don't like talking about it around him. I know it sounds silly, but I feel like he hears me. I don't want to upset him," I admitted.

"Fine, I have the truck. You want some dinner? I got off a plane a couple hours ago and haven't had nothin to eat all day," he confessed.

I hadn't gone anywhere with anyone for so long. At first, I wanted to say no, but this was Colt, someone who knew me before I was with his cousin. He knew I wouldn't hurt anybody intentionally. "Okay, we can grab something to eat."

I leaned over and kissed Ty before following Colt out of the hospital room. When we got outside, I recognized the old pickup truck immediately. It was Ty's fathers. I assumed that Colt borrowed it to come see Ty. We both climbed into the old clunker and headed down the road.

Colt pulled over at an old diner on the edge of town. They were known for being open twenty-four hours and having the best pies around. We found a small booth in the far corner of the place and sat down facing one another. Once the waitress got us drinks and we both ordered food, Colt got right down to business.

"You gonna start explainin' soon?" He asked.

I played with my paper place mat, never looking up at his face. My sexual dream with Ty was still fresh in my head and I felt myself blushing just thinking about it. I took a deep breath and focused on the guy sitting across from me. The one that made fun of me since I was around ten. "A month before the accident I told Tyler that I needed some time. I was struggling with my courses and figured if we just spent some time apart I could focus better. I swear it was not because I didn't want to be with him. My feelings for him never changed," I promised.

Colt took a sip of his beer. "Did you explain that to him?"

"Of course I did, but he just assumed it was something else. Anyway, after a week or so, he stopped calling me so much. I missed him, but I figured he was just giving me some space." I fell silent for a moment, because the next part of the story was like stabbing myself in the heart.

Before I could even open my mouth, I felt the tears building in my eyes. "He found other ways to deal with the breakup," I confessed in a quiet voice, just hoping he understood.

"Other ways? Or someone else?" He asked calmly.

"Yes," was all I could get out.

Colt took another sip of his beer. I still couldn't look at him. "Are ya sayin' he had another woman?"

"Women. Plural," I said with my hands over my face. This person across from me knew me and I should have been okay with letting him see me like this, but I was so ashamed.

"I don't blame him. I can see how he would be all messed up over you," he blurted out.

I removed my hands and looked right at him. One of his eyebrows was cocked. "What's that supposed to mean?" I asked angrily.

He held up his beer to motion to our waitress that he needed a refill, then he leaned in closer to me. "All I am sayin' is that I can see how the breakup would hurt him. You both have been together for a long time. He was just tryin' to forget ya that's all."

I hated him. I hated his words, even though I knew he was just being honest. I wanted to get up and leave. He had to know how awful he was making me feel.

"So, what happened that night? You catch him with his pants down?" He asked.

"Yeah, I did." I swallowed back the tears and tried so hard not to picture the last time I spoke to Tyler. I could smell the liquor from the time I opened that bedroom door. His little blonde conquest was sprawled out on all fours on the bed and he was on top of her, riding her into tomorrow. I shook my head. "His pants were off actually and he was very drunk. He tried to talk to me, but I couldn't stand there watching them together. I just needed to leave, to get as far away from Tyler as I could."

When I stopped talking, Colt started. "Let me guess. He got in that car and went lookin' for ya. Ya see, alcohol is a funny thing. It makes you do things you wouldn't never do, but it always makes you tell the truth. It heightens your emotions."

"I get it, really I do. I know it was my fault. If I would have just stayed...."

He cut me off. "No. You didn't do anything wrong Van. He messed up. Sure, you broke his heart, probably tore it into pieces, but he made his bed that night."

I looked up at him. I was shocked. "You believe me?"

"Look Van, it's easy for my aunt and uncle to blame someone. They see their son and have no answers. You can't blame them," he explained.

"I miss them though. I miss them so much Colt. They were a big part of my life. I feel so empty without all of them. I feel like I don't want to live anymore," I confessed.

He reached over and pulled my hand away from my face. "Don't ever say you don't want to live."

He was serious. His face was stern, almost like a parent to a child.

I quickly changed the subject. "So what are you here for Colt? Are you just visiting Ty?"

"Na, I am here to help with the summer crops and some of the livestock. Uncle Mitch can't do it himself. Dad has plenty of help at home, so I offered to stay through the harvest."

"Can I ask you something?"

He stared at me for a second and took another sip of his new beer. "Shoot!"

"Do you think you can help me see Daisy? I am not really welcome at the farm right now and I miss her something fierce. I don't want to sneak around, but I think it would be better if I visit when they are not there," I admitted.

He waited a minute. "I reckon I can do that. Just give me your number and I will text ya."

I had to laugh. "A country boy like you knows how to text?"

He gave me another cocked eyebrow. "Look here Van. I may be from the country but it aint the ice age Darlin'. We have indoor plumbing at home as well," he added with a wink.

We didn't say much more when our food came and as soon as we were done, we both paid and went our separate ways, once he dropped me back off of course.

I watched him pull away before getting into my own car and calling it a night.

Chapter 3

Colt

I never knew what my cousin saw in Savanna Tate, but that was before she became a woman. The girl had acquired never-ending curves. Her grey eyes that used to be so big, now fit her face perfectly. Even her lips and cheekbones had changed. When she was younger, she had her haircut like a boy and never even dressed like a girl. Now, if I hadn't seen the pictures on my parent's fridge, I would have never believed it was the same person. She had become quite beautiful. It's no wonder that Tyler assumed there was someone else. It would have been my first assumption as well. With the way she looked, she could probably get any guy she wanted.

For some reason I believed she was telling the truth, not that it even mattered anyway. The past couldn't be changed.

Tyler was far from perfect, in fact, when he came to visit me just last year we went to a bar, where he hooked up with one of the local girls. He claimed that being in a different zip codes gave him the right to 'sample the land'. I could only assume that he never came clean about that to Van.

My cousin looked like shit. I imagine that was from being in a bed for months. I hadn't believed my aunt when she said that Van spent all of her time there. How could they doubt her love for Tyler? I had never known someone to be so devoted. It was sad. She had to know that he may never wake up. Was she going to sit there day after day until she got so old she couldn't anymore?

I was the last person to question her intentions. My dang girl had up and left me. I reckon it had to do with my drinking and the fact that I couldn't be bothered with entertaining someone that I had nothin' in common with. If I had extra time, I was going to spend it fishing or hunting. I did miss the hot meals at night, but I could just head to my parents for dinner.

It was just me and Sam now. Sam being my lab of course. When I offered to come work on the farm that had been my only stipulation. I couldn't leave my dog back in Kentucky.

I didn't always want to be a farmer, but the truth was that it was in my blood. For four generations my family had lived off the land and provided for their families. My father had never been too keen on me getting my college degree, but like my cousin Tyler, I was pretty damn good at football and got a scholarship. Had I not torn my ACL junior year, I may have been drafted. My major was business, but jobs in my small town of Kentucky were hard to come by, and even though my parent's farm had enough workers to manage itself without me, my father wanted me to be around to do the books. My father's ranch was well known and he and my mother never had to worry about money. They had the best cattle in the state.

I didn't want to be a part of my father's money, even though I knew eventually it would all go to me, if the old hard ass didn't live to be older than me. Knowing him, he would. I swallowed my pride and built a small cabin on the edge of my parent's farmland. It probably wasn't small to some, I mean eventually I wanted a family of my own. It gave me enough space to have my own life, but enabled me to be close enough to my family in case anything happened. There had been many nights where the cattle got out, we had to go out, and round them all back up. Even the high tech chicken houses that we had, managed to break down every now and again.

Still, my uncle was desperate for help, and thought I would be put to good use if I came here to the Carolina's for the summer. The fields had already been seeded when I arrived, and for the next week there weren't any chickens to attend to. The last shipment had gone out last week in fact. After visiting my cousin at the hospital and having a meal with Van, I found myself having nothing to do.

Since I still had my uncle's truck, I decided that it would be fine to stop by the one and only town bar on the way home. It was just about eight in the evening and the beaten up bar wasn't very crowded. Several people sat around the wooden bar in the center. I found an empty spot at the bar and ordered a beer.

I was just sitting there minding my own business when someone came up beside me and tapped me on the shoulder.

"I thought that was you," she said. "How the heck are ya Colt?"

I remembered this girl from when I spent summers here as a kid. I was trying to think of her name when she interrupted my train of thought.

"It's Sabrina remember?" She asked.

Trying to play it off I answered. "Of course, I don't forget a pretty girl's face."

She blushed and gave me a second smile. She signaled the bartender to bring us two beers and turned to face me again. "So what brings you back here?"

"Just helping out my uncle with the farm."

The red head took a sip of her beer. She had always been pretty attractive, but the problem was that she knew it. I hated cocky girls. "Have you been to see Ty?"

"Yeah, I saw him today. Looks like shit," I added.

She looked at me with a curious grin. "Was Van there? Don't tell me, of course she was. So how did that go? You better have been nice to her. Ty's parents have been horrible."

"Yeah, she was there. We uh, we had dinner and she told me about everything," I replied.

She cocked her eyebrow at me. "Were you nice? I know your kind Colt Mitchell and being nice to a lady is not how you roll," she implied.

I chuckled. "How I roll?" This was the second woman today to accuse me of basically being a dick.

"Yeah. You know exactly what I am saying, so don't act all innocent. Just tell me you didn't leave her even more depressed. That girl can't take anymore. Did she tell you about her own hospital stay?" She asked.

"No. She didn't. What happened to her?" I didn't know why I wanted to know, but something made me ask.

She looked straight toward the bartender. Her eyes seemed so serious. As she began to talk she never turned to face me. "She wanted to kill herself."

"Well hell. She mentioned that."

"She doesn't leave his side. It isn't healthy. None of this was her fault," she explained.

I lifted my hat off my head and then put it back on. It seemed I did that a lot when I was at a loss for words. "No, I reckon it wasn't. Why don't you take her out? Get her to do something. Take her mind off of things."

"She won't Colt. I try. I try like every day. I don't know what to do with her. Tonight is a big bonfire and she refuses to come out. I know since it's the weekend she will be coming home, and even then she just sits around in that house and mopes."

"Maybe you need to drag her ass there," I suggested.

She gave me a half smile. "Maybe you could ask her to come?"

"What? Why would she come for me? We aren't exactly friends Sabrina, in fact the last time I came to town she made it clear that she hated my guts," I explained.

She pushed me on my shoulder. "That's because you called her a buck toothed boy. You know how much she hated that."

"Yeah, well in my defense she did look like a boy for a long time," I added.

She pulled out her cell phone and started texting while she was still talking to me. "Trust me when I say that there is nothing boyish about that girl now. I am sure you noticed if you spent time with her earlier."

She was right. It was the first thing that I had noticed. That little awkward duckling had turned into a real swan. "Yeah, I noticed," I said with a sly grin.

Sabrina got quiet. "Call her. Make her come out with us. Tell her you want to go out but don't know anyone. Don't even tell her I saw you here," she suggested. "Please?"

"I don't see how me calling can make any bit of a difference, but I reckon it don't hurt to try."

Sabrina grabbed her gemstone-covered cell phone and started looking through it. "Here is her number," she said.

I held up my own phone. "I already beat ya to it Darlin'. She gave it to me earlier."

She started smiling while shaking her head. "Well then get to callin'," she urged.

I creased my brow while I hit send on the phone. Sabrina continued to drink her beer, while she intently watched for me to respond to the person on the other line.

Hello

Hey, um Van, it's me Colt.

Oh. Hey. What's up? Did the Mitchell's leave and I can come see Daisy?

No. Actually, I was wonderin' if you would want to come out to this bonfire with me. I don't know anyone here, but I can't just sit around in that house.

I don't think so Colt. I don't really do that kind of thing anymore.

I don't think I can take no for an answer.

I can't Colt.

I am asking for you to do me a favor just like I am doing a favor for you with Daisy. It's just one night Van.

Are you saying you won't help me if I don't go?

Maybe I am.

You are an asshole Colton.

Meet me at the old barn in an hour Van.

She hung up before agreeing, but I had a feelin' she was gonna show.

Sabrina was busting. "Tell me what she said."

"She aint happy, but she will be there," I said confidently.

She started clapping her hands. "Oh yay! Thank you thank you!" She said as she hugged me. Before I could pull away, Sabrina brought her lips up to my ear. "I will personally thank you for this later." When she pulled away her eyes were focused on mine.

"You have a deal Sugar," I winked as I got up from the barstool.

Sabrina explained where and when to meet and we parted ways at the bar. I had no idea what I was getting myself into, but as long as I had two pretty ladies by my side, I figured it would be an okay time.

Worst case was that I took the pretty redhead home and gave her some good lovin'. She seemed all too eager to oblige anyway. I wasn't usually that type of guy, but I was single and a grown damn man. The summer was going to be boring enough being by myself.

Chapter 4

Savanna

I could not believe that son of a bitch was forcing me to go out with him. Ty would be kicking his cousin's ass if he knew he was doing this. I didn't want to be around all of Ty's friends. They had all given up on him. Not to mention the fact that everyone blamed me for his accident.

This was a bad idea.

I grabbed some low-rise jean shorts and didn't even bother changing out of the button up short sleeve shirt I was wearing. Instead, I just tied it up at the bottom. I had braided my hair while it was wet this morning, so I just took it out and let the waves fall down my back. There was no way I was going to apply any extra time on myself. This was going to be a miserable night. I wished I never saw Colton earlier today.

Since it had only taken me ten minutes to get ready, I sat on the bed and started sulking. Being in public places where people knew me had gotten to be unbearable. People were mean and they had no problems talking shit.

When Ty had been in the hospital for only a month, a bunch of girls stopped by to see him from one of the female fraternities. I could see them coming from all the way down the hallway, almost like they walked and bounced in sequence. I rolled my eyes as they entered, but they just ignored the fact that I was in the room. Finally after the first minute, I had to leave and wait outside. I didn't know how all five of them were able to visit together, but they crowded in the room and started gabbing about parties he had attended.

It was hard to hear about Ty having a life without me. One of the little bitches even made a point to mention the tattoo he had on the top of his upper thigh. I could feel the vomit rushing into my mouth. They never turned to face me, but were fully aware of who I was and why I was there with him. They didn't care.

From outside I watched the busty blonde talking and stroking my boyfriend's cheek. She took her fingers and brushed them over his perfect lips, while she was clearly talking about how she had messed around with him. Of course I hated her, I hated them all.

When I called Brina to talk about it, she finally confessed to all of the rumors she had heard going around campus. Ty's accident was at the top of the gossip chain, so anyone that had been a part of his life was sharing their stories. According to Brina, he had hooked up with a bunch of different girls. It hurt me, like someone was stabbing me directly in my heart. She never said an exact number, but it didn't matter if it was one or forty, it still hurt the same.

The thought of someone touching something that had always only been mine was horrible. After she told me I refused to even speak to her for a few days. She called and texted me non-stop until I finally gave in. I knew it wasn't her fault for keeping it a secret. Ty was lying in a hospital bed, and I didn't need that added stress.

Brina ended up staying with me for the next two nights. At the time, Ty's mother Ann was still talking to me, but I couldn't tell her why I had been so sad. Finally, after drilling me for two weeks she cornered me and accused me of sleeping around on her son. When I denied it and told her it was Ty, she slapped me across the face. After that, our relationship was strained and now it was non-existent.

They had been my second family. I had played with their son since we were children and I had loved him for almost that long. I would never have cheated on him. No guy ever compared to the way I felt about him. Making her believe that now was impossible.

I grabbed my cowboy boots and purse and headed out the door. I got my things and drove to the old barn where Colt was meeting me. I was sure about only one thing tonight. I was going to make sure that Colton Mitchell never blackmailed me again.

Instead of waiting in the car, I walked inside and looked around.

When my phone started to vibrate, I took one look and saw the message.

I am here.

Colt

On the drive over to pick up Savanna, I actually felt bad about manipulating her to come with me. She had explained in detail about how people treated her now. I was certain tonight was going to be filled with a bunch of animosity. At least that pretty redhead was willing to make things better for me.

The pickup truck hadn't had AC in years and by the time Savanna finally came outside, I had started to really sweat my ass off. The first thing I noticed about her was the short shorts and cowboy boots. Her navel was showing out of the bottom of that tied up shirt and a small ring was displayed in the center of it. Her long brown hair bounced as she walked toward the truck. She was not the girl that I remembered.

When she reached the truck door, I took the stupid smile off of my face. She did not look happy to see me.

"I just want to thank you ahead of time for making me do something that I don't want to do," she said as she hooked her seatbelt.

I started the truck back up and began driving before I responded. I needed to ponder on what exactly I could say to make her feel better, but I didn't really care. That little ginger was waiting for us at the party.

When we got there it was already dark. A bunch of trucks were parked around a big circle and the fire was at least a hundred foot away from us in the center. Music played from someone's radio and people were already dancing and mingling. I got the truck backed up and looked over toward Van. She hadn't said a word since we pulled out of the lot. This was a bad idea, I just knew it.

"You ready to have some fun?" I asked trying to break the ice.

She looked over at me. Her lips were pressed firmly together and her eyes were squinted. It was a face where a woman was getting ready to go all bat shit on someone.

"I told you before that I did not want to come. This isn't going to be a good time."

I grabbed the old John Deere hat from my dash and put it on my head backwards. My cooler was in the back of the truck and I needed a beer. When I jumped out of the truck, she stayed in it, refusing to cooperate. I decided the best thing to do was ignore her. She wasn't my problem anyway.

I had no sooner grabbed a beer, when I saw Sabrina heading toward my truck. "Hey sexy. Where is she?" She said as she approached.

"Where do ya think?" I said as I handed her a beer and pointed toward the truck. I jumped up on the tailgate, while Sabrina made her way to the passenger side of the truck.

"Get your ass out here with us," she said as she opened the door.

Van didn't give her a second to say anything else. "This was your idea? You are such a bitch! You knew I didn't want to come and you have him manipulate me? How could you do that? And how did you even know he was in town?" Savanna asked.

"We ran into each other earlier," she said as she turned my way and bit down on her bottom lip.

I gave her a wink and tried not to watch she and Van having it out.

"Get over it Van. You need to get out. Your life is wasting away. He wouldn't want you to be like that," Sabrina suggested.

Van wasn't having it. "Don't tell me what he would and wouldn't want Sabrina! Seriously, back the hell off!" I felt the truck shift and then saw Van standing in front of the cooler. She helped herself to a couple beers and took off away from the circle of vehicles.

Sabrina came over and sat on the tailgate next to me. "Should we go after her?" I asked.

"No, she's being a bitch. Let her have a beer and calm down. She will be fine," Sabrina said.

I finally noticed that she wasn't dressed nearly as sexy as Van, in fact she was wearing just normal jean shorts and a t-shirt that said flirt across the chest. Her red hair was up in a ponytail and she had feather earrings in both ears. She didn't waste any time with her seduction. Her hand went from my knee to my inner thigh within seconds.

"Darlin', I suggest you slow down."

She leaned into my face. "I have wanted a piece of this since before I had tits." She whispered.

I was midstream with my beer and almost choked when I heard her say that. That mixed with her hand reaching the waistline of my pants was enough for me to stand up. "Listen here. I am all for taking you someplace and letting you do whatever your pretty little heart desires, but I brought my cousins girl here tonight and it's my job to get her home safe."

She seemed annoyed from the moment her hands left my crotch and she hopped off the truck. "Fine!"

I grabbed us two more beers and we made our way through the crowd of people. A few guys recognized me immediately and came up to say hello. Sabrina wrapped her arms into mine as if we were an item. Finally, I pulled myself free and started to ignore her. I had just got out of a clingy relationship and I was not about to start a new one with this chick.

All at once I heard someone screaming the word "fight" and watched as the entire crowd of people ran in one direction away from the fire. I wasn't concerned about watching a fight. I was getting too old to be dealing with things that did not concern me, but something in my gut told me to walk over there anyway.

I was much taller than the people in front of me and could see that the fight was between a bunch of girls. Three blondes were yelling, but I couldn't make out what they were saying from the back of the crowd. I could hear the people around me yelling "hit her". I tried to spot Sabrina in the crowd, but couldn't find her. I pushed my way closer just as I got a glimpse of Van being held down by two blondes, while the third was punching her and kicking her. She was trying to kick her way free but the other blonde sat on her legs. She was crying and screaming underneath them.

Anger filled me and I managed to push everyone in the crowd away from me. When I reached the girls, who hadn't seen me coming I pushed two of them at once off of Van, while the other continued to kicking her in the side. She got one look at me and backed away from me.

"Get the fuck away from her, all of you!" I yelled as I picked her limp body up into my arms and carried her away from the crowd. I didn't walk toward the truck, she didn't need another audience. Instead, I carried her away and sat her down in a patch of moss on the edge of the woods.

Her shirt was ripped and she had scratch marks across her chest. I moved her hair away from her face and noticed her cheek was bleeding, and all around her nose and lips were covered in blood too. "Van, I am so sorry. What happened?"

She just started crying worse, so I held onto her and let her cry it out. "Shhh, you are safe now. I won't let them touch you."

She clung to my shirt and I let her. I had been a fool to have forced her to come here, obviously people were being far worse than I originally thought.

When I couldn't kneel any longer, I stood up and picked her up again. She let me without a fight and I carried her to the truck. Sabrina was waiting there for us. "Where did you go? Oh my God Van, I had no idea. I am so sorry," she apologized.

Savanna didn't speak. She just clung to my chest with her eyes closed and the tears pouring out.

"I'm gonna have to take a rain check on that alone time, Sugar," I said as I got Van into the truck.

"I can meet you later," she offered.

"No can do. I think my cousin would expect I made good on taking care of Van tonight. I can't take her to her mommas like this."

She nodded but looked disappointed. "Fine, your loss though."

Right then I was glad I hadn't taken her home. She was not someone I wanted to associate with no matter what special skills she may or may not have had.

Chapter 5

Savanna

I knew it was a bad idea going there, but I had no clue it would be that bad. I was walking away from everyone just trying to get to a place where I could sit alone, when Heather and her band of bitches came walking toward me. I looked around the truck and knew I was finally safe.

"Van are you okay?" Colt asked as we were heading away from the party.

"Not really," I admitted.

I was balled up against the window of the truck. I didn't look over at him, but I could hear him hitting the steering wheel. "Dammit. I should have never let her talk me into bringing you out."

"It's not your fault Colt."

I could taste the blood on my lips and my face was stinging like crazy. I was afraid to touch anything that hurt in fear that it was worse than I could imagine.

"What the hell happened?"

I shrugged even though I didn't know if he was looking in my direction. The tears ran down my face. "They came out saying I killed him. They said he was planning on telling me we were through for good. " I started crying so bad that I couldn't get any more words out.

"Aww hell, you didn't kill anybody, Sugar. You know that right?"

I wasn't sure if I believed him. I wanted to, but Tyler was basically lifeless. If it weren't for my decisions, he would be fine.

When we had drove without words for more than ten minutes, I let myself fall asleep and I only knew it because when I opened my eyes next I was in Colt's arms, being carried to the carriage house at the Mitchell farm. He got me inside and took me right into the bathroom. I sat down on the seat of the toilet while he rummaged through the first aid kit.

"This is going to sting," he said as he started wiping my face.

"Ouch!" I said when it first touched my skin. I could smell the alcohol on the pad he was using.

He stuck out his tongue like he was concentrating on all of the scrapes and bruises. "Just tryin' to clean you up so I can assess the damage." he explained.

"Can't I just tell you every place that hurts?" I asked.

"Just keep sittin' there." He was focused on my cheek for a longer than normal amount of time. His hands started scrambling around the kit again. "Van, do you trust me?"

"Should I? Why are you asking me that?" I wanted to know.

"I need to give you a couple stitches," he said confidently.

I stood up in a panic. "No way!"

He smiled. "No to the stitches, or to trusting me?"

"Maybe both," I said hesitantly.

"You do know that I have stitched up every type of farm animal that exists? I am fully capable of mending your cheek without you having to go to the hospital or worry your family tonight."

I was scared, but he was right. I couldn't let them see me like this. I had put them all through Hell. There was not much more that they could take. "Fine," I finally said.

He left the room for a moment and as soon as he did, I looked in the small mirror above the sink at my face. It was worse than I thought. My one eye was almost swollen shut. My cheek was busted at the tip of my cheekbone and blood was still coming out of it. My lips had doubled in size and dried blood was at the base of both of my nostrils.

That was just my face.

Colt came back in the room and sighed. "I knew you would look," He shook his head and handed me a bottle of whiskey.

"What's this for?" I asked.

"Well I reckon this is going to hurt some. So, I figured you could get a few shots in you and numb the pain. I promise I won't touch you all night," he said and winked when he did it.

I hated the taste of whiskey, but after seeing my face, I knew it would hurt like a bitch. I opened the cap and started taking big gulps. It burned so bad and I struggled to keep it down at first. Colt leaned against the bathroom wall and watched me as I drank.

"You want some of this?" I asked handing the bottle to him.

He smiled. "I think it would be best if I operated on your face sober, don't you?"

I laughed. "Yeah, you're probably right."

He shook his head and laughed again. "Keep drinkin'."

I took some more large sips. It was starting to not burn so bad going down. I could feel my body starting to relax after a few minutes, but Colt waited patiently. He walked toward the sink and got a clean washcloth. His eyes were focused on my face, but only at what he needed to do to take care of it.

"I bet you didn't come to this town to deal with my shit," I implied.

"No big deal Darlin'. Me and Sam weren't doing much else anyway."

Sam? So he did have a girlfriend. I wonder where she was tonight. I hadn't seen her at the bonfire and he hadn't mentioned her at all. "Where is this Sam? Is she pretty? I bet she's a beauty," I admitted.

He laughed again. "She's up at the farm house and yeah she's pretty darn cute."

I imagined him being with this beautiful blonde. He was such a handsome man and any girl would have been lucky to be with someone like him. Colt acted rough on the outside, but he had a big heart and his family was always the most important thing in his life.

"I can't feel my tongue anymore," I confessed.

He knelt down in front of me. As his strong hands began working on my face, I closed my eyes and felt his warm breath against my cheek. When I opened them again, I noticed how focused he was on my face. I could feel him touching it, but there was no pain.

"Try to hold as still as you can Van. Okay?" He asked.

"Okay," I said slurring my words. I looked at him as he worked on me. I liked the patch of hair that sat just under his bottom lip and the small remnants of a moustache that could only mean he hadn't shaved today. Colt had lips like Ty's and I couldn't help but notice them. His hair was so dark and it was so thick coming from underneath his green hat. Being this close to him, I could see a few small freckles he had across his nose from being in the sun all the time. His green eyes were like crystals and just as I was admiring them, he caught me looking.

"You doin' alright?" He asked, causing me to blush and feel embarrassed.

"Yeah, I am."

It must have been the alcohol, because my mind was not on my injuries at all.

Colt

I had managed to get myself into trouble after only being here for one day. Not only had I gotten myself involved with drama, but I had my cousin's girl in my bathroom. Her face was beaten to a pulp and her clothes ruined. I was doing my best to take care of her after forcing her to come out in the first place. Her friend was of no help and I was positive that we would never be hooking up in the future.

Everyone in town might be mad at Savanna, but she didn't force the football star to make the decisions he made. None of this was her fault. I felt sorry for her. She had loved him for so long and now she was the one suffering the most.

When I got the final stitch finished up, I stood up. I could tell Van was pretty drunk and it was a good thing, because she looked like Hell.

"Let's get you into bed," I suggested, not realizing she read too much into that comment. I smiled. "Van, I am sleeping on the couch. You need to rest. I will give you something to change into and you can lay in my room."

She smiled. It was one of those drunk looks that girls do when they start to get all sloppy. "Oh," she said before she started laughing uncontrollably. Seeing her like this, even with the beaten up face was cute. She was relaxed and not uptight. "Lead the way Doctor Colton," she slurred.

Van followed me into the bedroom where I gave her a clean shirt and pair of boxers out of my bag that I hadn't even unpacked yet. "Go ahead and change into these," I said as I handed them to her.

"I can't!" She said as she stood there swaying back and forth.

"Why not?"

"I can't feel my fingers. I haven't drank in a long time," she admitted and giggled some more.

I rolled my eyes. This was bad, but at the same time, I wasn't doing anything wrong. I was taking care of her. It was what Ty would want.

I walked up to her and took a breath. I had to focus on her face. I couldn't look at her as nothing more than Ty's property. Without really touching her skin, I pulled off the shirt that hung on by a thread anyway. Her white lace bra was still intact. Thank God. She started to lose her balance and pressed her hands into my chest to regain her composure. When she went to stand back up her face was within inches of mine.

This was harder than I thought. I closed my eyes and took a deep breath. "Savanna please try to stand still. I am trying to be a gentleman here."

She started laughing again, but then she bit down on her lip and looked me right in the eye. Her finger pointed toward my chest and she poked me with it. "Why did you call me names when we were younger Colt?"

I rolled my eyes. Of course she would bring this up. "Because I was an asshole."

I got her shorts unbuttoned and she started stepping out of them, using my shoulders to balance herself. I hadn't realized that once they were removed, my face would be straight even with her very revealing panties. I stood up as fast as I could.

She just stood there looking at me. "You said I was a boy." She took her hands and waved them from her head to her feet. "Do I look like a boy to you now?"

She was drunk. Completely trashed, but I looked at her figure anyway. I was human and she was gorgeous. Her waist was so tiny but her hips accented her backside perfectly. When my face actually looked at her chest, I tried to focus on the scratches and not her breasts. I closed my eyes. "Van you are drunk. I am not going to answer that."

I grabbed my shirt off the bed and pulled it over her head. She stepped into my boxers without arguing, but as I got her into my bed and tucked the covers up, she looked at me again. I gave her a smile and turned to walk out of the room but she grabbed my hand.

"Thank you Colt," she whispered.

I looked at her, at the girl who I used to tease about being a boy, and the one that was possibly the prettiest woman I had ever seen. "Goodnight Savanna."

I knew from that moment I would never call her Van again and restraining myself from wanting to touch her was going to be difficult.

Chapter 6

Savanna

I woke up and didn't remember where I was and after having an awful dream that I was falling into nothingness, I felt like I couldn't catch my breath. I took a look around the room and started to panic, until I felt the pain all over my body, reminding me where I was and what had happened.

I climbed out of the bed and walked toward the bathroom. Since the carriage house was small, it was basically a wide open lay out besides the bathroom and bedroom. I spotted Colt asleep on the couch with half of his body hanging off the end and sides. I was going to ignore it, but I felt terrible that he was on that old ass couch without even a blanket to cover him up.

He stirred when I approached him. "Savanna? Are you okay?" He sat up and asked.

"I am fine Colt. Why don't you just come and sleep in the bed with me. We can separate with pillows between us and use different covers. We are both adults and there is no reason you need to try to sleep on that hard ass couch."

I watched as he considered my suggestion. "I don't think that's a good idea."

"You are being ridiculous. I promise not to touch you Colt. To be honest with you, I can't sleep either. I had a horrible dream and think I would feel better if I wasn't alone. Besides, we have known each other for half of our lives. It's not a big deal." I meant it innocently. The alcohol was wearing off already and I just wanted to sleep. He helped me tonight, more than anyone else would have done. It wasn't really a big deal if we slept in the same bed. Colt would never think of me like that anyway. To him, I was probably still that girl that looked like a boy.

He kept shaking his head. "Savanna, I can't do that."

"Why? I am not going to try anything if that's what you are worried about!" I blurted out rudely.

He laughed and scratched his head. His hair was sticking up all over the place. "I aint worried about that Savanna."

The way he said it made me mad. It was almost like if I were the last person on the planet, I still wouldn't be in his league. "Well you don't have to be rude Colton. I was just trying to be nice. So sorry that I repulse you that much that you can't be near me without feeling all weird about it. Geesh, you're an ass."

I don't know if it was the way I said it, or him just realizing the couch sucked, but he stood up and stretched and followed me in the room. "I didn't mean it like that," he climbed onto the bed on the other side of me and got himself situated so he wasn't facing me. After about five minutes of silence I heard him clear his throat. "You don't repulse me Savanna."

I didn't answer him. It felt so nice not being by myself that I closed my eyes and let myself sleep.

When I woke the next morning, I was surprised to find Colt still asleep. The clock read seven, but I remembered him saying he didn't have work until next week. Sometime during the night, he had turned over and he was facing me. I lay with my head on my pillow staring at his beautiful face. It made me miss Ty so much. I felt so lonely even though I was with him all of the time. It was hard to be with someone that couldn't talk back to you, that couldn't even look at you. He just lay there silent and still.

I watched Colt's chest rising and falling. His hair was a mess and his mouth half open, but he was still handsome. Colt had a tiny scar just above his right cheek. I was there when he got it. We had been riding four wheelers and somehow he flipped his. He refused to get stitched up and said it would make him look tough for the ladies. Funny thing was that he was right. Girls were on him like glue. When he and Ty used to talk, Ty would turn around and tell me about all of his crazy hook ups. We even fought about it sometimes, because Ty seemed like he was so interested in it, almost like he wanted to live like that himself.

I continued to watch Colt as he slept, focusing on his chiseled chin and his slightly crooked nose, possibly from braking it at some point. It was silly because you could barely notice it, until you were as close up as I was.

Before I could even snap out of it, Colt opened his eyes. When he focused on me watching him, he jumped out of the bed. Colt turned back to look at me, before heading out of the bedroom and into the bathroom. He never said a word. I sat up and looked past the door waiting for him to come out. Finally, when I heard the water running, I lay back down and stared at the ceiling.

I had been in this room a zillion times with Ty, in fact in this same room was where I lost my virginity. He had waited for his parents to go out one night and set up candles all around the room. All of my friends had awful first times, but mine was with the guy I loved and was going to marry.

My head was pounding and every part of my body was aching. The water was still running in the bathroom, but I need to pee and get some medicine. I knocked on the door. "Colt, are you going to be much longer?" I asked.

I heard the water immediately shut off. When the door knob moved, I took a step back. A cloud of steam came rushing out, revealing Colt's chiseled wet body wrapped only in a small white towel. My mouth dropped open. I couldn't help it. He was like an incarnation of some Greek God.

"Are you okay?" He said as he stood in front of me smiling.

I tried to keep my eyes focused on his face, but I had never noticed how well toned his body had gotten. Perhaps it happened in the years I hadn't seen him, but damn he was gorgeous. Like the kind of gorgeous females talk about licking up and down gorgeous.

I had to snap out of it. What was wrong with me? I couldn't be thinking the things I was thinking about Ty's cousin. "Sorry, just not awake yet I guess," I lied.

He gave me a weird look and walked past me. "All yours."

I rushed into the bathroom and shut the door. After relieving my bladder, I wiped off the steam covered mirror and assessed the damage to my face. My right eye was black and purple colored but it wasn't swollen shut anymore. On that same side, my cheek had two or three stitches at the top and a few scrapes were more prominent as they scabbed over night. My lips weren't as big, but they were all busted still. I backed up away from the mirror and buried my hands into my demolished face. The tears came and soon turned into full blown sobs. After a few minutes I felt the door pushing open.

Colt came in and pulled me out of the bathroom. He sat me down on the couch without saying a single word to me. He left for only a moment and came back with a warm washcloth. I felt it rubbing across my face but refused to open my eyes.

"The stitches look good today. I was hoping they wouldn't get infected." At the sound of his voice, I opened my eyes. He held a bottle of water and cupped two pills in the palm of his hand. "Take these."

I grabbed the tiny white pills and took them. "Thank you."

"I want you to stay here for a couple days," he said.

I looked at him confused, but he held his hands up for me to wait while he explained.

"Savanna, you look like Hell. After seeing exactly how cruel people are treating you, I don't think it's a good idea for you to go back to the dorms. I also don't want your parents to see you like this. Your daddy would beat me to a pulp if he knew I took you to that party and let this happen to you. Since it's the weekend my aunt and uncle will be at the hospital. Just please consider it."

I looked down at the bottle of water. I hated being a burden, but he was right. I had no other place to go for the time being. Explaining myself to anyone would just be more painful. "Okay," was all that I said.

He stood up and started walking toward the door. "I need to go into town and grab some groceries since I didn't do it yesterday. When I'm done, I will grab Sam and be back here to check on you. It's probably best if you try to sleep," he said.

"Will Sam care if I am here?" I asked.

He smiled. "Nah, she likes everybody," he said as he walked out the door.

I wondered why Sam hadn't come over to check on Colt today. She must not have known that he brought me home last night. There was no way I would let someone who looked liked him out of my sight. Not that I felt like he was a cheater, in fact it was the opposite. He seemed like he was the kind of guy that didn't do relationships at all.

When I could finally feel the pain medicine working, I went back into the bedroom and tried to go to sleep. It was going to be a long couple of days.

Colt

It only took me about an hour to run into town and grab some basic things I needed for the small carriage house. I still couldn't believe I was in this situation. I was half tempted to tell my aunt and uncle what was going on, but they wouldn't understand me helping Savanna. I hadn't believed her yesterday when she told me about how mean people were, but I couldn't make the same mistake with my family. If they really did blame her than she needed to stay away from them.

Her face was a mess and every time I looked at her, I felt guilty. I had let that little vixen friend of hers talk me into something that I should have known not to do. I owed it to Savanna to help her until she was better. For the next couple of days she was going to be in a shit load of pain.

When I pulled back up at the farm, I noticed that my aunt and uncle were gone. I walked into the main house and was greeted by Sam jumping into my arms. "Hey pretty girl. I have someone I want you to meet. Yeah, come on girl," I said to my dog.

Sam followed me while I got the bags out of the truck and headed toward the carriage house. When I got the groceries in and had them put away, I made my way into the bedroom. She was sleeping, but stirred as I walked in. "Sorry I woke you," I said while trying to leave the room.

"It's okay. So is Sam here? I really want to meet her. I don't want any weirdness if I am going to stay here."

I looked at her like she was crazy. Sam was a dog. What was she talking about? I shook my head and faced the direction of the door. "Sam!" I yelled.

My giant yellow lab came running into the room and immediately jumped on the bed. Savanna looked up at me. "This is Sam?"

"Yeah, why are you asking me like that? I told you about her," I said.

She started laughing. "I thought she was a girlfriend."

I took off my hat and ran my hands through my hair while I laughed. "Seriously?"

Savanna nodded. "Sure did," she said as she pet and let Sam lick her face.

I grabbed her by the collar. "Be gentle Sam. Savanna is already banged up. Get down girl."

Sam jumped off the bed and sat like the good girl she was. "Well, obviously she's my dog. I don't have a girlfriend," I confessed.

"Wow that's surprising," she said.

"How so?"

She looked down at her hands. "Someone like you always has a girlfriend."

I smiled and shook my head. I sat down on the edge of the bed near her feet. "Someone like me? Well, I hate to break it to ya, but I aint nothing special. I put myself first and women don't like that. My last girl walked out for that reason."

She smiled at me. Her face was such a mess. "I happen to know firsthand that you don't always put yourself first. I wouldn't be here right now if you did."

I shook my head again. "You are different. You're...like family," I admitted.

I knew I hit a nerve after the words left my mouth. Savanna put her head down and looked at her lap. "Right. Family," she said in a depressed voice.

I reached my hand over and placed it on her arm. "Hey, they will come around."

She just nodded and I could see that she was starting to cry again.

I needed to change the subject.

"Savanna, I think Sam and I are going to go fishin' later. You think you might want to come with us?" I asked.

She shrugged her shoulders but never looked up at me. "You don't have to babysit me Colt. I think I am being enough of a burden on you. I will probably just go out and spend time with Daisy."

I had almost forgotten about her horse. "We could bring her with us. I was only going out to the hole. I can ride Thunder and Sam can get some exercise."

She shrugged again.

"Tell ya what. I am going to make us something to eat and you can decide if you want to come with us, or stay here. Just so you know, you are never a burden. Did you ever think I might enjoy the company?" I asked while heading out of the

bedroom. I didn't give her a chance to reply.

Chapter 7

Sam was a dog.

I shook my head and lay back down in the bedroom. My body was still achy, but being with Daisy and at the hole seemed like it would be a good time. I didn't want to be in public, but the hole was at the back of the property on the farm and I knew that we would be the only two people there. Nobody would be there to bother or judge me. Besides, Daisy would really like the ride. She was cooped up during the week and I hated it.

I climbed off of the bed and located my shorts. There was no use trying to salvage the top I wore last night, so I just left Colt's t-shirt on. I looked down at it and saw that it was just a white t-shirt with a beer bottle on the right breast. I was sure the back had some saying or logo, but I never bothered to look. I found my boots near the bathroom door and made my way out into the kitchen.

"Can I still tag along?" I asked.

"Hell yeah. Hey, I got you something at the store," he said not answering my question. He reached into the bag and handed me a small bag. Inside I found a toothbrush, a hairbrush, and a pack of hair bands.

I looked up at him curiously. "How did you know I was going to stay here for sure?"

"I didn't, but I wanted you to have some things in case you did. Now as far as a new bra and panties, well I wasn't about to buy that," he joked.

I shook my head and walked into the bathroom with the bag. After I looked in the mirror I realized how horrible my hair looked. I had to wet the brush to get out all of the knots. I needed a shower, but since we were going out to ride the horses and fish, it was kind of a waste. After throwing my hair up into a ponytail, I managed to brush my teeth. My lips were sore and the toothpaste stung when it entered into the cuts. I looked horrible and couldn't understand how Colt was keeping a straight face. He hadn't even said a word about it.

When I walked out of the bathroom, Colt was nowhere to be found. The bag of food that he had made was also gone, so I hurried out toward the barn. It was a surprise to see Daisy all saddled up waiting for me just outside. Colt was coming out of the barn with Thunder and Sam was jumping and running around like crazy.

"You ready to ride?" He asked.

I started to get up on Daisy, but the pain was so bad that I couldn't get my legs up into the stirrup. Colt saw my dilemma and hopped down off of Thunder. "Hold up Savanna. Let me just help you with that."

I put my hand on his shoulder and let him pick me up so that I could get my foot hooked in the stirrup. His hand was on my butt as he helped get me onto the horse. It was nothing to get excited about, but for some reason I had noticed and it made me smile.

"Thanks Colt. I didn't realize how sore my legs were," I admitted.

He hopped back up on Thunder and lightly gave her a kick. "Yah," he said as they took off in front of me. I followed suit and soon we were away from the farm and making our way through the woods.

I hadn't been out here in a few weeks, but I knew these trails like the back of my hand. Daisy and I explored every inch of these woods and the hole was our favorite spot to relax. There was a large patch of grass just a few feet away from the pond, so that Daisy could graze while we fished or sometimes swam. Going here with Colt made me think about being here with Ty. I am sure that he didn't intend for it to bring up sad memories, but there was little in my life that didn't remind me of Ty.

When we got to the opening in the woods, I spotted the pond. It was funny how as we were approaching I could see the turtles and frogs jumping in the water when they heard us coming. The pond itself was pretty big and years ago Ty's family had anchored a floating dock in the center. We would get a bunch of people out here and sunbathe for hours out there. Just seeing the dock reminded me of last summer being here with Ty.

We had come out for a swim, but ended up having wild sex on that dock. When we heard his father calling, we jumped in the water and hid under the dock until he finally left. The worst part was that our clothes were laying on the grass at the water's edge. He either noticed and was embarrassed or never even saw them there, because he never mentioned it to either of us.

Colt had already jumped down from Thunder and was tying his line to a tree near a patch of shade and grass. The horse immediately started ripping out large chunks of the fresh green grass. Colt was standing there waiting to help me off of my horse. Once again, I felt funny about him touching me but I knew it was necessary. I got Daisy hooked to a tree close to him, but not close to where they would get tangled up.

Last year Ty's dad had bought one of those giant plastic sheds and put it at the edge of the pier so that we didn't have to carry all of the rods and floats back to the barn. Colt knew exactly where to go, and I wondered when the last time he visited was. Obviously he had been here and I didn't know.

"How did you know we had the rods here?" I asked.

"Well, I looked for them in the barn and when I didn't find them I asked Harvey," he explained.

Harvey was the farm hand that lived in a trailer on the property. I was pretty sure he didn't have legal papers to be in the country. Most of his family was still in Columbia and Ty had mentioned that he sent most of what he made to them.

"Oh, I was thinking that you visited and didn't say hi," I confessed.

Colt just laughed and shook his head.

He picked out two good poles and handed one to me. "Here this one is pretty good. Do you need me to bait it for you?" He asked.

"Hell no! I can do this with my eyes closed," I said confidently.

He attended to his fishing rod while I got mine ready to go. I had already cast my line into the water before he had his baited. I giggled when I looked back at him and saw he had pricked his finger with the hook. "Do you need me to help you instead?" I asked sarcastically.

"Shut up! I got this smart ass!" He laughed.

For the next hour we sat side by side fishing and talking about the past year. It was so nice to finally have someone listening to me. I didn't cry, in fact it felt so good to get out.

Colt

When I asked Savanna to go fishing, I immediately had regrets. She looked terrible and needed to rest. Being in the sun couldn't have been good for any of the abrasions on her face. I had packed lunch, but not sunscreen and I hadn't found any in the small shed.

I handed her my one and only favorite hat. "Here, put this on your head so your face doesn't get too much sun," I offered.

She smiled and held the hat in her hand. "Are you sure you don't want it? I mean your hair looks like a hot mess," she joked.

We both started laughing as I tried to pat down my hair. I needed it cut, but just hadn't had time. "If you want to talk about hot messes we can start with your hair this morning. I mean, it was so bad that I had to drive to the store and get you the brush. I was afraid that by tomorrow we may have lost the TV remote in there," I said sarcastically.

"Ha ha! It wasn't that bad."

"Okay, if you say so," I said as I stared out at the water.

Since I wasn't expecting it, Savanna took her hand and pushed me over, causing me to get my hands and my rod all muddy. When I turned to face her and she saw the mud, she held her hand over her face while she laughed.

"You better get up and run, because paybacks are a bitch," I said as I picked up a large handful of slimy mud.

Savanna threw the pole on the ground and started running away from me. The problem was that the pond was a large circle, so as long as she stayed away from the woods, she couldn't hide.

Just as I suspected, she tried to hide behind a bunch of cat tails growing out of the water. I spotted my white shirt and tossed the wad of dirt up high so that it disbursed all over her head and unfortunately my hat.

She screamed as it came down on top of her. "You suck Colt!"

I started laughing as I bent over to grab another chunk of mud, but as I came up I got slapped right in the forehead with a cold chunk of earth. Before I could say a word, I heard her laughing uncontrollably.

I looked toward the sound of the giggles, but couldn't spot her. Suddenly I saw another bunch of it coming my way and I tried to move out of the way. It slapped me on the shoulder. I caught a patch of white moving quickly and I ran after it. As I came up behind her, I tossed the mud at her back. She screamed as it hit her, but kept running, knowing I had to stop for more.

As I ducked down, she must have done the same, because we both came up and had a handful cocked back. She started walking toward me with a smile on her face. "I will put mine down if you do the same," she said.

"Okay, on the count of three," I agreed.

We both counted.

"One."

"Two."

"Three."

At the same time instead of dropping the mud we threw them at each other. I closed my eyes and let the mud cover my face. When I opened them I saw Savanna hunched over. She was being really quiet and I started to wonder if I hit her in the face by accident. I was sure I aimed way lower. When I came within inches she smacked me on the chest with more mud. Her laugh was contagious and I couldn't help but push her down and try to get her back. Unfortunately, my body was now on top of her and I froze as our eyes met each other's gaze.

I pushed her muddy hair away from her face with my fingers. She closed her eyes as I did it. She was still gorgeous, even with the black eye, busted cheek and fat lip. Her mouth was so close to mine that I could feel her breathing. I wanted to kiss her, in fact I wanted to do a whole lot more.

She closed her eyes again and started moving her head up toward mine. I pulled away and stood up quickly. "I am so sorry. I didn't mean...Why don't we eat some lunch," I said changing the subject.

She sat up and just like me, pretended nothing happened between us just now. Maybe I had just imagined it, but I swear she wanted me to kiss her.

We ate most of our lunch in silence and it seemed uncomfortable for a while. Finally she just started talking about normal things.

"Wanna play some Rummy tonight?" She asked.

I finished the last bite of my sandwich. "You do know that I am the Mitchell champion right?"

"I can beat you at that game any day Colt. We aren't kids anymore you know," she replied.

"Well I aint doing shit until I get a shower. This mud smells like ass," I admitted.

She started laughing as she picked at the meat on her sandwich. "You think it's the mud. Maybe it's you."

I flung some of the cold bottle of water at her. She tried to cover herself from being hit by it and yelped as the cold water hit her neck. "That's so cold."

"You deserved it. I was sittin' here being nice to you," I replied.

"Actually, we really do stink now," she admitted.

I gathered everything up and put it in the bag. "How bout we head back and get cleaned up. It will take us awhile gettin' the horses cleaned up anyway," I suggested.

I held my hand out to help her up and when I pulled she ended up losing her balance and falling into my chest. She looked up at me and again our gazes met. For a few seconds we both just stood there staring at each other. Her eyes were staring at my mouth and I couldn't help but lick them. I wanted to feel how soft her lips felt.

I opened my mouth to say something and she pulled away and started making her way toward Daisy. I had to shake it off. There was nothing going on between us. It wasn't possible. I didn't know what was wrong with me. I had known her since we were kids and she was going through a tough time. It had to just be that I felt sorry for her. It had to be that.

Chapter 8

Savanna

After two close encounters, neither Colt or myself spoke much on the way home. I didn't really understand what had happened. We were just joking around and having a good time, which was something I hadn't done in forever, in fact I couldn't even remember how long it had been.

Maybe it was because it had been over six months since I had physical contact with anyone, especially a guy. I just felt so comfortable around Colt after knowing him for so long. It didn't make it any easier considering he was so damn hot. Part of me wished I could see him shirtless again, but the other part felt like it would be cheating on Ty. I was just so lonely.

We got back to the barn after taking the long way home. Colt helped me get Daisy back into the barn and fed. Thunder gave him a heck of a time, but he managed to get him calmed down. He only acted that way when a storm was coming. His name used to be Dusty, but even as a small colt he had issues with thunderstorms. Ty changed his name a few months later.

Sam came rushing past us and I could hear the thunder rolling in as we walked back to the carriage house. I stopped Colt when we got about halfway there. "Hey can we get into the main house?" I asked.

"Yeah, why?" He said as he leaned over to pet his dog, who obviously didn't like the storms either.

"I have a change of clothes there. I keep them in Ty's closet. Can we go see if they are still in there?" I asked.

"Of course. How about you run in and I keep a look out for my aunt and uncle," he suggested.

I nodded and ran into the house. I hadn't been in there in months and it was hard walking through and seeing all of the pictures of Ty. Something did however catch my eye and cause me to freeze. Every single picture that I had been in, had been removed. There were no Homecoming photos, no Prom, not even the professional ones we took last year outdoors. They had gotten rid of everything that had to do with me. I ran into Ty's room and started crying as I looked through his closet. In the back corner was the book bag. I grabbed it and ran out of the house as fast as I could.

Colt stopped me when I met him back out next to the carriage house. He grabbed both of my arms. "Calm down Savanna. What's going on Darlin'?" He asked.

I fell into his chest and continued to cry. I couldn't talk about it. It just hurt too much.

At first he didn't wrap his arms around me, but as I cried I felt his arms wrap around my back. "How about we get inside and get you cleaned up," he suggested.

I nodded my head and pulled away from him. He opened the door for me and pointed toward the bathroom. I followed his lead and headed directly in there. Colt was patient with me as he helped me get the water going.

"If you need me I will be right outside the door. All you have to do is call," he stated.

"Thanks!" It was all I could manage to get out.

When I finally stepped into the shower, I let the beads of water beat down all over my face and back. My body still hurt, but not as much as last night. The soap burned my face, but I had noticed that my lips were almost back to normal size. They still had one scab on the bottom, but everything else was just from the swelling. The soap smelled fresh and I took my time washing my hair.

I stepped out of the shower and felt like a new person. I knew my face was a mess, but I was clean. I took my time brushing my hair and my teeth and then I slowly got dressed. The clothes had been in the closet forever in Ty's room, but they were still the only clean clothes I had. Luckily, I had a pair of sweat shorts and a tank top, plus another t-shirt. The best part was a fresh pair of underwear and a bra, which happened to match and were also white. Geesh I was so predictable.

I had managed to calm down by the time I made it out of the bathroom. The first thing I noticed was the smell. The place was filled with the aroma of spaghetti, which I loved. As I turned the corner to the kitchen area, I noticed something else. Colt stood over the stove without a shirt. It was the first time I had really seen his back. In big fancy letters across the top of his back he had a tattoo with the name "MITCHELL". It was done perfectly and accented his broad shoulders. He turned around as I was standing there admiring him.

"Hey. You feel any better?" He asked.

"Yeah. Thanks for letting me go first. I didn't know you had a tattoo."

He smiled and turned to face me. "There is a lot about me that you don't know Savanna," he laughed. "I have one under my bicep." He lifted his arm to display a mustang horse running. It was clearly noticeable if he was in a t-shirt and lifted up his arm, but I hadn't noticed before. "And I also have one somewhere else that you can't see." He winked.

"Eww, I don't want to know," I said as I walked away.

I heard him chuckle. "Well you will be the first woman who hasn't wanted to take a peek."

Oh..... I wanted to peek!

I shook my head and turned on the television. If I stood in the kitchen and stared at his chest any longer I might have an orgasm standing up. It had been a really long time for me after all and he was just so freaking hot.

The thunder and lightning were becoming intense outside. I brought my legs up into my arms as I watched television. I still couldn't believe I was here with Colt. I didn't belong here, but felt happier than I had in months.

Colt finally walked past me and headed into the bathroom. He gave me a quick smile before closing the bathroom door. I tried to ignore the fact that he was naked in there, but I couldn't do it. After a few minutes, I heard the water stop running.

I glanced as he came walking out in just a towel. As I looked over to peek, he caught my eye and gave me a half smile.

Was he teasing me? Ty would kill him.

Colt

Something happened to Savanna when she went into that house, but I didn't have the heart to bring it up after she seemed to have finally calmed down. I was trying to do the right thing with her, but the more I was around her, I was starting to wonder if it was a bad idea. She was my cousin's girlfriend, or she used to be, hell I wasn't even sure what they were. All I knew was that she wasn't mine. Several times I had been in situations where I felt like there was something happening between us.

I didn't know how I even felt about that. I was a man and I had needs. She was a beautiful girl who had been depriving herself of a life for a long time. She deserved to be happy, and to be satisfied. I just couldn't be the one to do that. I couldn't do it to Ty. I had to stop thinking with my dick.

I found Savanna setting the small kitchen island for two. I walked over behind her and grabbed two glasses out of the cabinet. "What do you want to drink?" I asked as I leaned in the fridge.

"What do you have?" She asked.

I went to turn around to answer her, but didn't realize she was right behind me. Our chests brushed and we both froze. Without saying anything, she turned around and started talking about drinks again. "Do you have any tea bags? I can make us some tea."

"Actually, I bought a gallon. Is that alright?" I asked, trying to forget about touching her again.

"Yeah, that's fine. You get the drinks and I will make our plates."

We decided to eat while sitting on the couch, so we could watch television. I let Savanna pick the movie and thankfully she picked a comedy. I got up and put our plates in the sink and got us two beers. The first movie finally ended and a love story came on. It ended up being about a couple who were forbidden to see each other. After the first intimate scene, I grabbed the remote and changed the channel. I couldn't even look at Savanna.

"Want to play some cards now?" I asked.

She pulled her legs up on the couch and rubbed them with her hands. "Sure. If you' re ready to get beat that is."

We both smiled and I got up to get the cards, pen and paper. When I got back she was cracking her knuckles and pretending to have a game face. I sat on the floor across the coffee table from her, so that she couldn't see my cards. Rummy was a serious card game for my family.

We played three hands and our scores were almost identical. After having three beers each, we were both feeling more comfortable. "How about we play for shots?" Savanna suggested.

"Girl, I can drink you under the table. Did you forget I saw you last night?" I teased.

"I don't plan on losing," she replied confidently.

"You're on. I am just warning you now, I draw the line at holding your head when you're puking later."

She just smiled and started shuffling the cards, while I grabbed the bottle of whiskey that was in the bedroom. The bottle was still half full, so we had plenty for this game.

After four more hands, Savanna and I were dead even with two shots each. She was starting to slur her words like last night, but was convinced she was going to continue. I felt relaxed, but not drunk at all. When she lost the next hand, she stood up from the table.

"Are you cheating?" She asked as she pushed her finger against my nose.

I laughed. "No, you silly little drunk. I am just that good."

She stood there giving me that look again. "Do you know that I haven't had sex in over six months. I went from having it like every day to never. Do you know what that's like?" Before I could open my mouth she kept going, slurring away. "Of course you don't. Someone like you probably gets ass every day. Hell, you probably have a little black book, or do they just each have a day of the week?"

I tightened my lips and creased my eyebrows. She couldn't have been more wrong. "You are drunk. It would be best if you just stopped talkin'. You obviously have no idea about how I live my life," I said defensively. "And just so you know, I am just a regular guy. You keep saying guys like me like I am some special breed. I aint Savanna. I am just as normal as you. I had one girlfriend in the past year and I have never had a fuckin' black book."

She looked directly into my eyes. I stood still for some reason. "Why do you keep calling me that?"

"What?"

"Savanna. Nobody calls me that."

I ran my hands through my hair and turned to walk out of the room. I needed to separate us. Drinking was obviously a bad idea.

"Tell me Colt."

I turned around and found her less than a foot from me. Her eyes looked up into mine. "You should probably go to bed Savanna."

She never looked away. "You said it again. Tell me why."

I smiled and looked away. "Fine. I can't call you Van anymore. It doesn't fit you," I confessed.

I went to walk away but she grabbed my arm. "It's my name, how doesn't it fit me?"

"No, it isn't your name. Your name is Savanna and it's beautiful, just like you," I said in almost a whisper.

I couldn't look her in the eyes. I knew what would happen next if I did. I walked into the kitchen and started doing the dishes, trying so hard to focus on anything but her. When I got the last plate cleaned and turned around I found her standing there.

She had tears in her eyes. "Colt. Will you sleep next to me again tonight?"

Awe Hell!

I leaned against the countertop. "That really aint a good idea. Last night was different, but we both have been drinkin' and I can't promise that I will be a gentleman," I confessed.

I put my head down so that she couldn't see me reacting to her. Instead of saying something she approached me. I looked up at her as her hands touched both sides of my cheeks. They reached up and ran through my hair. "Savanna," I whispered, wanting to tell her to stop, but the words wouldn't come.

Her finger brushed over my lips and she traced them with it. I watched her bite her lip. It made me lick and bite mine. I leaned my forehead against hers. "We can't do this," I said hesitantly.

I closed my eyes but kept my head against hers. "I know," she whispered.

With my hands on her shoulders I backed her away from me and turned her to face the bedroom. She looked back at me and started walking, but suddenly stopped. "Will you just please sleep next to me? Please?" She begged.

I shook my head. *This was trouble.* She needed to leave tomorrow. I couldn't do this after tonight. Every part of my body wanted her, and it was becoming hard to restrain when she was in front of me offering.

I waited a few minutes before going into the bedroom. I hoped that she had passed out, but instead she was still standing on the side of the bed. She hadn't seen me come in and I froze as she removed her shorts and climbed into bed. How in the hell was I supposed to sleep next to her when she was only wearing her fucking panties? I pulled off my shirt and made sure not to remove my shorts before climbing in the bed next to her. We were far enough apart where I didn't have to touch her at all. I tried to get comfortable on the edge, but soon needed to lay on my back. As I was turning, I saw that she was laying on her side, just looking at me. "Sorry for earlier," she said calmly.

I propped my head on a pillow and looked at her. I shouldn't have, but I did. "It's fine. I can't imagine the stress you been under for all this time. I can understand that you are lonely, hell I get lonely a lot," I confessed.

"Everyone blames me. I just can't take it anymore. Sometimes I just wish it was me in that hospital bed," she confessed.

I reached over and touched her cheek. "Please don't talk like that Savanna. What happened wasn't your fault. Shit, he wasn't the angel they think he was."

I wish I could tell her the truth...

She sat up and I realized I stuck my foot in my mouth. "What does that mean? If you know something tell me?"

"I just meant that he was hooking up with all those girls instead of just waitin' for you." It was partially the truth. I didn't have the heart to be the one to tell her he had cheated while they were really together.

"Oh. Do you think it's stupid of me to pretend like we are together even though he's lying in that hospital?" She asked.

We were so close and answering this could change things. We had already taken things too far. But, I couldn't see her wasting away in that hospital room having false hope that he would ever wake up. It wasn't fair to her. "You aren't pretendin', but if you ask me, I would say he wouldn't want you to be miserable. When you love someone you want them to be happy."

She smiled a little. "I do want to be happy again. I just think it's never going to happen. I don't know if I can let myself go through with it"

"Well when the time is right you will know. You will feel it in the pit of your stomach and thinking that you will never have the chance will tear you up inside. That's when you will know for sure that you are ready to move on," I said confidently.

I watched tears fall down her eyes. "I want you to kiss me."

You can't ask that!

Her request caught me off guard. "What did you just say?"

She got even closer to me. "I've never kissed anyone besides Ty. I just want to know what it feels like and since I don't have any other guy friends, I was hoping you would do it." I opened my mouth but she started talking again. "Never mind, it was a stupid idea. I am so…."

I pressed my lips against hers, first gently while waiting for her to respond. I pulled away and looked at her. Savanna dug her hands into my hair and pulled my lips to hers again. I tried to be gentle with her busted lip, but she wasn't even paying attention to it. Her tongue slid across mine for the first time and it was like fuel for the fire. My hands came up and grabbed her face as my tongue played with hers. I teased her lips with mine and licked them before sliding my tongue back into her mouth. When we finally pulled away we separated quickly, neither of us wanting to say anything.

I was about to turn over and go to sleep when I felt her hands touching my back, and then I realized it wasn't just her hands. Savanna's lips kissed the top of my back and I felt her tongue as she did it. "You asked for a kiss Savanna. You know we can't do anymore than that," I whispered.

I turned to face her, to make sure she heard me.

"Was I bad at it?" She asked.

It was perfect and I want so many more.

"Are you kidding me? You were great Savanna. Please can we go to bed?" I begged.

"If you answer one more question."

"Fine."

"If I was never with Ty and my face didn't look so bad, would you have wanted me then?" She asked curiously.

She was so close to me and I could still taste her on my lips. "Savanna, this is so wrong. We shouldn't be here together. We shouldn't have kissed."

"Just tell me the truth," she begged.

I looked at her again. In the dark it was hard to see her black eye anymore, not that it mattered to me at all anyway. I knew how she really looked and that it was just temporary. "Even if I tell you yes, it doesn't matter because it can't happen. So why do you need to know so bad? It's just going to make things harder."

"I just haven't been around people in a while especially a guy, but being around you has been so different. I feel like there is something happening between us. I just need to know if I am going crazy."

Shit. Do I lie and break her heart or tell her the truth and throw caution to the wind? I wanted her, but the problem was she wasn't like other girls. I had known her for so long. I spent my summers here as a kid and she was always a part of them. She wasn't the kind of girl that you fucked and forgot about. That's probably why my stupid cousin couldn't seem to just let her go.

"I am going to say this once and I don't want you to ask again. I think you are gorgeous. I don't want to call you Van because you are a beautiful woman who deserves a beautiful name. If you were never with Ty, you would be all I thought about until I had you for myself. Now can I please go to bed?"

"Yes," was all she said.

Chapter 9

Savanna

There are times when someone drinks where they wish they could forget what their drunk self did or said the night before, but last night just wasn't one of those nights. I remembered everything that was said. Mostly, I remembered every word that came out of Colt's mouth. I was almost afraid to open my eyes to see if he was still lying in the bed next to me. I opened my eyes just as Colt stirred next to me. When I turned to look in his direction, he was already looking in mine.

"Hey," he said.

"Hi."

Obviously he was wondering what to say next. Something had happened between us and as much as I should be upset with myself over it, I couldn't help but to feel happy.

"Your eye looks better," Colt said as he reached over and pushed the hair away from my face.

"Is it still black?" I asked.

"Eh, it's kind of like a faded brown and purple now. Your face isn't swollen though, and your lip is barely noticeable."

Since he was clearly looking at every aspect of my face, I started to blush. It was weird, being here like this with him, but at the same time, exciting.

I needed to change the subject. "So what are your plans today?"

"I don't know. What did you have in mind?" He asked.

I was shocked that he asked. I figured he would be the first one of us to bolt out of this bed and drop me off at the dorm. "I am pretty comfortable right now," I admitted.

"Me too," he said as he looked at me and smiled.

I smiled back and we just lay there looking at each other for a long time before either of us said anything.

For the next two hours Colt and I laid in bed across from each other talking about everything under the sun. It started as a joke, but soon progressed to an intense conversation. I thought it would be awkward talking about such personal stuff, but after a while I realized it was easy. Colt hung on to my every word and he seemed genuinely interested in everything I was saying. Whenever he would ask a question, I would have to answer, but he would have to answer the same one too. After two hours, I felt like I knew so much more about him.

His favorite color was gray. He preferred Country music over any others. His favorite food was hot wings and anything breakfast. He talked about college and jobs that he had. We even talked about funny things we did as teenagers.

Colt only got out of bed because we were both starving. I offered to make pancakes, but he claimed he made the best in all existence. After they were served, I had to admit that they were pretty dang good. Not being around other people had become so normal to me in the past few months. I had shut everyone out in fear of being hurt or rejected. I honestly wanted to be around Colt. He made me smile and always said the right things. He made me feel like we were kids again and that it was alright to smile and want things.

I insisted on doing the dishes and Colt didn't argue. He was sitting on the couch with Sam sprawled out over his lap. Once again he wasn't wearing a shirt. I caught myself glancing over and just looking at his body. He wasn't giant, like over muscular, but he was well defined. I thought about the way his skin felt last night when we kissed and I felt my cheeks getting hot. As much as we were trying to fight it, I wanted to kiss him again, even more so today. I kept replaying what happened last night in my mind and all of the things he said to me.

That was one thing that neither of us brought up so far today, and part of me worried that he may have regretted it. He was right about me needing to be happy with my life. Ty wouldn't want me to be miserable. Was I wrong for wanting to move on? Was I an awful person for being attracted to someone that saved and took care of me? He was the first person who had treated me with respect since the accident. Even if he didn't want me for more than a friend, I would be okay with that. Except for my so called friend Brina, he was all I had.

Once I finished in the kitchen, I headed over to the couch. We sat on opposite ends and started watching a movie. After a while he sat a pillow in his lap and offered me to lay down. At first it was innocent, but as the time passed I felt his hands stroking my hair. I wanted to look up at him, but I didn't have the nerve to do it. I was afraid he would stop and I didn't want him to.

"Savanna?"

"Yeah?"

"I know you have to get back to school tomorrow for finals, but I need to talk to you before you go." He stated.

"Okay. Just so you know, I don't have finals until Tuesday," I said as I smiled up at him.

His face was serious so I sat up and faced him. "What's wrong?" I asked.

"I um. Well I didn't really sleep much last night. After what happened....the kiss I mean, well it got me thinkin'. Then after this morning I knew for sure I needed to bring this up."

"I'm not following you Colt. Just tell me." I said wondering what was going on. "Do you want me to leave now? Are you mad about the kiss?"

He looked down at his knees. "I really enjoy your company and I don't want you to leave. I was kind of hopin' you would stay," he said in a calm voice.

My mouth dropped open. I didn't know what to say.....

I had loved Ty since I was fourteen years old, but the past two days with Colt had made me feel alive again. So much had happened to get me to where I was right now. I didn't want to turn my back on Ty, but how long could I wait? For countless days I had done nothing but cry and want to end my life. Finally, someone made we want to smile again. At first, I thought it was through pity, but I could see the fire for me building in Colt's eyes and just knowing it sent sensation through my body that I thought would never exist again.

I wanted more...

I wanted him...

Colt

I shouldn't have said it, but I did. I just wanted to be around her and it wasn't because of some kiss, even though that was pretty hot. It was because I genuinely enjoyed her company and seeing that she enjoyed mine, well it made my decision making easier.

She was like a lost little puppy and I wanted to save her. I wanted to see her smile and I especially wanted to feel those lips. Even if this was a temporary attraction, I wanted to explore it more.

At one time, she may have been my cousin's girl, but right now she was all alone. Maybe I was being a horrible relative, but I was a grown man. I'd been so horrible to her in the past. I couldn't help but want to make it up to her, to spend time with her and show her that she was allowed to smile again.

"Say something," I said in a panic when I saw the look in her eyes.

She closed her eyes and shook her head. "I don't know what to say Colt. I mean, what's this thing that's going on between us? Is it real or is it just something new and exciting? I want to tell you that I can't stay. I want to say that I regret kissing you." Her eyes locked with mine. I could feel my heart beating in my chest. She was going to tell me we weren't on the same page and that she just couldn't do something like this, with me of all people. How could I expect that she would. Of all the people in the world, why would she want to start something with her boyfriend's cousin?

Before I could tell her never mind, she shocked me by taking my hand. "But it would be a lie Colt. I don't know what's happening, but I don't want it to stop. I haven't felt this way in so long. I haven't let myself live. And if you don't kiss me right now, I might pass out from all of this excitement."

Without hesitation, I pulled her into my arms and pressed my lips against hers. There wasn't anything gentle about it this time and I could sense her sudden eagerness. We went from something innocent to an explosion of lust.

I ran my hands into her hair and pulled her in closer. With my other hand I touched her thigh and ran my hands slowly at the base of her shorts. Savanna grabbed the collar to my shirt and pulled me even closer into our kissing. She held me tightly as her lips drug over mine. Her soft tongue played with my bottom lip before she bit it gently with her teeth. When her hands found the edge of the bottom of my shirt, I pulled away. "Are you sure about this Savanna, because if we go any further, I won't be able to stop," I admitted.

I put my forehead against hers and waited for her to reply. She reached for my lips again, but I pulled away, awaiting her answer. She kept her eyes closed but I watched as she licked her lips. "I want you Colt," she whispered.

I didn't reply with words, instead I grabbed her shirt and pulled it over her head. I could feel the heat building as I caught my first glimpse of her bra. Her perky little lips found mine again as one of my hands caressed her breast. I finally let her pull off my shirt and our mouths only separated for seconds as it left my head. Savanna slowly kissed my chin and I held my head back and absorbed how amazing her tongue felt as she drug it against my neck. With both of her hands she began feeling my chest, paying close attention to my nipples. When she reached them she pinched them both while she kissed my shoulder.

I pulled her onto my lap and let her straddle me. Just having her ass in my hands made me rock hard. I had felt it a few times in the past couple days, but this time she was offering. Her shorts made it easy for me to slide my hands up them. I pressed firmly as I made my way up her thighs and when I touched the fabric of her panties she giggled. "Are you okay?" I asked.

"It just tickles. Don't stop though," she whispered in my ear before biting on the lobe.

My fingers grabbed the fabric to her underwear and I pulled them away from her tender skin. I could feel her soft skin on the back of my fingers. She giggled even more than before as my fingers rubbed against her smooth skin. I could already feel how much she wanted me by how wet she had become.

I pulled my hands away and grabbed the back of her again. "We need to get these off," I said as I quickly removed her shorts.

She scooted back on the couch and before joining her, I remained sitting up admiring her tiny stomach and beautiful curves. Her underwear were so small they almost didn't exist and I couldn't help but lick my lips again. "You are so hot Savanna. God, I want you so bad," I admitted while sliding my hands up her thighs again. I watched as she lifted her hips a little as I got closer to her center.

My mouth touched her inner thigh and she retracted giggling again. "Sorry, it tickles when you touch me Colt."

I smiled and focused on her soft skin. Her creamy thigh just wanted to be kissed and it was exactly what I did. When I got to her panties, I kissed them and stroked my tongue over them. Her hips lifted again. "Oh my God that's so hot!" She spat out.

Her eyes were focused on mine, so I never took mine off of hers as I licked the fabric again, this time aiming for the direct center. Savanna gasped and I knew she liked it. With my teeth I grabbed the fabric and pulled it away from her skin. I used my hand to hold the fabric out of my way as I gently kissed her wet skin for the first time. She tasted sweet and part of me wanted to stop fooling around and be inside of her. My dick was starting to throb from not getting attention, but I wanted Savanna to be satisfied. She needed to be.

I slid my tongue inside of her again and found the tiny nub at the base. I let my tongue go a little crazy when her body started to convulse against my face. When she finally began screaming out I took it into my mouth and sucked hard. Savanna's hands were in my hair and she was pulling me up to her face. I grabbed my shirt and wiped it off before kissing her, not knowing if that was something she was in to.

As my body lingered above hers, she reached for the button to my shorts and yanked my pants down off of my ass. I felt the edge of her fingernails digging into my skin as she pulled my body against hers. With one hand I reached down and threw off my shorts. I found her mouth again as I reached behind her back and unhooked her bra. She sat up and let me slip it off her arms. I cupped her breasts in my hands and sucked on one of her nipples. Her soft moans filled me with hunger to be inside of her, but when her hand found my shaft and began stroking it, I knew it was only a matter of time.

"I don't have protection," I confessed realizing I hadn't thought this through.

Her lips found mine again and God she tasted so good. "Bedside table in the back," she said between kisses.

I was using Ty's rubbers...what the fuck?

I pulled away far enough where I could see her face. "Are you sure about this?"

"Yes please hurry."

I jumped off of the couch and ran into the bedroom. At first I thought I was out of luck, but then I noticed the familiar feel of a plastic wrapper all the way in the back. I suppose it was hidden in case my aunt was being nosey. Considering that this was a reminder of her being my cousin's girl, I sat down on the edge of the bed and considered that I was making a huge mistake, possibly something that I would never be able to forgive myself for.

As I was about to chicken out, Savanna came walking into the room. She stood right in front of me naked. Just looking at her took my breath away. "You are worth it," I said as I pulled her into my arms.

She pulled away for a moment, maybe to question what I meant, but I cupped my hand between her legs and used the palm of my hand to rub against her. I started kissing her stomach and noticed a tiny butterfly tattoo that had been hidden by her underwear. I wondered why she hadn't mentioned it, but considering where it was located kind of answered the question.

Savanna grabbed the wrapper out of my hand and took it upon herself to apply it to my hard shaft. She pushed me on my back and sat on my knees. I had to smile when her eyes took their first real look at my whole body. I sensed the hint of a smile cross her face when she looked at how ready I was for her. I felt the condom sliding slowly down my shaft and Savanna's hands sliding up and down it a few times before she came up to kiss me again. My tongue found hers and I licked it outside of our mouths. My head made its way to the center of her neck and I sucked it before licking my way to a new spot.

Savanna's eyes found mine as I shifted her into position. When I slowly slid inside of her, she let out a small cry. It had been a while for her and I could really tell. I moved slow at first, but soon her hips moved in sync with mine.

I flipped Savanna on her back and looked into those pretty eyes of hers. My lips brushed against her black eye and then her cheek that I had stitched up. I kept my nose on hers and let our lips brush as I felt her climax. When her body tightened with me inside, I could feel myself letting go. I collapsed on top of her and buried my head into her long brown hair. We lay there holding each other trying to catch our breath.

I grabbed one of her hands and held it against my lips. When I felt her body shaking I turned to look at her.

She was crying.

Chapter 10

Savanna

I never thought I would sleep with someone other than Ty, especially his cousin Colt, who had been so out of my league my whole life. Colt held onto my hand as he looked over at my tear filled eyes. It was so emotional for me, and I didn't know how to explain it to him. I didn't even know if he would understand. The last thing I wanted was for him to get mad at me for crying.

It had been amazing. The way he touched me and how perfect his lips felt when he kissed me. I loved every second of it. I couldn't help but feel like I was betraying Ty and I didn't know what to say when Colt was asking.

"Savanna, did you hear me?" He asked again.

"Sorry. It's been a while, that's all. I guess I just wasn't prepared for it to be so......so emotional," I admitted.

Colt rolled over and ran his hand down my chest and in between my breasts. "Did I hurt you or make you feel uncomfortable?" He wondered.

I let out a small laugh. He had no idea how wrong his assumptions were. "No, of course not. It felt wonderful. I feel …….amazingly wonderful Colt. I swear," I confessed.

I did feel wonderful. I wanted to stand up on the bed and scream how amazing it was to be laying naked next to him. I wanted to shout out to everyone how I had just slept with the hot guy everyone lusted over as a kid.

"Are you having regrets? I won't be mad Savanna," he said.

I closed my eyes for a second and turned on my side, propping my head up with my hand. His fantastic chest was inches away from my face and I finally gave in and let my head lay against it. I ran my fingers across the top of it. "If we didn't have some kind of guilt for what we just did than we would both be heartless, but I don't regret it. It was so perfect Colt. I didn't want it to end honestly."

Colts arms finally wrapped around my back and pulled me back into his arms. I felt his lips kiss the top of my head and he held his face in my hair. "I don't regret it either."

"What do we do now?" I asked.

I heard him sigh. "Do you really want to talk about this right now? My body feels like jello and having you laying here naked prevents my brain from working properly," he joked.

We both let out small laughs. I stroked a tiny patch of hair in the center of his chest.

"I can't believe we just did that," I confessed.

"Yeah, I didn't see that comin', but it sure felt nice," he agreed.

I kissed his chest and closed my eyes. "It felt great."

Colt and I must have fallen asleep, because when I opened my eyes again I was still in his arms. I felt so safe here with him. After all of the brutal things people had said and done to me, I had finally found a safe haven. He wanted me to stay and I couldn't bear to leave, not when he was being like this.

I think every girl I knew at some point had fantasies of Colt Mitchell and here I was lying naked in his strong arms. It was surreal.

I couldn't stop thinking about his lips and how good they felt as they kissed every part of my body. He knew how to touch a woman and I admired that he made a point to pleasure me first. Ty had never worried about that, in fact I couldn't think of one time he had done that before taking care of himself first.

I hated comparing them, and it was probably some unforgivable sin, but I just couldn't help it. It was the only thing I had to compare to. I was just so amazed at how passionate our encounter had been. Perhaps it was because he was an adult and had been with other adults. A feeling of jealousy rushed through me as I thought about Colt being with other, more experienced women.

I started getting myself upset, thinking he was just being nice. I didn't have much experience, so

I just assumed that I couldn't compare to some of the women he had been with. I hated that and I couldn't help but think I could never be good enough for someone like Colt.

Colt

So I did it, I slept with my cousin's girlfriend. I should of known better to involve myself in her problems and spend the past couple days alone with her. Now, I didn't want to let her go. I understood why she was so special to him and how he couldn't do it either.

I wanted to feel guilty, hell I wanted to regret it, but I just couldn't. Every inch of her skin was like kissing heaven. Savanna was beautiful and my most favorite part about her was that she didn't really know it.

I didn't understand how everyone could turn their backs on someone like her. I wanted her to know she could count on me as a friend. I really hoped that having sex with her didn't ruin that friendship. In the past I had treated her meanly, but now I wanted to make up for it. She deserved to be happy and to smile.

I kissed her on the head again and felt her stirring. "How do you feel?"

She sat up and stretched her arms before looking in my direction. She seemed so relaxed. "I feel better than I have in a long time actually. How bout you?"

I started to laugh. "Yeah, I kinda feel great myself."

She started to climb out of the bed and I grabbed her and pulled her back. "Wait! Where are you goin'?"

She pushed me away. "I have to pee." I got a smile as she kissed my lips. "Is that okay?"

I brushed my lips against hers. "As long as you come right back." Before letting her climb out of the bed again, I kissed her once more.

She turned around and smiled at me as she made her way out of the bedroom. She looked so beautiful naked. I shook my head, still in shock that we had just had sex. I tucked my arms behind my head closing my eyes and replaying how every inch of her body felt. I think I would be okay if we never left this bed.

I hadn't heard her come back in the room, but I knew it when she jumped back on top of me. "I'm hungry," she said as she bit down on my chin.

I flipped her over on the bed and tickled her sides. She began laughing hysterically. "Stop it, please!" She begged in between my tickle attacks.

I grabbed both of her breasts and shook them in my hands. She tried to get free of me, but I was too strong. Finally she yelled, "Stop it or I will put my clothes back on," I stopped immediately.

"We can't have that now," I said as I winked at her and climbed out of the bed. She propped herself up and watched me walking toward the door.

"What's that?" She asked as I turned away from her.

I knew what she was asking. "I am surprised you didn't notice it sooner."

"Oh my God Colt does that say 'YOUR NAME'?" She burst out laughing.

"Well, yeah, it does," I admitted.

"What the hell would you do that for?"

"It was my first tattoo. I thought it would be funny to tell everyone their name was on my ass," I confessed.

She put her hand over her face and tried to hide the laughter.

"Shall I put on some shorts?" I teased.

"No way! I could watch you walk around all day," she confessed while biting down on her lip.

I smiled and felt my cheeks warming up. It was funny that someone like Savanna could make me blush. I didn't remember the last time I had felt embarrassed. "Keep talkin' to me like that I will come back in here and kiss you all over again," I threatened.

"Please do!" She yelled as I headed to the bathroom.

Before heading back into the room, I ran into the living room and pulled the cowboy hat off of the mounted deer head on the wall. I set the hat atop my head and leaned my naked body against the bedroom door. "I hear someone in here was looking for a cowboy to tame her every desire," I kidded.

She stuck her fingers in her mouth and giggled. The best part was how her eyes lingered up and down my body as I stood there posing.

"So do I have the job?" I asked while still standing in the same spot. "Gettin' kind of cold here Darlin'"

She shrugged her shoulders and gave me an ornery look. "I guess you will do."

I ran onto the bed and grabbed her body, pulling it into mine. "I will do huh?"

She kissed me softly and grabbed the hat off my head. I watched her sit it between my legs and giggle as she did it. "Can I take a picture of you just like that?"

"You're being serious aren't you?"

She had already climbed out of bed and went rummaging in her purse. She pulled out her phone and got a weird look on her face.

"What's wrong?" I asked.

She shook her head. "Nothing. It's just Brina and my mom checking on me. I texted them both that I am fine." She held the phone toward me as she began smiling again. "Say cheese you sexy cowboy."

I tried not to laugh, but I couldn't help it. "Should I worry that my naked body will be all over the internet in the next hour?"

She bent over laughing and shaking her head. "I wouldn't do that to you, well unless you really pissed me off. Then maybe I would," She teased.

Savanna climbed back on the bed, lifted the hat away, put it on her head and climbed on top of me. "Maybe later I can see how many seconds it takes for you to buck me off."

"So now I am some wild bull?" I said as I sat her body up straight and placed gentle kisses around each of her breasts.

"Actually you may be too tame," she snickered and looked down at my growing shaft."Then again, I think you might have a little fun left in ya."

"I will show you fun you little tease." I reached in the drawer and grabbed another condom quickly ripping the wrapper with my teeth. I saw her wicked smile as I did, and immediately I flipped her over and slid right inside. She gasped in shock because it happened so fast. Savanna was on the bed on all fours, still wearing that hat. I pulled at her hips and grinded myself into her as hard as she could take. She screamed out in pleasure, but never asked me to stop or slow down. I reached out and cupped both of her breast into my hands and continued.

"Don't stop!" She screamed.

I kept grinding against her. "Oh God Savanna, I can't hold it," I yelled.

I heard her cry out too just before I collapsed over her back. I grabbed the cowboy hat that had fallen on the bed and put it back on my head. "Looks like there is a new sheriff in town pretty lady." I winked before falling on the bed next to her.

We both busted out laughing.

Chapter 11

Savanna

Colt and I spent the rest of our day in bed. We only got up to make something to eat and drink, and go to the bathroom. I had to admit that spending the day like this was another thing I had never experienced. Ty and I never had enough time to do those type of things, but since everyone else in my life had pretty much cut me off, I had all the time I wanted.

Colt held me in his arms all night and we talked until both of us finally fell asleep, mid-conversation. He was so easy to talk to and even on topics where we didn't agree, he was still understanding of my opinions.

The next morning he got up and made us breakfast. He tried to serve it to me in bed, but I insisted on getting up. We sat and watched some sport network that he seemed to love for quite some time. I finally got up and washed the dishes before hopping in the shower.

I was shocked when I heard the bathroom door open. "What are you doing in here?" I asked feeling uncomfortable.

"Well I was gonna join ya, but your acting like I never saw you naked before," Colt said as he closed the curtain back up.

In a panic that I made him upset, I ripped the curtain back open as the hot water was falling over my naked body. "Touchy! Geesh. Hop in. There is plenty of room," I said nervously.

I had gotten one shower with Ty and the whole time I felt so uncomfortable, but after everything I had experienced in the past twenty four hours, I couldn't believe that I was even considering being modest. Colt had touched parts of my body that I had never seen before; surely I could handle standing under some falling water with him.

He finally climbed in with me and cleared his throat. "Is this your first time being washed by someone since your mamma did it when you were little," he joked as he lathered up his hands and started washing my back.

I had to laugh at his smart-ass comment. Shaking my head, I tried to focus on where his hands were and what they were doing. "No, it'sn't my first time. But, in all the years I was with Ty, I never experienced anything like we have in the past day. You are just so attentive with everything you do. I love it and am also scared to death by it."

His soapy hands reached around and started massaging my breasts. I closed my eyes and felt his chin sit on my shoulder. "If you are ever scared, you just need to tell me and I will stop. I don't want to hurt you."

I turned around and wrapped my arms around his shoulders. "I don't want you to stop Colt. I am having such a good time with you. I just hope you can be a little patient with me. This is all so new and moving so fast. I am not as experienced as you," I admitted.

He pulled away and started washing himself. Within seconds he was rinsing his head and climbing out of the shower.

"Colt, Are you mad at me?"

He was wrapping his towel around his waist when I opened the curtain. He immediately handed me a towel by wrapping it around me. "No! Of course not. I just, well I feel so comfortable with you and it makes being with you feel so natural Darlin'. I guess I should have considered it wasn't the same for you."

I jumped out of the shower and came within inches of his glistening wet chest. "Colt, I don't want to slow down. I promise that I don't. I feel the same, well kind of like we have known each other for so long and that's why this is so easy for us."

He placed his hand on my cheek and leaned down to kiss me. "I'm sorry if I did rush you though. I have this problem with seeing things I want and thinking I can just take them. So Darlin' if you are ever feelin' overwhelmed, well then you just tell me."

I grabbed the edge of his towel and pulled him closer. "Colt, will you take me out to eat before I have to get back to the dorms?" I confessed.

He smiled. "Are you sure you are ready for that? What happens when people see us? You know they are goin' to talk."

This probably was the wrong place to have this conversation, but it needed to be done. "I have spent the last six months trying to make up for breaking your cousin's heart and causing something terrible to happen to him. I have prayed and I have wept. I have begged and pleaded for forgiveness. But, nothing happens. Maybe he will never wake up. Everyone thinks that I deserve to be miserable."

Colt put his arms around and held me tight. "I don't"

"I know you don't, but everyone else does. I have become afraid to interact and associate with people in fear of what they were saying about me. I have heard the rumors about how many girls Ty was sleeping with weeks before the accident, but I stood by and spent every moment by his side. How long am I supposed to wait? It has been six months and there hasn't been any change Colt. I will love Tyler forever, but you're right. He would want me to live. I know that much. Maybe being with you isn't exactly what he would of had in mind, but you are the only person in months to give a damn about me. I'm not asking for some kind of commitment, but just a promise that you will be my friend. Because right now, you are the only one I got!"

Well I had Brina, but she wasn't exactly being there for me as much as I needed her to be.

I took a deep breath and looked into Colts eyes. He flashed a smile across his face and leaned his forehead on mine. "I will be whatever you need me to be Savanna. I promise you I will."

It was funny how Colt kept saying the right things. I wasn't sure about what I was going to say to him until the words came out of my mouth. Sure, I enjoyed being with Colt, but if I wanted whatever it was we had to work, I needed to let go of hoping that I would ever have something again with Ty.

I wanted to believe that someday he would wake up and everything would be the way it was supposed to be, but I had given up so much and lost everything that meant anything to me. I just wanted to breathe again. I needed to. I'd obviously just jumped into the biggest step by being with Colt. Part of me wondered if I would be considered a whore. I kept trying to rationalize what I had done. I was an adult and I made an adult decision to sleep with a beautiful man. I didn't understand how I could feel so good and so sad all at the same time.

Colt

Savanna was hinting around that maybe we had rushed things. She hadn't come out and said it that way, but I felt bad that she thought it.

I shouldn't have gotten involved, or kissed her for that matter, and everything after that, well that was all on impulse. The truth was that I really liked Savanna. She was beautiful and witty and such fun to be around. Anyone that couldn't see that was a damn fool.

After following Savanna into the bedroom, I watched her looking around through the bag she had gotten from the house last night. She seemed content with what she had and scurried back to the bathroom. I shook my head and laughed as she walked by. I sure wasn't used to someone being so modest around me. Hell, most of the time girls were all but trying to rip their clothes off in front of me. I think that's why I really like Savanna. She was nothing like anyone I had ever been with.

My ex, well she wasn't someone that your parents are proud of. She grew up in a double wide outside of town, with her alcoholic daddy and younger brother. When I met her, she was bartending, and trying to keep her and her brother from having to move out. Her daddy was collecting disability and the checks didn't last long once they came in.

I felt bad for her and ended up helping her get caught up before she moved in. Her little brother had joined a band after graduation and went traveling around to different towns in our surrounding states. Her daddy stayed in the trailer and as far as I know, still lives there. I could only assume that's where she went when she had had enough of my shit.

Maybe I just had that natural attraction to charity case women. This was the second girl in a row that I had put myself out there for. I'm not saying that my ex and Savanna are similar, because they are nothing alike. Savanna is different and we have a past. Sure, we were just friends, and rocky ones at that, but she was still there in my life. Her beauty overwhelmed me and her hidden sense of humor that she kept bottled deep down inside of her was amazing.

My cousin was a damn fool. Part of me wanted to go to that hospital and just stand there giving him a piece of my mind. I knew for a fact that he fooled around on her. Every time Savanna brought up me being "that guy" I wanted to turn around and tell her she was talking about the wrong cousin. She couldn't have been more wrong about me.

Being with Savanna was different. She was sweet and innocent and her laugh was contagious. I didn't know what was going to happen between us, but I was willing if she was, to at least try to make something out of this.

After the past few days there was one thing I knew for sure. This summer just got a hell of a lot better, as long as I had her in my bed.

Because it was Monday, I knew that my aunt and uncle were back on the farm, so I needed to take precautions when I took Savanna to the truck to drive her back to her car. My relatives had just about shunned her from their life and the last thing they needed to see was that she had been here with me.

I didn't even know how they would react. Hell, my uncle might even try to brawl with me over it. Sure, what we did was probably wrong, but it didn't feel that way to me. I felt guilty, but also happy and excited. I had made Savanna smile and showed her that she had a reason to look forward. Even if this thing between us turned out to just be one crazy weekend, at least she made the first step to taking back her life. I loved my cousin, but Savanna being at his bedside every single day was just wrong. The truth was that he wouldn't want her living the life she had been living.

Savanna and I managed to sneak off the farm undetected. I had her duck down on my lap as we drove down the dirt road adjacent to the property, just in case.

We drove straight to the old barn where Savanna had parked her car the other night to meet me. She hadn't said much about what was going to happen next between us. I had brought up the topic and she seemed liked she was interested, but women had trouble making up their minds sometimes.

As I put the truck in park I looked over at Savanna. She had brushed her hair after her shower and let it air dry. It resulted in natural waves all over her head. I couldn't help but reach over and run my hand through it. "You still feel like getting' somethin' to eat?"

She turned to me and smiled. "Of course Colt. Why would you think I would change my mind?"

I shrugged. "Just makin' sure Darlin'. I don't want to make you upset."

She scooted over on the bench seat so that she was closer to me. Her hand played with the collar of my t-shirt. "How about we drop off this hot ass truck at my dorm and grab something in town?"

I smiled and stroked her cheek. "I reckon that's a fine idea."

She smiled and looked down for second. When her eyes lifted to meet mine she bit her lip. "Sounds like a plan." She started to scoot over and grab the handle to open the door.

I grabbed her arm. "Wait. You forgot my kiss."

She kept climbing out of the car and turned around once she was out. "I didn't forget. I just want you to wait for it." She closed the door and walked over to her car. I laughed at her comment and watched her cute little ass walking away. Someone like Savanna could make me crazy.

Chapter 12

Savanna

I don't think the reality of what I had done actually set in until I started my car. Colt was following me to the dorms, so I had to pull out first. Flashes of what had happened over the past couple of days flooded my mind. I wanted to feel ashamed for what I had done and the things that I had said. I knew it wouldn't be easy if I ever decided to move on, and I didn't purposely hook up with the one and only person Ty looked up to in the world.

It just happened.

I was attracted to him from the start. Anyone that wasn't, was a fool. His calm personality and southern drawl made him irresistible. Not to mention that the guy knew his way around the bedroom. He did things to me that I never knew could be done and when he was all but spent; he turned around and did them again.

Tears started to run down my face and I just let myself cry. I needed windshield wipers for my own face, but never made an effort to wipe them away. I loved Ty, so much that it hurt, but Colt had awakened something deep down inside of me, something that I had lost so long ago.

I kept looking in the rearview mirror, almost hoping that he had decided pursuing something with me was a big mistake. Maybe if he made the decision I could just let it go and try to move on. Seeing his truck close behind my car made me realize just how real all of this was. This connection that we were feeling was mutual and it scared us both, but neither of us could walk away from it.

When I finally pulled up at the dorm, Colt parked next to me. I looked over and saw him wink before he noticed my wet eyes. He jumped out of the truck and rushed to the driver's side of my car. "Darlin' what's the matter? Do you want me to head back to the farm?"

I didn't even hesitate. "No! Please Colt. I don't want you to leave. I swear. I just needed to have an emotional moment," I admitted.

"Are you sure you just don't want to go out some other time? I won't be mad Savanna."

I reached my arms around his waist and let my head lean against his chest. "I don't want to be away from you yet. Please don't leave."

His hands rubbed my back. "I will be here as long as you want me to stay."

"Thank you." I pulled away and grabbed his hand. "Why don't you come up to my room so I can change." I suggested.

He walked along with me. "Do I get to watch?"

I gave him a smile. "Maybe." I giggled.

It took me about five minutes to get changed and I opted to do it in the bathroom instead of in front of Colt. It wasn't that I cared if he saw me naked, obviously he had already seen everything I had to offer, but I still wanted just a little bit of privacy.

When I walked into my room, I saw him laying on my bed looking at pictures that I had on my nightstand. Of course all of them were of me and Ty and I felt awful for not thinking about them sooner. "I um…"

"Savanna, don't even go there. You love him. I get it," he said without even changing his expression.

"I don't want you to feel like I am using you. I would never do that," I confessed.

"Sugar, I haven't thought that for a darn minute. Stop worrying your pretty little self over it. In fact if you want we can stop by the hospital."

I was shocked that he wanted to include seeing Ty on our day together. Part of me felt like it was wrong and inconsiderate, but the other part realized how thoughtful Colt was being of my feelings.

"There is a restaurant near the hospital. I would like to just stop by for a second if it's really okay with you." I shook my head and reconsidered. "Never mind, maybe it isn't a good idea."

Colt sat up and pulled me into his arms. "Savanna, I want you to do what you want to do. I don't regret being with you for a minute, but I know this is a big step for you. We can go there and I can wait outside. It doesn't bother me or even make me the slightest bit frustrated. I love the kid too you know."

Why did he always know what to say?

"Well, I would like to just stop by. I usually spend the whole day there, so it would be nice if I just say hello real quick."

He stood up and grabbed my hand. "Shall we go then?"

I squeezed his hand. "We shall."

Colt

Savanna had a bunch on her mind, I understood more than anyone about it. Her decisions over the weekend had caused her to have a painful reality today. I hadn't thought that today would be the first weekday she had not spent at the hospital. That's why I had to offer to stop by. I wanted her to feel like she could still be there for Ty, even if we were spending time together. Above everything else that happened sexually between us, she had become a very good friend. I had told her secrets and shared things with her that I never told anyone else. I wanted her to know that I trusted her.

Pulling up at the hospital was harder than I first thought it would be. Savanna didn't speak the whole way there, but she did hold my hand for the ride. We had decided on taking her car because she had air conditioning and the truck did not.

"Do you want me to wait here for you?" I asked kindly.

She looked down at her lap and then finally over to me. "Actually, I think I want you to come. I need to be able to do this. I need to get over this guilt I am feeling, because I know for a fact that I don't want to stop whatever this is. Does that make sense?" She asked.

"Sure it does Savanna." I lifted my hand to her lips. "I am ready when you are Darlin'."

We walked into the hospital hand in hand, but once we reached the elevator Savanna let go. I didn't think too much of it. Hell, she had probably made friends with all of the nurses on Ty's floor. They didn't know I was his cousin, not that it would make any bit of a difference who I was if they saw us walking up together holding hands.

I walked next to Savanna as we made our way to Ty's room. She nodded and waved to a few nurses as we walked by them.

Ty looked exactly how he had the last time I had been in. He lay there hooked up to all kinds of tubes and devices. The constant beeping let us know just how serious his condition was. Savanna stood at his bedside but never touched him. I could tell she was crying but I stood back and let her have the time she needed. When her body finally collapsed over his, I felt the pain in my gut. I had been stupid to assume this was a good idea. It was like I was flashing it in front of his face or something.

I walked out of the room and stood with my back against the wall. I didn't know what else to do, or what I could do. I had done this. I had let things get this far. Heck, I wanted it so bad I just couldn't help myself.

I heard Savanna talking but I couldn't let myself listen. I focused on everyone walking around the halls of the hospital instead of her voice. It was hard to ignore her sad tone and soon I heard her saying my name. I lifted up my head and made my way back in the room. She looked over at me with tear-filled eyes. "I told him you were taking good care of me." She said.

"I'm doin' my best," I admitted out loud.

Savanna only wanted to stay for a few more minutes and once we got into the elevator, she seemed to relax. When the doors shut she threw her arms around me and I pulled her in tight. "You okay?"

"I am now," She confessed.

I kissed the top of her head. "Savanna you can tell me anything. I want you to know that. I promise that I will always be your friend. If you need anything you just tell me."

Maybe it was wrong for me to assume she needed anything from me. Maybe I had caused her more pain than she was already experiencing, but I couldn't help it. I just wanted to be there.

She looked up at me and smiled. "I am so glad that you came to town Colt."

"You sure? I think I may be making things harder on you Darlin'," I admitted.

"In the past three days I have smiled more than I can remember. I am so grateful to have you right now," she said.

I couldn't help but smile. It seemed a bit immature of me, but knowing that she appreciated my kindness meant a bunch.

We climbed in her car and she drove us to a little restaurant off the beaten path of town. It was nestled on a small side road and looked more like a log cabin than a place to eat. When we walked in, I took off my hat and nodded to the hostess. I noticed right away that she was trying to play the seduction game on me. I reached down and grabbed Savanna's hand and kissed it as we walked. The girl finally rolled her eyes and led us to a table, before leaving.

"She was totally flirting with you," Savanna said with a big smile.

I looked back in the direction of where the girl walked. "Really? I didn't even notice." I lied.

"Yeah right!"

I smiled and leaned into the table. "Maybe I don't care, because I am here with someone else," I pulled her hand up and kissed it again.

"Good answer cowboy."

We were interrupted by the waitress and soon ordered our food. Savanna ordered a burger and when it came it was bigger than her whole head. She gave me half, minus the bacon that she stole as I was taking a big bite.

"What? It's my favorite part," She confessed.

I shook my head and continued to eat my fried chicken meal. There was nothing like eating homemade food. I could tell right away.

Savanna squirmed when a couple of people, who looked her age, walked by and made comments. I gave her a quick wink to let her know that she wasn't alone. Nobody was going to hurt her again on my watch.

After we finished eating, we sat there and talked for a long time. The waitress got frustrated since we were keeping her from more tips, so I left her a little extra for her troubles.

The truth was that I didn't want to call it a night. Savanna had finals in the morning, but she didn't seem to want to leave either.

We got back to her dorm room and she invited me up. I was hesitant considering more people might see us and start running their mouths, but she assured me it wouldn't be a problem. When we got to her room a girl was busy filling a duffle bag.

"Who is this?" She asked as I walked into the room.

"This is Colt Mitchell. He's Ty's older cousin. He's here for the summer," Savanna explained.

"Well I was going to head to the frat house for the night, but maybe I could stay here and keep you company," She offered, looking directly at me.

Savanna got this mean look on her face. "He has a girlfriend," She spat out.

I smiled and couldn't help from chuckling as her friend said her goodbyes and walked out of the room.

When we were sitting there alone finally, I turned toward Savanna. "What was that about?"

"Did you want her to stay?"

"Of course not."

"Explaining everything was too much for tonight," she said as she hugged me again. "Besides, I didn't want the competition."

I kissed the top of her head. "There aint no competition Savanna. Not when it comes to you."

Chapter 13

Savanna

When I saw my roommate trying to hit on Colt, I felt jealous. I had no right to be. He didn't belong to me, but I couldn't help it. He was my savior and I didn't want to share him with anyone else.

After he said what he said to me, I felt better. That was Colt though. Always saying the right thing. Since we had the room to ourselves, I pressed my lips against his. The kiss started out slow, but progressed into something more intense. I grabbed the collar to Colt's shirt and pulled him closer to me.

His soft lips sucked on mine and I felt his tongue slide across them. Our mouths opened and I felt his tongue start mingling with mine. His kissing made me weak in the knees and I felt like losing all control over myself and giving in to his every desire.

Colts hands reached under my shirt and I could feel them moving up and under my bra. He cupped the skin under my breasts and squeezed my nipples as he continued kissing me aggressively. His tongue became a tool and soon he was running it down my neck, ending in small kisses as it traveled around my ears.

His hot breath gave me chills when he spoke near my ear. "Do you need me to leave so you can get some studying in?" He asked.

I pulled away and looked at him. "What would you say if I asked you to help me study?"

He sat down on my bed and shook his head. "I don't know how good I would be."

I laughed and sat down beside him. "Actually all you have to do is quiz me. I have all the answers written down."

He grabbed the notes out of my hand and started looking at them. After a few long minutes he turned to me and smiled. "I reckon I can help with this."

Knowing how much Colt distracted me, I chose to sit on my roommate's bed while he quizzed me. With every question I found myself staring at the perfect guy across from me.

After at least an hour we were both yawning. Between the past couple of nights we hadn't slept very much and I knew that I needed to get a good night's rest if I wanted to do well on my final. Colt started to get up to leave. "I better be goin'."

"Do you want to stay? I mean, I can't stay up much longer, but you don't have to leave," I asked.

He stood in front of me and took both of my hands in his as he talked. "I don't want to be a distraction Savanna. You need a good night's sleep for tomorrow."

"Well doesn't this friendship include cuddling?"

He let go of one of my hands and played with his hat. "Cuddling?" He put his hands over my face. "Stop givin' me those puppy dog eyes Savanna. I can't ever say no to them."

"It's fine if you want to go. I just wasn't ready to be without you yet. What happens if you get a flat tire on the way home and that hostess stops to help you," I joked, well kind of.

"If you are that worried, I guess I can stay. I wouldn't want you losing sleep over me," he replied.

I pulled off Colts shirt and took off my jean shorts before we climbed into my small bed together. He was so tall, I knew he couldn't be that comfortable. He never complained though, instead he buried his head into my hair and wrapped his arms tightly around me.

After a few moments I heard him starting to snore. It wasn't an annoying snore, but something more subtle, almost like it was letting me know he was there. I wrapped my arms into his and closed my eyes knowing that I was in the safest place.

His arms.

The next morning, I let my alarm go off for ten minutes before I shut it off. I refused to get out of bed and Colt's strong hold. I tried to climb out without waking him, but it was impossible.

When I got myself ready for class, Colt was standing up putting on his shoes. "You going to call me later?" He asked.

"I thought you would stay and sleep," I assumed.

He shook his head before giving me a hug. "I gotta go let Sam out. She has been in the house since last night. She's a good girl, but I know she has to go."

"Okay. Well I guess I will call you later." I reached up and pecked him on his lips.

Colt pulled me back for another kiss. This one was more passionate, and it made the heat rush between my legs. From the first touch of his tongue I thought I was going to squeal. Colt broke our kiss and looked into my eyes. "I really hope you do." After one more soft kiss he followed me outside and we parted ways.

From the moment I lost sight of him, I felt like something was missing. When I got to my class, it was even worse. I made it through my exam with little distraction, by forcing myself to give it my all. Finally, when my tests were all complete, I rushed out of the building and started searching for his number in my phone. I didn't have to search far, because he had already sent me a message.

Missin' your pretty face –C

The text had been time stamped for ten minutes after he left my dorm. I smiled and realized he sent it before my first final started.

I laughed out loud while I messaged him back.

All done. When can I c u? – S

Do you have any finals tomorrow? –C

Two more and then I am done for the summer – S

Supposed to have dinner with family tonight. Do you want me to come later? – C

No just call me. We can hang out tomorrow. – S

Call me if you need anything. – C

TY- S

Colt

Just to be kind, I sent Savanna a quick text as I left her dorm. She needed to be focused and not worried that I had used her for sex or anything else.

I felt really bad for not being able to hang out with Savanna, but I hadn't spent any time with my aunt and uncle. Since I had snuck Savanna into the carriage house over the weekend, I had avoided them like the plague.

My aunt had called me this afternoon and told me that they were having her famous chili and that I better be there. I hesitated for only a minute before agreeing to dinner. I was staying on their farm and they would soon figure out my secret if I kept dodging from seeing them.

I played with Sam at the swimming hole for over an hour and the whole time all I could think about was my time there with Savanna. Her muddy face and hair came flashing in my mind. Savanna needed to study for her last two finals, so I knew she would be busy for the entire evening. I walked into my family's farmhouse ready to chow down on some spicy good food.

As soon as I reached the living room, I noticed the difference. Growing up, my aunt had been a fanatic about having pictures that documented everything Ty had ever done in his life. Some pictures were there, but all of the ones of he and Savanna were gone. I'm not talkin' like small pictures, it was more like the eight by tens were missing from the wall, and you could see the spot that had been removed, because nothing replaced them.

My mouth dropped.

My aunt came into the room and cleared her throat when she realized what I had noticed. "I couldn't stand looking at her every day. It's bad enough I can't get her away from that damn hospital. It's a little too late to show him how much she cares, if you ask me."

I had never wanted to hurt my aunt, but at that very moment, was the first time in my life where I could have hurt a woman. How could she be so bitter? They both loved Ty. It didn't have to be this way.

"I don't really get it. I saw her at the hospital the other day. She seems to really love him," I said defensively.

"Colt, I really don't want to talk about that girl in my house anymore. Get on in that kitchen and wash your hands for supper boy."

Just like that, she ended the conversation. Once my uncle came in, we talked about the upcoming summer and what my job duties would entail. They didn't talk much about Ty, and I was actually okay with that, although my mind was elsewhere the entire time.

I was pretty thankful when supper ended abruptly with some game show that both of them watched every weeknight. I said my goodbyes and Sam and I left the farmhouse. I checked on the horses before heading into the carriage house. It seemed lonely without Savanna there, but the last thing I wanted to do was seem clingy, so I refused to call her.

After flipping through the television channels and playing fetch with Sam, I ran out of things to occupy myself. I couldn't explain the sense of loneliness that had overcome me. Even when my ex lived with me, I never felt like I had missed her when she wasn't around. Savanna was haunting my thoughts and I didn't know whether it excited me or scared the pants off of me.

Our friendship was more than we were both admitting and jumping in as fast as we both had, had thrown us into a place neither of us knew what to do with.

When I finally couldn't take it anymore, I went into the bedroom and called my dog up on the bed. She seemed like the only constant in my life. I was lonely, hell at home I could have called several young ladies to keep me company, not that I ever did. I was the kind of guy that preferred to be alone. Nobody had ever been that interesting to me. I never had a relationship where a woman was my friend.

Savanna was my friend, but she was so much more. The idea of knowing that was the scariest of them all. If I had any hopes of my cousin waking up, then I needed to figure out what the hell I was doing with his girlfriend.

The problem was that for the past few days, she was all I could think about.

Chapter 14

Savanna

The next few days' worth of finals seemed like they took forever. All I could think about was how little I had heard from Colt. I held my phone up in my hands several times a day just wanting to send him a text or give him a call. However, I didn't want to seem needy. It killed me to not talk to him, in fact.

In all the months and even years I had been with Ty, I had never once considered I would have any interest in someone else. I adored Ty and everything about our past, but Colt made me see that I could smile again. He made me look forward to my days and I feared that I could easily fall for someone like him.

Since I had just finished my last final, my summer was officially starting. I headed over to the hospital to sit with Ty for a bit, before making the drive back to town. I had been worried about summer break for months, knowing that I wouldn't be close to the hospital if I was staying home at my parents. I considered staying here in town with someone, but really couldn't afford to do something like that. After spending time with Colt this past weekend and taking a bunch of things into consideration, I decided that I would still make the drive twice a week.

My car was packed up with my clothes and important things from my dorm room. I didn't bring anything that I didn't need, since I would be returning in a couple months anyway.

I was greeted by several familiar nurses when I made it to Ty's room. Once I was inside, I stood over his hospital bed and looked down at him. His face was thinner, but he still was handsome. I admired his long eyelashes and reached up to touch his face. The stubble on his face was something that took me a while to get used to. His momma insisted on shaving him herself on the weekends. Since we weren't on speaking terms, I never argued with her about it.

I just didn't see how Ty would care if his facial hair grew.

I ran my fingers over his lips and found myself leaning over to kiss him. I could feel the hot tears running down my cheeks. "I miss you," I whispered as I pulled away.

I grabbed a chair and pulled it as close to the bed as I could get it. Even though he was hooked up to all kinds of equipment, I leaned my head on his chest, just sitting there stroking his hair. It didn't matter how many times I had come in this room, it still hurt just the same as seeing him in here for the first time.

I don't know how long I had been lying there on Ty's chest. When I woke up I heard someone across from me clearing their throat. When I looked up, I saw Colt standing there. His John Deere hat was in his hands and he gave me a nod.

He put his head down, looking to his hat when he first spoke. "I reckoned I'd find you here."

"I just wanted to come here before driving home this afternoon. I won't be able to make the drive everyday this summer. It's too much on my little car," I admitted.

Colt walked over to the opposite side of the bed and looked down at his cousin. "I was just stopping by. We needed some parts for the tractor and I figured since I was in town I would say hello."

I gave him a quick smile. It was weird for me to be here with both of them. I felt very guilty looking up at Colt as Ty lay here not knowing what we had done behind his back. It really had nothing to do with Ty, but my guilty conscience made me feel horrible about it anyway.

"Did you already pick up the part?" I asked trying to change the subject.

He winked at me, sending butterflies through my body. "Yeah, you hungry Darlin'?

"Actually, I am," I confessed.

He started heading toward the door. "How's about I give you some time alone with my cousin. When you are finished, I will meet you at your car."

"Sounds perfect," I said as I watched Colt leaving the room.

Me being here with Ty didn't seem to bother Colt and I appreciated that a bunch, considering everyone else thought I was obsessed. I just couldn't let go of hope that someday he would wake up. Colt kept telling me that I wasn't responsible, but indirectly I knew I was.

I leaned over to kiss him one more time before heading out. My lips pressed hard against his forehead and although it felt warm, there was no reaction from him.

I found Colt waiting for me outside at my car, exactly where he said he would be. He was leaning on the hood looking down at his phone. I snuck up behind him and yelled "HEY". He jumped about a foot in the air before turning around and trying to chase me. Once I sat down in the driver's side, he gave up and climbed in next to me.

"You okay Savanna?" He asked.

It still made me smile hearing him call me that. Unless I was in class or in some kind of trouble from the parents, I never heard someone use my first name. My mother was into nicknames when I was little and from as young as I could remember, she called me Van. My grandmother hated it and always called me Savanna, but everyone else stuck with the nickname. Even my teachers in elementary school called me Van. When I graduated, I almost didn't respond to my full name being called over the intercom. My friend behind me nudged me in the back to get me moving.

I turned to look at Colt. He was so handsome. His chiseled cheeks and five o'clock shadow made him even sexier. I couldn't help but immediately think about how his whiskers had tickled when he touched me. "I'm fine. Are you okay?" I teased.

"I gotta admit somethin' to you. I was hopin' you would be here today. I kinda missed talkin' to you."

I blushed and looked down at the steering wheel. "Why didn't you just call? I wanted to call you, but I figured you would call me."

Colt started to laugh and shake his head.

"What?" I asked.

"I guess if I hadn't stopped by here today, we would have both been waitin' for each other to call."

I gave him a half smile. "You are probably right."

He lifted his hand and ran the back of it across my cheek. "Would you be mad if I wanted you to follow me back to town?"

I was confused. " Don't you want to eat?"

"Well sure, but I would rather have both vehicles home so we can spend more time together tonight."

Relief washed over me. "I thought you just didn't want to hang out."

"Savanna, I came to the hospital in hopes of just seein' you. Why would I not want to hang out later?" He asked.

"Chalk it up to a stupid moment for me. So, shall I follow you?" I asked trying to change the subject of being a worrywart.

"Sounds good. See you soon," he said as he climbed out of the car.

I felt kind of sad with his dry exit, almost like being with me was a burden. He didn't even look back at my car as he climbed into his truck. I knew because I watched him in my rearview mirror.

Colt

I should have just leaned over and kissed her, but after she had just spent time up in that room with my cousin, I didn't know how she would react, and it just didn't seem right. I wanted her to enjoy my company, not feel like I was trying to replace him.

Maybe I shouldn't have even stopped in the hospital today for that reason. Me and Tyler needed to be separate parts of Savanna's life. I had no idea what was happening between us, but I was sure she wasn't going to give up on him.

I knew that whatever was going on with us was probably a summer fling. We were friends, enjoying each other's company. The problem with that was that I wasn't sure why I thought about her so much. Perhaps it was because I had been so bored the past couple of days. Without having things to do at the farm, I found myself going crazy. The idea of Savanna coming home to her parents meant we could hang out more. I knew I would have to work during the day, but we would be able to spend time together every night she wanted to. It wasn't like there was anyone else to hang out with in this town. The people had made it clear how they felt about Savanna. I wasn't about to hang out with the likes of them.

When we pulled up to the old barn, Savanna immediately jumped out of her car. She came rushing over to the truck and placed her hands on her hips. I slid out of the truck seat slowly wondering what in the world was going on.

"You alright?" I asked.

"Did I do something wrong to you Colt?"

"Of course not Darlin'. What would ever give you that idea?" I replied.

Her hands came down off of her hips and she lowered her head to look down at the ground. "You just seemed different than when I last saw you, that's all." She shook her head. "Never mind!"

I didn't walk toward her. Instead, I held up my pointer finger and signaled for her to move forward. "Come here."

She looked at me funny, but started to move toward me anyway. I grabbed her by the waist of her shorts and pulled her into my chest. Our mouths were less than an inch apart, and I held her gaze. "Well, I wanted to do this earlier, but I didn't want to make ya mad," I confessed as I brushed my lips against hers.

Savanna didn't let me take my time, instead she pressed her lips against mine. When she pulled away she took her time opening her eyes. "I waited days for that."

I held my arms around her waist loosely. She looked up into my eyes and gave me an ornery look. "Sorry that I made you wait. Just trying my best to go slow."

Savanna sighed, but didn't say anything. She reached her arms around me and laid her head on my chest. I couldn't help but kiss the top of her head as we continued to hold each other. I was glad I was still leaning up against my truck, because it made holding her like this weightless.

Finally after a few minutes of silence, I whispered into her hair. "You sure you are alright Darlin?"

I felt her shake her head. "I guess I just still can't believe that something is happening between us. I mean, I know we aren't labeling things, but there is something. I guess I am just wondering why being with you feels so good. Shouldn't I feel awful about what I am doing?"

Her question was kind of loaded. I considered what the right reply would be. I didn't want to come off as selfish, or like I was getting a kick out of stealing my cousin's girl, but in some ways that was exactly how everyone would see it.

"Savanna, you and I are adults. We aren't strangers. I put you into a bad situation and when I did my best to take care of you, something happened between us. It wasn't premeditated, so I find it hard to feel awful, especially when being with you feels so damn good. I've thought about how hard it must be for you. That's why I didn't pull you into my arms at that hospital. I need you to tell me what you want, because I will not overstep my welcome or ask you to choose. I already know your choice and I am alright just being your friend."

"What happens if we can't just be friends Colt?" Savanna asked while pulling away from me. She looked directly into my eyes.

I hated being cornered with questions about my future. I had lived every second of my adult life for myself. Even my ex would agree to that. "Do you want me to promise you that I won't want anything else from you? I really don't want to get into the technicality of whatever this is going on with us. Why can't we just enjoy each other while I am here? When the summer is over I am going back home, and you will be back to school here. Let's just have a great couple of months. What do you say?"

I couldn't tell whether my words put her at ease or made her frustrated. At any rate, she shrugged her shoulders and pressed her lips on mine. "Okay Colt."

I needed to change the subject. "You ready to eat?"

"I'm starving actually," she admitted.

I reached down and smacked her on the ass. "How about you get that fine ass of yours in the car, so we can go eat then."

I followed Savanna over to her car and climbed into the passenger seat. She started her car and looked over to me. "Ever had a buffalo chicken pizza?" She asked.

"Heck yeah, it's great. Why you askin'?" I wondered.

"I know just the place to eat," was all she said.

Savanna ended up taking us to a pizza joint in this new strip mall near her house. Her parents lived in a small community inside of the town itself. My family's farm was about two miles outside of town. She was used to having things she needed within walking distance, whereas my family enjoyed the idea of being far away from the congestion of a town, small at that.

Savanna had been right. The pizza was great, but being in the company of a pretty lady was the highlight of my evening. After dinner we went back out to the old barn and lay up in the hayloft. I opened the top hayloft doors so we could watch the sunset.

When Savanna cuddled her body into mine, I knew she was okay with being here with me. It was hard taking her to places that I figured she and Ty had gone to be alone. I was pretty sure every teen in town had come here to have sex at some point. I wasn't even from around here and knew that.

Chapter 15

Savanna

I never thought I was one to label things, but I guess I had just never been in the situation to have to do it. All I knew was that being around Colt awakened something inside of me that I had kept bottled up for months. Enjoying his company was an understatement and if he didn't want to label things I was okay with it.

After having pizza, I half expected Colt to part ways with me, but his warm invitation to the carriage house was surprising.

Of course I accepted his offer.

We still had to do the switcharoo with my car and his truck, but instead of leaving my car at the barn, we dropped it off at my house. It was nice because I was able to grab a bunch of things I hadn't had the last time I stayed, including clean underwear. My mother questioned me a million times about where I was going when she spotted an old truck that resembled Ty's fathers. I was worried she was going to run out to the road and see who was driving. Thankfully, she didn't and finally gave in to my story that Brina's new boyfriend drove a truck similar and he was taking us both back to her house. Her say didn't exactly matter much anyway, since I was nineteen.

My mother had no inclination about me wanting to spend the night with another guy, in fact I think if I would have told her the truth she never would have believed me. She always said my love for Ty was more of an obsession. It wasn't like I stalked him, but he was what I had based my life around for the past five years.

Even though I continued to think about Ty while I was spending time with his cousin, Colt didn't seem to mind. He always mentioned Ty, which I found so thoughtful.

When we finally got back to the carriage house, it was dark. The way Colt parked the truck made it easy for me to walk right in without having to duck behind things. I hated the sneaking part, but it beat having to explain why I was spending the night with their nephew.

Sam greeted us at the door and then made her way out to do her business. Once she was out the door, Colt grabbed my bag and tossed it on the floor. He took both of my hands in his and pulled me into the kitchen. Just hearing him clear his voice was so sexy to me. I found my eyes wandering to his perfect lips, but I didn't have to wonder when the next kiss would come. I watched as he drug his tongue over his lips right before placing them on mine. They were wet and slid easily from my top lip to the bottom. I tried to keep my eyes open, but one kiss from Colt was like being under a magic spell.

His kisses sent tingles down every inch of my body. He held my hands at my sides, but eventually I was able to free them and slide them under his loose t-shirt. I loved how smooth his skin felt and how he had two dimples on the lower part of his back. I slid my fingers over them just as I felt our tongues touching for the first time. Immediately, I could feel the heat conjuring between my legs. It was unbelievable to me that just a kiss from Colt could do this to me. I accidentally let out a small moan and felt Colt's lips stretching in a smile against my mouth.

When he realized that I knew, he pulled away and looked at me.

"Your laughing at me?" I asked embarrassed.

"I actually found it to be cute," he confessed.

Colt brought his fingers up and brushed them over my lips. I grabbed the neck of his shirt and pulled him toward the couch. "You have me all worked up already," I spat out.

"Do I now? Well don't expect me to apologize," Colt said sarcastically while slowly running his hands up the back of my shirt.

The stubbles on his face rubbed against my neck, tickling me, before I felt gentle kisses following. Naturally, my head fell back to give him more room to explore. I wanted to feel him kissing every inch of my neck. My hand started from Colt's perfect ass to the waist of his pants. I couldn't help but reach down his pants and feel the smooth skin beneath his boxers. Colt was the most well endowed lover I had ever been with, well considering I had only been with two, I guess it didn't mean very much.

He pulled away from me, but not far enough that my hand was removed. "You tryin' to seduce me beautiful?"

"If you keep calling me beautiful, I just might," I admitted.

His large hands ran up underneath of my shirt and slowly pulled it over my head. I hated that he'd moved my hand, but I knew it was temporary. I couldn't help but mimic him, by grabbing his shirt and pulling it off. Once his shirt was quickly thrown somewhere on the floor, I ran my hands over his cut chest.

When I reached both of his shoulders, I ran my fingertips slowly down his arms. We were sitting on the couch facing each other, but I had actually sat myself up on my knees. Colts hands grabbed me on my backside and I felt him squeeze my cheeks as he pulled me in closer against his body. Colt brought his head down and removed my bra strap with his hand before pressing soft kisses on my shoulder. I shuddered as I felt his lips touching my skin. When he brought his head up, I pushed him back against the couch, so that I could climb into his lap, instead of kneeling. With my body on top of him, he immediately reached behind my back running his hands up and down just before I felt the support of my bra disappearing. He grabbed it in the front and bit down on his lip as he pulled the bra away exposing my breast, inches from his face.

Colts hands cupped both of my breasts as his tongue entered my mouth again. With every stroke of his soft tongue, I could feel the tension building between my legs. My hands automatically responded to his kisses by reaching for the button to his shorts. Once I had them loosened enough, I reached my hand down and massaged him until he finally let out a groan. He pulled away from my lips, and I reached for one more kiss before I would let him speak.

"Stand up," he ordered.

"Why? What did I do wrong?" I asked in a worried tone.

"Shut up woman!" He said as he picked me up and pulled my legs up to wrap around his waist. "I am taking you to bed."

I didn't say anything, before his lips found mine again. He must have had his eyes closed, because we bumped into two walls before eventually making it into the bedroom. Colt released me on the bed, while he basically walked out of his shorts that had fallen around his ankles. With only a pair of boxers on, he climbed on the bed beside me.

My breathing became heavier when he ran his hands slowly from the base of my neck, in between my breasts, then finally to my navel. He circled around my belly button with one finger while he looked up at my face. I knew he could tell I wanted him. I couldn't remember a time in my life where I had wanted Ty the way Colt made me want him. Maybe it was the fact that we were doing something wrong, and I had never been the kind of person to break the rules. Whatever the reason, Colt's soft lips were like chocolate, and his hands were heaven. His eyes could melt me, while the other parts of him made me wish I never had to leave his bed.

I felt his face kissing me below my belly button. I licked my lips when his hands found the elastic part of my shorts. As the fabric began moving downward, I felt soft kisses on each of my hips. After removing everything, he ran his chin roughly over the smooth skin between my legs. As good as it felt, all I could think about was how happy I was that I had shaved this morning. Colt sat up, leaning on one of his arms. He made me feel uncomfortable when he just stared at my naked body, while dragging two fingers around each of my hips and in between. His fingers slid deep between my legs and when they entered me, I let out a soft moan. He cleared his throat as he focused on my face, while his fingers worked me on the inside.

"Do you want me to stop?" He asked while still moving his fingers slowly in and out of me.

"No, please don't stop Colt. It feels so good. Just please ......don't stop." I moaned.

I tried to sit up to watch him, but at the same time he started stroking the sensitive part with his thumb.

My body jolted up off the bed as I let out an uncontrolled cry and then collapsed on the bed, breathing hard, but still wanting more.

Colt climbed up until his face was even with mine and he kissed me full on the lips. As he pulled away he let the saliva from our tongues act as a friction as he drug his lips over mine. "I want you Savanna, but I won't take things any further unless you tell me to."

"Yes, oh God Colt...I want you so bad. Please.....please fuck me," I begged. I could not believe that it came out of my mouth. Ty used to ask me to say it all the time, but I felt ashamed.

I could tell from the look on his face, that he liked me using that word. I felt dirty, but he obviously loved it. Within seconds he had removed his boxers and was already biting into a condom wrapper. He positioned his body over mine, but held most of his weight with one of his arms. I gasped when I felt his hard shaft pressing over my own readiness. He was slow and gentle with his first movements, but after my body relaxed, I found myself pulling on his ass, so that he could thrust harder. He filled me with heat and the harder he gave it, the more I enjoyed it. I dug my nails into his back when I started to feel him finish inside of me, the idea of it turning me on so much that it started happening to me as well. With only a few more thrusts, he collapsed over top of me, breathing heavy into my hair.

Colt and I lay there naked for hours talking. I laughed so hard that I couldn't breathe at some of his stories. His sense of humor was contagious, and I found myself hanging onto his every word. There were even some moments where he would grab my hand and just passionately kiss the back of it again and again, while his green eyes were locked on mine.

I found it so comforting that he didn't hold back with me. If I asked him anything about his past, he would tell me. He wasn't one of those secretive guys I had always assumed he was. Instead, he was just living life enjoying himself whenever he could.

Colt told me about his girlfriend from college. He caught her with his best friend who was also his roommate. There was no need for him to explain how awful that was, just knowing Ty had slept with someone else, even if we were broken up, was hard enough. I couldn't imagine it happening while we were together. In fact something like that would just be unforgivable to me.

It was probably around midnight when we heard the front door opening. I looked over to Colt with giant eyes of concern. He sat up and threw the sheets over my naked body.

"Who's there?" He called.

"It's just me Colt. Sam was scratching at our door," I heard his aunt saying from the other room. He jumped up and wrapped a blanket around his waist, but before he could make it out of the bedroom, she was already noticing things out of place in the living room. "Do you have company dear?"

Colt whispered the word "shit", before walking out of the bedroom. "Actually, yes, I do. Ran into an old friend today. Sorry I didn't ask your permission."

I was lying in that bed shaking like a little scared kid. If she walked into the room and saw me, my life was over, for more reasons than just the obvious.

"Colt, you don't have to ask permission. You are twenty five years old. Sorry I interrupted. Have yourself a good evening," his aunt said before I heard the door closing.

Colt walked to the bedroom door and leaned against it. I had to admit, that although I was still shaking, he looked sexy as hell standing there with only a blanket hanging off his hips. "You want something to drink Darlin'?" He asked nonchalantly.

I shook my head, but remained quiet as I watched him exit the doorway.

Chapter 16

Colt

Leave it to my damn aunt to scare the willies out of Savanna. When I walked back toward the bedroom, her face looked like she had seen a ghost. For the life of me I couldn't figure out how in the hell I had gotten myself into this mess in the first place. I knew one thing though, I wasn't regretting one second of it. Savanna was an amazing person and I would be a fool to not want to spend every free moment with someone like her.

I walked into the kitchen and took my time getting something to drink. When I had emptied the glass, I refilled it for Savanna. Before making my way to the bedroom, I managed to lock the front door, something I needed to get into the habit of doing from now on. Although, as of right now, I wasn't sure Savanna would ever want to take the chance and be with me like this again. For all I knew, she was getting dressed and preparing to go home instead of staying the night.

I thought about letting the blanket drop and just delivering her a drink in only my birthday suit, but after seeing her shocked face, I didn't think she was in a mood for jokes. With one hand holding the blanket tight and the other holding the fresh glass of sweet tea, I walked back into the bedroom.

Savanna was sitting up in the bed. Fresh tears covered her eyes and she was holding the sheet up to her chin, covering every inch of her skin from my view. I set the tea on the table bedside the bed and knelt there next to where she sat. "Darlin' are you alright?"

She nodded her head, but at the same time I watched her scrunch her face up and start crying. I climbed up on the bed next to her and pulled her into my arms, tryin' real hard to keep the blanket from falling off my waist as I did it.

Savanna buried her wet face into my chest and cried her hardest. I stroked her hair and kissed the top of her head. There was nothin' that I could really say to her. We were in this situation, that neither of us planned, but both of us had to live with the guilt of it. I kept callin' Savanna my friend, and she was very much that, but with every moment I spent with her, I couldn't help but wonder if she could ever be more than that.

When it was obvious that she was gonna cry until she had no tears left, I repositioned myself to lay back on a pillow, while she was sprawled out still clinging tight to my chest. I stroked her hair until I heard the last sniffle sound coming from her nose and then I let myself finally fall asleep.

The next morning Savanna was still asleep on my chest. I half expected her to have gotten up and slept on the couch, as upset as she was. Part of me felt like I had gotten her into this awful situation and felt like she could never forgive me for it. Once she finally started to stir she looked up at me.

"Hi," she whispered.

"How you doin' Darlin'?" I asked.

I felt her arms move as she shrugged, but noticed that she never unwrapped them from around my body. Her face came close to my chest and I felt her soft lips pucker up against me. "I am so sorry I got upset last night. It wasn't your fault." She brought her hands up and propped up her head with them. Even with her elbows kind of grinding into me, I said nothing. "I chose to sleep with you, I mean, I wanted to sleep with you Colt. Maybe the alcohol helped make that decision at first, but obviously I enjoyed it. Just like I enjoyed it last night."

She turned over on her back and covered her face with her hands. "I don't think I will ever be able to let go of Ty completely, but I can't just linger around waiting for something that may never happen. He may never wake up and I know that. I'm so sick of crying and feeling like my life is over. The past week has been so eye opening for me. Spending time with you makes me happy. It's just when your aunt walked in last night, it was like I actually was doing what she accused me of doing months ago. It hit me right in the gut. Technically, I am not cheating on her son, but you have to understand that sometimes it sure feels like I am. I mean, I haven't been with anyone else besides you and Ty."

She started to talk again, but began to well up. If I were a stranger she wouldn't be feeling this way. I knew it was hard, but we were adults. We enjoyed being together, and at the moment, there wasn't much else to do.

"You don't have to explain Savanna. I kinda figured that you hadn't been with anyone else. I don't know if it means anything comin' from me, but you are not cheatin' on him. I have said this before. If you want to stop hangin' out, or just keep things plutonic, I am totally fine with that," I replied.

"That's just it. I don't want to stop seeing you. You are all I have thought about since you came back to town." Her head fell down on my chest and her hand ran up and down it. "I don't want to hurt anymore and I don't hurt when I am with you, in fact I feel the opposite," she confessed.

"You don't have to hide how you're feelin' from me. I'm a big boy. If you ask my opinion, I would say you are just tryin' to get through the hardest part of your life. If being with me makes you feel better, then I am not complainin'. If you need to cry, then let it out. Hell, I wouldn't expect anything less." I kissed the top of her head again. "Just so you know, I thought about you a bunch this week as well. Now how about we drop all this serious talk and get our suits on. It's supposed to get hot as heck today and I plan on spending my time in the swimmin' hole with a pretty lady at my side, if she will accompany me of course."

"I'm sorry I keep doing this," she confessed.

"You have been with the same person for the last five years. You do not have to apologize for being confused. I completely understand," I added before kissing her head and sliding myself off the bed. "Now how about that date?"

She sat up and looked at me. Her eyes gazing below my waist. I cocked a smile when I noticed and finally caught her attention. "How about we have breakfast?" She inquired.

Just to mess with her head, I put my hands on my hips. "What are you hungry for?" I teased.

She bit her lip, but did not stop staring at my naked body. The sheet had fallen down over her breasts and I couldn't help looking myself. Savanna got up and sat on the bed in front of me. Her hands grabbed around my ass and pulled me close so that her face was even with my stomach. She kissed it gently. "I can't get enough of you. I don't know what you did to me, but I feel like I am under a spell."

Her lips drug over my belly button, while her hands slid down my hips. I could feel my erection beginning with just her being where she was. "Sorry Darlin', these hands don't perform magic."

"I beg to differ. Your smell is tantalizing. I lust for your strong hands to touch me." She grabbed my hand and kissed the palm of it. "You are the most handsome man I have ever laid eyes on." She kissed the edge of my hip bone. "When we touch, it's electrifying, but when you are inside of me, I forget about all of the pain in my life. I love how you can make me forget."

I pulled her up to a standing position. "You don't have to forget Savanna, but I am glad I can make you feel better. I do aim to please, you know."

I reached down and kissed her softly on the lips. She didn't know how sexy she was with that gorgeous bed head and since I already had a semi erection from her touching me, I pulled away. "Let's get you some food so we can enjoy our day," I suggested.

I had enough of the serious talk for the day, but I knew it wouldn't be the last. I got that she needed it and I wouldn't deny her answers, but the fact was that I was the last person to give her advice about relationships. I couldn't deny my attraction to her or the fact that I cared about the girl, but I couldn't let myself become attached to her. I knew I was only here temporary, so taking our relationship to a new level just wasn't feasible. There was no denying that if things were different, I could see myself wanting more.

After grabbing some swimming trunks, I headed into the kitchen and started making us egg sandwiches. Savanna came out in a pair of shorts and a bikini top. The top was yellow and blue, and I could only assume that the bottoms matched. She had her hair up in a ponytail and a pair of flip flops on her feet.

When she saw me looking at her body she smiled and leaned against the counter. "See anything you like?"

"Darlin' there isn't anything about you that I don't like." Well there was one thing, but having her without baggage was impossible and it wasn't something I was willing to discuss.

"Keep talking and breakfast might have to wait," she joked.

I leaned over the opposite side of the counter and was about six inches from her face. "Don't threaten me with that body of yours. There are just some things that no man can resist."

In her sexiest voice. "Are you saying that you can't resist me?"

I waited a moment, tracing her face with my eyes. She was glaring at me, waiting for me to respond. I licked my lips when she bit down on her own. "I reckon' I am."

Savanna pulled herself up onto the counter so that she broke the distance between us. I pulled her towards me so that her legs hung down beside either side of my legs. Her arms wrapped around my neck as she brought her head in to lean against mine. "What happens when I can't resist you either?" She said as her lips were so close they were brushing against mine with every word.

"I think we already know the answer to that," I said before taking her bottom lip into my mouth and biting it gently.

When I let go of her bottom lip, she ran her tongue over mine. "Before dating your cousin, I used to imagine what it would be like to kiss you. I always pictured it would be amazing." She confessed.

I was shocked by her admission, so I pulled back and looked at her. "Seriously? Why me? I mean there were a dozen other guys here in town you could have pictured."

She shrugged. "I don't know. I guess it was because you were the guy who only showed up in the summertime. You were mysterious and gorgeous and every girl had you in their sights."

She was burying herself more and more, but I loved it. I backed up and leaned against the fridge, putting my hands on my hips. "So you had me in your sights?"

She tossed a grape at me. "Are you making fun of me, Colt Mitchell?"

I held my hands up, as if I were surrendering to the police. "Not at all Darlin'. I was actually flattered that you had eyes for me back then."

She put her head down and shook her head. "It isn't really a big deal. I mean, not only were you way too old, but I looked like a little boy."

I walked over to her and lifted her chin up with my hand. When our eyes met, I could tell she was embarrassed. Her cheeks were bright red. "None of that matters Savanna. There is nothing boyish about you. I may have done and said mean things to you when we were kids, but I am real sorry about that. Look, I don't have many friends. I mean, I have friends from college, but most of them moved away and started lives. I keep myself held up in that cabin when I'm not workin'. I guess I am telling you this so you know that you really are a good friend and I hope we can stay this way. I feel like I can tell you anything. You just never judge me and I appreciate that."

The color in her face returned to normal. "Thank you for saying that. Through everything I have had Brina, but she pushes me to do things every time we talk. I'm just not ready to go out. Being here with you, I feel safe, but mostly I don't feel like you are judging me. Even if we weren't having sex, I would still want to be here with you, hanging out and doing normal things. I missed my life and just being me. Every second with you lets me have that again."

I pulled her into a hug. "I hate that people have pinned all of this on you like my cousin was some angel. They all know how much he had to drink that night and how awful he treated you sometimes. They all just need to get their heads out of their asses and they would see that. As long as I am here, you have a place to stay. Besides, I kinda like how you look when you wake up in the morning. You know, your hair is all everywhere, and you have this look on your face like you have no idea where you are. It's real cute."

We both laughed.

"When we get back I am going to get those stitches out. I don't want the skin growin' over them." Her black eye had disappeared a couple days ago, and the small white stitches were not even noticeable unless you looked close enough.

"You changed the subject," she whined.

I grabbed her hand and pulled her forward. "Will you just come on? Let's get movin' so we can enjoy the whole day," I suggested while getting the food together.

Savanna and I got our butts into gear and got ready for a day at the swimming hole in no time flat. We packed us up a nice lunch and prepared for a relaxing day. Plus, I personally could not wait to spend the day next to her in that little bikini.

Chapter 17

Savanna

Being that it was a Friday, we had to sneak out of the carriage house and avoid taking the horses, in fear that Ty's parents would see us. It wasn't like we were really doing anything wrong going to a place that many kids went during the summer, but with Ty being in the hospital, there weren't many people coming to swim. Colt got this brilliant idea that he was going to go talk to his aunt and uncle while I ran as fast as I could to the path and waited for him. Once he went inside the main house, I started running. I never turned back to even look if anyone was behind me. The idea of having to explain how I had got here without a car was bad enough.

With the picnic basket in my hand, I waited for Colt. He seemed to be taking forever, but Sam was there sitting at my side keeping me company. Finally after a good fifteen minutes I spotted him through the paths opening in the woods. He had a big ole smile on his face.

"Sorry I took so long."

"I was thinking you weren't coming."

He took off his hat and scratched his head. "Well my aunt was drilling me something fierce about who stayed over last night. She wouldn't let it go."

"Do you think she suspects it's me?" I asked worried.

"I told her I picked up a girl in town and she got a ride home late last night. She gave me a lecture on easy women." He started laughing.

"Am I easy?"

Colt walked over and grabbed the cooler and bag with our blanket and towels out of my hand. He leaned over and kissed my head. "Darlin' there aint nothin' easy about you."

What was that supposed to mean?

"I don't like the sound of that," I admitted.

He started walking ahead of me and never looked back. "Will you just stop worrying about everything for one day. Live a little Savanna."

I sighed and followed behind him. He was right. I kept over-thinking everything.

It was summer and I was determined to let myself have a good time.

Colt didn't waste any time setting up our stuff before kicking off his shoes and jumping off the small pier. I watched him pop out of the water and throw his wet hair back away from dripping in his face. "You coming in or what?" He yelled.

The sun was hot enough, but the walk through the woods made us sweat more. I didn't even care if the water was freezing. Without answering, I let my shorts drop and threw them on top of our bag with my foot. I ran over toward the pier and looked around noticing Colt was missing. He was such a prankster and I remembered the last time we came here, we ended up covered in mud. I looked all around the water, but didn't see him. I figured that he had to be hiding under the floating dock in the center.

Without hesitation I dove into the dark water. Even with your eyes open, swimming under water was hard to see, plus I never really wanted to know what was in the water with us. In the past we had caught some real keepers in this pond. The snapping turtles had to be huge, not to mention the damn snakes. I came up above the water and started swimming toward the dock. When I came up underneath I didn't see him at first, but after looking through the sides I saw he was trying to hide on the outside. When he caught me catching him he started laughing and went under the water again.

I wanted to swim away, but by the time I got the inclination to do so, he was already grabbing me and coming up right in front of me. "It's about time you caught up," he joked.

Colt and I were completely hidden from anyone and everything being under the dock. It was about twenty foot long in each direction, so it was a great hiding spot.

"This was my favorite spot when I was a kid," Colt confessed.

His one arm was holding part of the dock, while his other was wrapped around my waist. "I bet you brought a bunch of girls here," I asked because Ty had told me all about it.

"Where do you hear these stories?" He asked.

I pushed him away. "You say you tell me everything, but you are going to deny that you had a slew of girls here every summer."

"Savanna, I never hooked up with anyone out here. Seriously, who told you that?" He asked again.

"Ty did. You going to deny it now?"

"Yes, actually I am. I swear to you Darlin' I never hooked up with any girls out here. He must have been talkin' about some other guy cause it sure as hell wasn't me. As much as I would have loved to have a summer fling when I was younger, I had a girlfriend. In fact I had the same girlfriend from the age of fifteen to seventeen. I never cheated on her. Not even during the summers here."

It didn't make any sense. Ty idolized his cousin for being a womanizer, but Colt seemed to genuinely be offended that I thought those things about him. "I don't get why he would lie."

Colt smirked and shook his head but he said nothing.

"What?" I asked.

"Nothin'. Can we just enjoy our day?" He asked while trying to get me to shut up.

I grabbed the front of his trunks and pulled him to float over until he was touching me. "I believe you, but it's a shame," I said right before kissing him.

He was still holding on to the dock so I let go and wrapped my legs around his waist. I ran my hand through his wet hair and made it stick up in all directions. He could be a total mess and still be perfect looking. I ran my nose over his cheek and felt the stubble against my skin. It reminded me that Colt was a man now, a strong hard working man with a kind heart. Any woman would be so lucky to have him.

"What's a shame?" He asked while breaking my fantasizing about him.

I bit his ear and pulled away as my tongue slid against it. "That you never got to experience what it feels like to have sex out on this dock, where anyone could walk up and see," I whispered.

"Maybe I was waitin' for the right girl to experience it with," he said as he teased my lips with his.

He pushed me back, but kept my legs hooked around him, so that he could run his wet hands under the water over my breasts. When his fingers reached my bikini, they slid under it easily and the top lifted right over my breasts. Once he had both of my breast out, he stroked each of them, playing with my nipples and pinching them until they were hard. I bit my lip as I watched him concentrating on each breast. I used my legs to rock my body against him more. His hand grabbed the small of my back and pulled me toward his face.

I found his lips and immediately located his long tongue. While our tongues stroked against each other, our kisses intensified. I couldn't get enough of his mouth. I teased it with my tongue and he teased me back. Even as we floated in the water, I felt hot between my legs. I had this burning desire for Colt every time the man touched me. I couldn't help myself, even if I tried to fight it, I knew it wouldn't go away until I had him.

My hand grabbed the string to his trunks and I pulled them until they loosened. His mouth found my neck and I turned it to give him more access. My hand slid with ease down his shorts and I soon found just what I had been looking for. His hard erection filled my hand and I began stroking it. With only one hand available, Colt pulled away from kissing my neck. His breath was on my ear. "Let's get out of the water. I need to touch you."

"Oh yes." Was all I could get out before he pressed his mouth over mine one more time. I didn't want to let go of his hardness, but it was required for me to climb onto the dock. Colt pushed me underwater and followed as we both found the ladder. I climbed out first, not even caring about my breasts being out of my top. Once off the ladder, it only took a second for him to come behind me and pull me down on the wooden dock. It felt hot against my back, but I didn't care. Colt started to kiss me and sat up abruptly. "I will be right back. Do not move!" He ordered as he dove into the water with no explanation.

I turned over and watched him swim to the shore. He grabbed something from the bag and jumped back in the water. Once he got to the dock I realized he had two towels in his hand. Of course they were soaking wet, so I shook my head.

"Stand up!" He said.

He took the towels and spread them out over the old dock. "I don't want you to get splinters," he said as he got on his knees and waited for me to join him.

"That was really nice. Thank you," I said as I kissed him.

I needed to add more to his already huge list of perfections.

Colt ran his wet hands slowly down my abdomen. My breathing was heavy and I couldn't control it. His touch tickled me and I felt goose bumps forming all over my body. My nipples were like little rocks and I knew he noticed. His mouth found one of them and I watched as his tongue stroked it. It moved so fast back and forth over it that the sensations were driving me wild. "Oh.....it feels ....so ...good," I managed to get out before he took the next one into his mouth and sucked hard.

He reached behind my back and untied my suit, tossing it beside us. When he sat up and let go of my nipple, a gust of breeze hit it and I gasped. I wanted him so bad. I reached down and grabbed the waist of his pants. When his body was close enough I reached my hand back down his pants. My dry hand stroking his semi wet shaft caused an undeniably different kind of friction. I watched him close his eyes and I knew he was enjoying it. I bit my lip and stroked harder. "I want you," I cried.

Colt opened his eyes and started pulling off his trunks. I pulled him so that he was sitting down, while I slid down between his legs. I just wanted to touch him, to taste him.

"Savanna, you don't have to.....oh God!" He said as I bobbed my head up and down his hard shaft. I was not very experienced with this, but seeing Colt naked made my mouth literally water. I wanted to satisfy him in every way possible. His hands ran through my hair as I sucked and kissed every inch of his hardness. As my cheeks started to burn, I began to wonder if I could continue much longer. Then he pulled me up to his face.

"Your turn," he said before making me lay down flat. I looked up at him over top of me. His hands slid up each of my thighs. When he reached my bikini bottoms, he grabbed them and quickly pulled them off. I paid no attention to where he threw them, in fact I didn't care. Colt buried his face between my legs and when his tongue reached the top of my burning flesh, I let out a scream that the whole state may have been able to hear.

Satisfied that he did well, Colt slid up beside me. He pulled me on top of him and I didn't waste any time guiding him to slide inside of me. He teased me at first, but slowly made one more thrust until his whole shaft filled me. It felt so tight and my muscles down there began to contract right away. I sat up and pressed my arms against his hard chest. He watched me with those green eyes. He didn't stare at my breast, or say sexy things, or even close his eyes. He just looked into my eyes. I couldn't stop watching him and I moved my hips back and forth against him. It was turning me on so much. Just the way he was watching me. I felt my body contracting again and couldn't control my burst of ecstasy. The friction felt amazing between us and soon I felt his hands griping both of my hips. With just a few more small movements, he was holding me still, closing his eyes tight as his release came the same time as mine.

I collapsed over top of him and felt him kiss my head, before wrapping both of his arms around my naked back. As he stroked my hair, I felt his body move as he chuckled. "That was a great first experience."

"It was amazing," I added. I really appreciated that he didn't ask me about my times here with his cousin.

Colt and I managed to part enough to lay side by side on the dock. The sun was shining down on us, and the breeze gave us the hint of honeysuckle when it blew. We could hear the birds and the sounds of the woods, but all we cared about was each other. We managed to get our clothes on, mostly because I think we both knew that when we were naked we couldn't keep our hands off of each other.

For the next couple hours Colt and I lay out on the dock and talked about everything under the sun. He had so many hilarious stories to share and I enjoyed just listening to him telling stories with his strong southern accent. I kept imagining him in a football uniform while he told me the stories. I knew he didn't walk around in one every day in college, but I couldn't help the sexy fantasy I had created in my head.

It was funny how I thought I knew so much about Colt, but everything Ty had ever told me about him seemed to be the opposite. He admitted to the handful of women he had access to at home, but said he never told Ty stories like he repeated to me. Colt's explanation was that a few times when he was lonely, he would pick up a woman. He said it was not often and that he barely ever did it to begin with.

He even admitted to me about the night Brina had offered herself. I felt jealous when he told me about it. I had no right, but it still pissed me off. It didn't matter about the women he had been with. What bothered me was that he seemed offended when I assumed there were many more. I hated thinking that one of them was lying to me, but I was more afraid to know which one of them it was.

Chapter 18

Colt

First, my aunt gave me the third degree about someone spending the night. I was pretty darn sure she wasn't going to let me leave the house this morning without giving her the girl's name and social security number. Part of me wondered if Harvey had told her Savanna had been here last week.

Then, I get to the hole and Savanna told me how Tyler used to tell her about all of these women I had supposedly bedded. I was starting to think I couldn't catch a break, until Savanna made all of my worries go away. When we were together, my only focus was her. She did somethin' to me and I wasn't about to let her go. Our relationship might be temporary, but I was going to make it memorable.

The more time we spent together, the more I admired about her. She was such a nice girl, who only wanted to be happy. She sacrificed everything for the people that she loved. She was misunderstood and mistreated, but somehow she claimed I made her forget about everything else. My problem was that she was getting under my skin more than any woman ever had. After one week, I was beginning to think that maybe there was something between Savanna and I that I needed to worry about. I was already crazy for her. What made it worse was that we weren't strangers. We just weren't close enough to know who each of us really was, and the closer we were getting, the more we liked about each other.

An innocent agreement between two friends was becoming something more overnight. I wanted to touch her. Hell, I needed to touch her.

We made it to shore and had a lunch picnic style. I was doing all of these nice gestures not even realizing it. A picnic lunch, grabbing towels to make her comfortable, saying all the right things, but when she was with me, I couldn't help myself. It started out as protecting her, but it was already more than that. I really liked her.

We spent the afternoon laughin' and foolin' around. When the sun started to set, we lay on the blanket I brought and watched it. I held her hand and made sure her arm was touching mine. When it really started to get dark, we gathered our things and made our way back to the farm. At the woods edge, I looked in the farm house and saw my aunt and uncle sitting in the backroom in front of the television. They were headed to the hospital in the morning, so Savanna and I could ride the horses and not have to sneak around.

That's exactly what we did too. I talked her into spending another night. Her mother was beginning to ask questions, but Savanna didn't seem to care too much. That night we rode out to the old barn. We watched the stars and talked about the things we wanted in life. She had so much going for her, if she would just let herself live.

I wondered what would happen when I left in the fall. Would she go back to spending every second at that hospital? Would she want to still talk to me, maybe even come and visit me?"

We ended up sleeping in the hayloft at the old barn. It wasn't the best night's sleep, but waking up with something beautiful in your arms is pretty damn nice.

Savanna could turn a bad farmin' day into the best day of the year. She made me smile like when it rained during a drought. Her sweet smile and innocent sense of humor were contagious. How could people not love her?

For the next few weeks we spent all of our free time together. When I had to work, I thought about her every second. It wasn't just the sex, in fact I hardly thought about that when I thought about Savanna. Of course I loved that the sex was pretty amazing, but I wanted to hear her voice and hold her in my arms. I missed her when she wasn't around. Now, I was an adult and I knew exactly what those feelings amounted to. No matter how hard I tried to fight them, they just kept coming up. Every touch, every word, led to me wanting her in my life.

Savanna made me want something with a woman that I had never had before. She made me want a family. I'd had several dreams about us being married and having children together. Then I would wake up and realize that was the future she had saved for my cousin, not me.

She talked about him less, but she still loved him the same. It wasn't like I was giving her hope that we could ever be more. I felt like I didn't have a right to do that. Above everything else, I wanted her to be happy, and to have the future that she deserved. If that future was to be with my cousin, then I wished her the best. It hurt like hell to think about, but it was the truth.

I never had a chance when it came to her choosing me. It would never happen. She confessed so much to me, there was no way she could ever love someone else. She had made it clear that he was her future. She would never let go of him.

Each night it didn't stop me from holding her in my arms, wishing she was my future instead of his.

Chapter 19

Savanna

The next month went by faster than I wanted it to. During the day Colt would work the farm with his uncle, while I went to work, stopped by the hospital and even made my appointments with my shrink. We spent our evenings together either at the carriage house or at the old barn. When the weekends came, we had free reign over the farm. There was a mess of skinny dipping and even more hot showers.

Being with Colt was an addiction. I no longer worried about hiding from people, in fact we often headed to town and ate in public. We ran into a few younger kids at the old barn one night and it never bothered me. As long as I had Colt by my side, I didn't care about anyone else.

He gave me a reason to smile every day. On nights that I couldn't stay the night, we would talk for hours on the phone, like little teenagers. Everything about Colt was a breath of fresh air. He was kind and always made sure I was safe. He never questioned my feelings and I found myself wondering what my feelings really were for him. Was it possible that a summer fling had turned into something real between the both of us?

I wanted to tell him, to let him know how I felt.

I wanted him to know that I thought I was falling in love with him.

The idea of him having to leave in two months made me sad. I hated being without him for more than a day. I couldn't imagine being without him completely. When I thought about it, I felt a hole in my heart that I recognized from before. I never wanted to feel that lost again. I couldn't lose him too.

I planned it all out. Colt needed to work in the chicken houses one Saturday afternoon. There had been some fan malfunction and even his uncle and aunt stayed home from the hospital to get it fixed. While they did what they needed to do, I bought two big steaks, some potatoes and a salad. I lit candles and cooked all of the food. After I finished, I headed into the bedroom and changed into the skimpiest little outfit I picked up in town, then added my cowboy boots for a finishing touch. I sat there at the kitchen table waiting. The excitement of seeing him was killing me.

When Colt walked in the door, his mouth dropped open. It was dark in the room, but the candles illuminated it. He wasn't looking at the table, the lighting or even the food. His eyes were fixed on me.

I crossed my legs for an extra touch. "Hey," I announced.

"Savanna." That was all he said before heading in my direction. I stood up and turned around for him. "You look so hot."

"Thank you baby," I said.

He kissed me then pulled away. "Did you call me baby?"

"I did. Actually, I wanted to celebrate. Are you hungry, because I got us two great steaks?"

He looked over the table, then back to me. "I'm starvin'."

"Well I made your favorites, so I hope I did them justice. Go wash up and I will make your plate," I offered.

I was getting nervous. I wanted him to attack me with kisses, but he seemed a bit caught off guard at me calling him *baby*. I didn't think it was a big deal, and I hoped he didn't either."

After ten minutes, Colt walked out from the shower in just a pair of shorts. His hair was still wet. He kissed me again before sitting across from me.

"You look beautiful and this food looks amazin'. Are you alright Darlin'?" He asked.

I smiled and started cutting my steak. "Actually I am more than fine. I want to talk to you about something."

Colt was in the middle of cutting his steak. His knife dropped on his plate making a loud noise. "Are you pregnant?"

I gagged on my first bite of food. "No! I'm not. Is that what you thought this was about?"

He held up his hands. "Wait before you get all upset. Just for the record, I wouldn't be mad if you were. We haven't been very responsible lately. I mean, most of it is my fault, but you don't help when you attack me like you do," he laughed.

"I'm not mad. I am actually shocked you thought I would be dressed all sexy to tell you I was with child. That's kind of screwed up don't you think?"

He smiled. "When you say it like that, it's pretty jacked up. So what's goin' on?"

"Eat your dinner and then we can talk. I want you to enjoy every bite."

He put his fork down and began chewing. "It tastes great. Thank you for cookin'. So, I gotta ask. Do I get to watch you take that little number off for dessert?"

His smile made me want to crawl across the table of food and candles and attack him. He was so damn sexy I couldn't control myself.

"Maybe if you eat all of your veggies," I teased.

"I will lick the plate clean if I have to," he noted.

"You can lick something," I replied with a wink.

I watched Colt eat his food like a Neanderthal with all intentions of watching me rip off my clothes. I thought I was excited, but the idea of being naked with him made me so hot between my legs. I was on fire with anticipation.

He got up from the table and put his plate in the sink. He leaned against it watching me take the few last bites on my plate. I took my time, knowing it was driving him crazy. Once I finished, I walked slowly to the sink. When I started to wash the dishes, pretending I didn't notice him waiting, he picked me up and carried me, only stopping to blow out the candles.

When he got me in the bedroom he tossed me down on top of the bed. He climbed on top of me. His naked chest called out for my hands and I immediately felt every ripple of his stomach. I reached down and kissed his nipple, biting it before letting go. He cupped one of my breasts and used his teeth to pull at the fabric. The tiny bra hooked in the front and Colt took no time at all discovering that. He grabbed the bra and tossed it behind him. He found my lips and ravished me in a hungry kiss. As our tongues mingled our kissing became so forceful that our teeth were touching. He only pulled away from my mouth to tease me with his tongue. I grabbed it with my lips and sucked on it hard.

"Woman, you are making me crazy," he announced.

His mouth found mine again, but his hand traveled down between my legs. He cupped my sex and used his palm to rub against the sensitive spot at the top. I bucked my legs and he rubbed harder, never letting go of our kissing. Colt's head dove for my neck and I could feel his slippery tongue lapping up my skin, heading toward my ear. His other hand cupped one of my breasts. Just when I was about to explode. He sat up and played with my panties. His fingers slid beneath them and I watched him watching what he was doing. He was turned on, steady licking his lips as he slid his fingers inside of my wetness.

I gasped when I felt myself losing control. The euphoric moment of ecstasy overwhelmed me. I closed my eyes and let it happen. The next thing I knew Colt's lips found mine again. I grabbed both sides of his face and held him close. His hands found my waist and started pulling down my panties. I lifted up my butt so he didn't fight with them. I wanted them off. My hands reached down and unbuttoned his pants. I used my feet to slide them down over his fine ass. When I reached down to feel his erection, I noticed it was already wet on the tip. Knowing he was already that turned on, made the fire between my legs get even hotter. The orgasm I had just moments ago was out of sight and a new one was building up. I turned my body around so that my butt was facing him. He started to position himself behind me, but slowly turned me back around.

"I don't want it that way Savanna. I want to see you. I need to look at you." He confessed as he entered me. I entwined my legs into his as we began moving in sync. As he thrusted in and out of me, he continued kissing me all over my face and neck. I gripped my hands in his hair and pulled him into my aggressive kisses. When he started to climax, he put his head against mine and let out a moan. His lips rested over mine as he tried to calm his breathing.

I wrapped my arms around his broad shoulders. "Colt, I need to tell you something."

He kissed me on my shoulder. "You can tell me anything."

He slid out of me and lay beside me, stroking my hair. I reached up and touched his face. "I love you."

Before he could respond, or I could say anything else, loud knocking came from the front door, followed by a bunch of yelling.

Colt sat up, just when he heard the door opening. Guess he forgot to lock it.

"Colt," his uncle called frantically.

"Coming," he yelled, but it wasn't in time.

"He's awake Colt. We need to get to the hospital right away. Did you hear me? Ty is .....," his uncle froze as he made his way to the bedroom door. His mouth dropped open when he saw me lying there naked in bed with his nephew.

If that wasn't bad enough, his aunt came into the doorway. She came after me, before she even said a word. "You little tramp. My son was bad enough, but now you want my nephew? Colt, how could you be with such a little whore? You know what she has done? How long has this been going on?" She screamed.

Colt stood up, while still buttoning his shorts. He walked toward his aunt and pushed them both out of the room without speaking. I could hear them screaming as I searched through my bag for normal clothes to wear. Within seconds I made it to the living room.

"She's not coming with us!" Ty's mother yelled.

"I will drive separately then," Colt threatened.

Ty's dad just stood there shaking his head at me. Tears ran down my face, but I was speechless. I couldn't deny being with Colt. For over a month I had lived in his world.

Finally the older man spoke. "Get your things and follow us to the hospital. Whatever this was....it aint happenin' anymore. He's never to know about this. Do you understand me Colton Mitchell? Savanna?"

I nodded my head before burying my hands into my face. I couldn't look at Colt. I didn't want to see him agreeing to never be near me again. As excited as I was about seeing Ty, it killed me to hurt Colt.

Ty's parents walked out without saying a word and rushed to their car. To be a fly in that car would be worse than being in a warzone.

Colt and I climbed in the old pickup. By that time I was balling. I couldn't help it. So much had just happened. Tonight was supposed to be about me letting go of Ty and finally committing to Colt. I wanted him to know how I felt. Instead, I confessed my feelings only to find out that Ty woke up. Almost like my confession to Colt made him wake up.

We had gotten about five miles before Colt said a word. I felt his warm hand reaching for mine. I didn't hesitate taking it. I unhooked my seatbelt and climbed over to be next to him. He let me cry on his shoulder, but never mentioned what I said to him.

"Savanna, I'm not going to stop being your friend. You have to know that."

I couldn't look at him. I was so confused. Ty was awake. For the first time in a month I reached in my purse and pulled out my bottle of Xanax. Colt looked over at me and smiled as I popped one small pill into my mouth and swallowed it dry.

"You gonna be alright Darlin'?"

I nodded my head yes and leaned back on his shoulder.

When we got into town, Colt leaned down to kiss the top of my head. He rubbed my shoulder and held me close, but still said nothing about my admission earlier. I was starting to feel calmer, but could feel my heart beating five hundred miles an hour the closer we came to the hospital.

Ty's parents were already running inside as we pulled into the parking lot. I knew they were thrilled to have their son awake. I wanted to see him too. I just didn't know exactly how to act or what to say.

Colt and I got out of the car. We kept our distance and said nothing until we got in the elevator. Before the door flew open, he pulled me back. He seemed stressed. "Savanna....I....I'm here for you."

We rushed out of the elevator and headed toward Ty's room. I started walking slow, but began to almost run. I didn't look back to see Colt, maybe I should have, but I just couldn't. I got to the doorway and saw him. He was sitting up. His mother and father at both of his sides. When he saw me the world around us stopped.

"There's my girl," he announced.

I just stood there frozen in place. I couldn't move.

Chapter 20

Colt

An hour ago, she was mine.

There was no going back. I had the whole drive over to plead my case, to fight for what I wanted. Instead I let her slip through my fingers. I felt the dagger stab through my heart when I heard Ty calling her into that room.

I couldn't even walk in there at first. I stood outside with my head down, tryin' not to listen to them talkin'. I could still hear them, like my ears where only tuned into them instead of everything else going on around the hospital.

At first Savanna seemed reluctant to go to him, for a second I had hope. Once he called her over, my hope went away. Through the glass I watched Savanna run to his bedside. My aunt and uncle did not seemed thrilled. They gave me a dirty look, like I wasn't even part of the family anymore. I couldn't imagine what they thought of Savanna now.

Ty did his best to hug her. I wasn't sure what it was like for him. I mean, the last thing he remembered was being in an accident I reckon. He didn't have to go through the long days and nights wondering. He didn't have to suffer the way Savanna had.

Even after their first embrace, and me turning away so I couldn't watch, I still listened to him talking to Savanna as if nothing had changed. When I finally couldn't take it anymore, I decided to go in and say goodbye, before I headed out. I couldn't stay there, not knowing that I could never have her.

The room got quiet as I approached my cousins bed. Savanna never looked at me, which sent pain straight to my heart. My cousin held out his hand and actually pounded me like we did something cool. I gave him the best smile I could fabricate.

"I have my four favorite people in the whole world here with me," Tyler announced.

I tried to smile, I really did. One glance at my aunt and uncle and I could tell that the tension in the room could actually kill someone. I tried to ignore the hurtful looks from them, and the fact that Savanna refused to look at me at all. "It's really good to see that you're doin' better cuz. We have all been waiting for you to make your return."

"Yeah, the nurses said this lady here was with me almost every day," he said as he held Savanna's hand and kissed it, while she gave him her beautiful smile.

Even as a grown man, I felt stinging in my eyes. I shook my head and tried to smile again.

"Looks like you are goin' to be home in no time at all."

Ty looked over at Savanna. "The doc is going to let me know how much rehab I need and where I need to go. I hope I can come home, but I won't know until we talk to him."

For the first time I heard Savanna speak and it crushed me completely. "We just can't wait to get you home babe." Her smile was real and her tears proved it all.

"I just wanted to stop by and wish you well cuz. I need to get back to the farm."

Ty let go of Savanna's hand and shook mine. For the first time in my life I couldn't stand my cousin. He may not have known it, but he had what I wanted. He had her.

Savanna

Everything was happening so fast. From the romantic evening, to getting caught, then finally being here. It was like a dream. The whole ride over I wanted to say something to Colt, but I couldn't. I wanted him to tell me that he loved me too, and that no matter what we would find a way to be together.

I had waited so long for Ty to wake up, but now that he had, I didn't know where my heart was. Colt had come into my life when I was at my lowest.

In a way he had repaired what was broken and made me want to love again. We never fought, which was something Ty and I had done even on our happiest of days.

Now, I didn't know what to do. Ty was awake and his parents had threatened Colt and I to never see each other again. I couldn't live with myself for hurting Ty, or for him finding out that Colt and I slept together. As soon as I entered that room, I knew I never wanted him to find out, but I also knew that deciding that ended my chances of ever being with Colt again. I tried to hide my feelings, but as I stood there holding on to Ty's hand all I could think about was hurting Colt.

Being in the room with his parents was overwhelming and even after taking the pill earlier, I felt like I couldn't breathe. When Colt decided to leave, I didn't know what to do. I couldn't run after him, knowing that Ty would wonder what had gotten into me and his parents might just spill the beans about my affair with his cousin. I needed to figure things out. I wouldn't be able to let Colt go without at least talking to him. When I told him that I loved him I meant it. He had to think I was being such a bitch right now. I just let him walk out of there anyway.

For the next hour Ty went on and on about what he had missed. How the team had done. How school went for me. How I got by. With his mother still there, I was unable to express the pure Hell I had endured for the past seven and a half months. He had no idea what my life had been like. The worst part was that I had waited so long for him to wake up, to have him back in my life and to tell him that I was sorry, but Ty didn't even seem to care. He was in a fine mood, even acting like I had never caught him having sex with someone else. To make that even worse was the fact that I didn't even care about Ty and that girl. I realized standing there that I didn't care at all anymore. I had fallen completely in love with Colt and he made me see exactly what I wanted.

However, wanting something I couldn't have was just the story of my life. As I stood here with Ty and his parents, I realized that my happy little ending was not going to come. Ty's parents didn't let me get a word in edgewise and I couldn't interrupt. My fear of Ty finding out about Colt and I kept me from doing anything to piss them off.

When the doctor finally came in, his parents stepped outside with me so he could be examined. At first, we stood in the hallway not speaking, but finally his mother pressed her angry lips together and came walking toward me.

"We need to talk," she said as she pulled me further away from Ty's room.

She got me standing in the opposite hallway and began pacing in front of me. I half expected her to slap me. "I don't know what kind of games you are playing with my family, but it will stop now! You will not see or speak to Colton anymore young lady. My son has been through Hell and if you have a decent bone in your body, you will be there for him. I hope he finally opens his eyes and sees you for the little tramp you really are, but until that day, you will do whatever he wants. Do you understand me?"

I swallowed the vomit forming in my throat. "Yes Ma'am."

Tears streamed down my eyes. I refused to argue with her. She had her mind made up. There was nothing I could say or do.

Before heading back toward the room, she turned around. "If I find out that you even spoke to Colton, I will tell Tyler everything," she reiterated.

I nodded my head and collapsed on the cold concrete floor. My hands were buried in my face and I kept them there until I had no more tears left to shed. My head was spinning and the nausea was overwhelming. I contemplated walking all the way back to town. It was late at night and pitch black outside. With no street lights for most of the way, I was sure to be killed and left to the animals living in a country ditch somewhere. Maybe that's what I deserved.

Realizing that my purse was still in Ty's room, I knew I had to go back in there. Thankfully when I went in, his parents weren't there. Ty pulled me as close to him as he possibly could. When he pulled me in to hug him, his lips found mine. For all of the months that I missed his kisses, and all of the fantasies that I had played out in my head, it was nothing compared to how Colt kissed me. I closed my eyes and let Ty kiss me as the tears, I didn't know I still had, began to fall. I couldn't believe that I had spent all of my time just waiting for this moment and now that it was happening, I didn't even think I wanted it.

Ty let me pull away and he wiped off my tears. "Don't cry babe. Everything is going to be fine now. I promise."

I wanted to believe that it would be, but things were so far from fine. "I am so glad you finally woke up. Do you remember anything?"

"I remember fighting with you. You catching me with that blonde. I remember taking the car.. I even remember the car rolling. I didn't believe the nurses when they told me it had been months. When my mom and dad came in and I saw the look in their eyes, I knew it was the truth. While I waited for everyone to arrive, the nurses told me about my girlfriend spending almost all of her time here. I never knew how much I loved you until I heard them saying that Van. Thank you for standing by me and taking care of me. I want you to give me another chance. Let me prove to you that I can be that guy you need."

When I saw Ty's parents rounding the corner, I squeezed his hand and had no choice but to agree. I was digging the hole deeper for myself every second.

His parents came in and acted nicer to me. They pretended to be on good terms with me and even asked if I wanted to get something to eat on the way home. Ty wanted me to stay, but realized it would be uncomfortable. Knowing they were my ride home, I smiled and said all the right things. I hugged Ty goodbye and told him that I loved him, because it was true. I never stopped loving him as a person, but my heart beat for his cousin and I couldn't believe it took me seeing Ty awake to realize it.

Before walking out of the room, I turned and waved one more time. He would see me tomorrow, I didn't plan on not being there for him. He was very important to me and I wanted him to be better before I told him we couldn't be together.

The ride home was horrible. We stopped and got something to eat at a little fast food place on the way home. Nothing else was really open. Ty's father talked about sending Colt home right in front of me. I knew he was saying it to get a rise out of me. At one point I put my fingers through the door handle and considered just jumping out of the car. Remembering having to get stitches made me rethink injuring myself.

When we pulled up at the house, I climbed out and said nothing. The window in the passenger seat rolled down and Ty's mother stuck out her head. "If you know what's good for you, you will not cross me young lady."

They abruptly pulled away and I sat down on the curb in front of my house. When the sun started to come up, my mother came rushing outside in her bathrobe. "Van? What are you doing out here honey? What's wrong?"

I fell into her arms. "Everything is a mess Mom. Ty woke up tonight, but before that his parents caught me with Colt and they threatened to tell him about us if we didn't stop seeing each other. I don't know what to do. I love him Mom."

"You were with Colt? Ty's cousin?" My mother finally asked when we were in the kitchen and she was making coffee. "Is that who you have been hanging out with? Cause I gotta tell ya honey, I saw Brina the other day and she claimed she hasn't seen you in weeks. I just figured you would tell me if something was wrong."

"It started out as friends. I got beat up at a party." I held my hands up. "Mom wait! It was still during school. I am fine now. Anyway, Colt saved me and took me back to the farm to rest. I didn't want you seeing my face so I stayed there for a few days. Things started happening between us. I slept with him."

My mother was shocked at my confession, but to be fair I was an adult and she knew for a fact that I was not promiscuous.

"Then what? Because, obviously you didn't stop seeing him."

I shook my head. "We decided to be friends, but we couldn't keep our hands off one another. Mom being with him is like nothing I have ever experienced. I found myself thinking about him all of the time, even when I was at the hospital visiting Ty. We treated it like a summer fling, but something changed for me this week and I wanted Colt to know how I really felt about him. Just as I was confessing to him, Ty's parents burst in the door, catching us without clothes, and telling us that Ty woke up. Mom, they said they would tell Ty if I had any contact with

Colt ever again. Ty can't know Mom. He can't ever find out what I did. He would never forgive Colt."

My mother pulled me into another one of her hugs when she didn't know what to say. I was used to them after all these years.

"If you don't want Tyler to know then you have to let Colt go."

I shook my head. "No!" She held me tight and let me cry more. I knew my eyes were completely swollen, but I couldn't help it. I thought I cried when Ty had the accident, but this was so much worse.

Chapter 21

Colt

I sat in the hospital parking lot for over an hour, hoping Savanna would come running out. I had this idea in my head that she would realize she loved me and we could just drive off together. With me not telling her how I felt, she was free to jump right back into Ty's arms. I punched the dashboard so hard, I busted my knuckles. The burn took away from the fact that I knew I lost the girl.

I watched as she and my relatives came walking out of that hospital. They never even looked my way as they exited. I didn't follow close behind them and when they turned to drop off Savanna, I kept going until I reached the farm. Sam greeted me, but I wasn't in the mood to play catch with her. I walked straight into carriage house and looked around at what was meant for a perfect night. The candles were still on the table and dishes in the sink. Savanna's little outfit was lyin' on the bedroom floor. Her overnight bag was in the corner. I let my body fall back on the bed while I considered how the hell I was going to get out of this mess.

I saw the headlights pulling up out front and knew that my uncle was not going to go to bed until things were settled. Sure enough, as I tossed Savanna's clothes in her bag and threw them in the closet, my uncle came rushin' in. "Colt, where are ya boy?"

I walked out into the living room. "I'm here."

"Sit down Son. We need to talk."

I put my hand across my chest. "I think I'd rather stand."

"Suit yourself. I'm not going to beat around the bush here. I am not very pleased with you right now. We are family and that's about all we got when we look at the big picture. Now this thing between you and Van is over. I don't know how you got involved with that girl, but from what I have noticed, it seems to have been goin' on for quite some time. I think it would be best if you left town. Now it will take me a few days to get ya a flight back home, so I would appreciate it if you would not contact her. My boy doesn't need to ever find out about this. He has been through enough."

"You aren't going to tell me who I can and can't talk to!"

"If you know what's best, you will walk away. There are other women out there. Go find your own. I don't know what this girl has going for her, but obviously she gives herself out to anyone who is askin'"

"Don't you dare talk about her that way! She isn't how you are sayin'. She's nothing like that at all. Do you have any idea how many women your son bedded while they were together? You might not know, but I was the one he called to brag about it to. She doesn't deserve that. Then after everything he did to her, you blamed her for his accident. That little bastard drank more whiskey than we both have in our whole lives. He shouldn't have even had a license."

"Mind your words Son. You are talkin' about my boy."

"Look, he's my blood and I don't want him hurt, so I will walk away. You need to know one thing first. I love her. I just want her to be happy. If she wants to be with him, then I wish her the best. Now, if you will leave me be, I think I want to be alone."

My uncle shook his head and walked out the door. I picked up a candle stick and threw it across the room, putting a large hole in the wall next to the bathroom. It was bad enough that Savanna chose Ty, but now I couldn't even say goodbye. I dug through every cabinet in that carriage house looking for something to drink. When I found nothing, I headed out to the barn where Harvey had a room. I felt bad about waking him, but I pushed the man until he woke anyway. "Harvey, where is the whiskey?"

He wiped his eyes before pointing to a small wooden cabinet in the corner. He shook his head and closed his eyes as I made my way to the cabinet, and grabbed the first bottle I found. It wasn't whiskey, it was tequila. This particular brand was straight up from Mexico, worm and all. I opened the bottle and began drinking it before I had even made it out of the barn. The slow burn made my eyes water, but I just kept hitting that bottle.

In no time at all, I couldn't feel my fingers. My body was numb and that's just how I wanted it to be. I didn't want to think about Savanna and how I would never be able to touch her again. Her pretty face would only be a memory to me from now on. My cousin would never let her go, and that's what she wanted all along. I never had a chance.

I woke up with a bottle in my hand and a massive headache. It took me a few minutes to access what had happened the night before. When I finally was awake enough, I wished there was more tequila left in the bottle. I grabbed some shoes and decided the best thing to do was work. I had to keep my mind off of things until I could get a flight back home. I should have just called myself, but there were no taxis here and my uncle would have reported the truck stolen if I tried to take it.

There was one field that still needed to be tilled and reseeded, so I took the tractor and started working. A few hours passed and the sun was really starting to get to me. My body was dehydrated from all the liquor and I could have passed out at any time. I noticed one of the farming trucks heading in my direction, so I turned off the tractor and waited to be yelled at again.

My uncle stepped out of the truck and headed in my direction. In his hands were two large bottles of water. "I may be pissed at you, but you are my blood boy. Harvey told me about the tequila and when I heard you out here, I knew you were needin' some of this."

I took the bottles and started downing them. The beads of sweat were now stinging my eyes, so I took some of the water and poured it over my face. "Thanks!"

"We got a call this mornin' about your cousin. He can come home next week. Your aunt is goin' to throw one hell of a party and Tyler wants you there. Now, I know what I said last night, but for the sake of my son, I am willin' to let you stay. I need your word that you will keep your hands off of his girl Colt. I appreciate everything you have done with the farm and I can't say I don't need the help. I know I was stern last night, but what you did wasn't right. At any rate, there aint nothin' we can do but move forward."

"I will stay as long as you need me." It was all I could say.

My uncle walked away and I started up the tractor. As much as I wanted to be able to see Savanna, it wasn't going to happen. She had her boyfriend back and I was certain that there was no way she was going to give me the time of day. Besides, my uncle did need my help. My cousin couldn't work and the farm was their only source of income. I needed to stay to get things going for them.

For the rest of the time here, I needed to focus on work instead of Savanna. She wasn't mine and being around her would probably make her frustrated. She had other things to focus on now.

Savanna

I didn't feel any better when I woke up. In fact my eyes looked like I had been in another fight. My mother brought me in a wet rag and I laid in the tub for over an hour tryin to relax. My cell phone was going crazy with texts from Brina and calls from Ty. Apparently, he was already back to his normal self. He and his mother had already been up early planning a celebration. Brina heard it from someone else and wanted to know why the hell she hadn't heard it from me. I wanted to be able to vent to her, to tell her how I felt about Colt. I just couldn't do it. The more people that knew, the more chance Ty had of finding out. I couldn't put that strain on him. I hoped that Colt was feeling the same way.

I started to call him several times, but hung up before the first ring. I didn't know what to say. Last night in that elevator, I thought he was going to tell me that he loved me too, but he just said he would be there for me. Maybe he didn't feel the same way that I did about him. It wasn't like he ever said he loved me. In fact, more than one time he made it clear that we were good friends. Maybe imagining we were on the same page was just another fantasy of mine.

After a few more calls from Ty, I got myself up and headed to the hospital. His mother was already there and greeted me with one of her nasty looks. I rolled my eyes and walked past her. Ty was sitting up and I noticed right away he wasn't hooked up to anymore wires. He still had a blood pressure cuff around his arm, but everything else was off.

"Hey babe. I been waiting all day to see that pretty face," he said as he pulled me in for a kiss.

"Sorry, I slept a little later than normal. You look great," I said, trying to be cordial.

He took my hand and played with it in his hands. "Did you hear about the party? I can't wait to get out of here."

"I heard about it. Do you need me to do anything?" I asked directing the question to his mother.

She smiled and pretended to be nice. "You have already done enough dear, don't you think?"

Bitch!

"So when are you getting out of here?" I asked, while trying to ignore that mean woman across from us.

"The doctors still have to run some tests. He estimated about a week. So far everything seems okay. I have some metal in my leg and my physical therapy is going to suck, but I'd rather be in a wheelchair than in this place."

His mother grabbed his arm. "The wheelchair is temporary Tyler. Don't get yourself upset about it."

Ty chuckled. "Mom, I'm not! Look, I know it has been hard for all of you. I can't imagine what you went through, but you need to understand that I don't remember any of it. To me, the accident just happened. As far as I am concerned, the past seven months never existed." He looked over to me and kissed my hand. "Well, except for the part that got my girl to come back to me. That part is all that matters."

I was pretty sure his mother wanted me dead. She tried to hide her hate for me, the best she could, but I was sure she was boiling inside.

For the next few hours I managed to sit with her and Ty and compile a list of everything we needed for his going home party. She seemed to calm down and actually treated me like a normal human being. It killed me that I used to be a big part of their family and now I was this person she hated the most in her life.

It was weird being with Ty. He acted like everything between us was perfect. I knew it was because he hadn't had seven months to deal with things like I had. He didn't know I wanted to end my life or that I had to be hospitalized for my depression. He didn't know how his friends had treated me and especially how his family had treated me.

In fact, Ty had no idea what I had gone through at all. He never even asked.

After hours of being in the same room, his mother decided she was heading out. I finally had time alone with Ty. I decided to be nice and walk her to the elevator. The doctors said to try not to stress

Ty, so we were both putting on our best poker faces. Once we got to the elevator she turned to me.

"One day my son will see you for what you really are," she said rudely.

"I never cheated on your son. In fact when the accident happened, I caught him with someone else. You can believe what you want, but you are wrong about me. I never once thought about another guy the entire time Ty and I were together. Do you have any idea what I have been through?"

She held up her hand and shook her head. "Don't you dare talk to me about my son. He would never cheat on a lady. How dare you, you little hussy!"

She climbed into the elevator and said nothing as the doors closed between us.

I huffed and puffed until I got back to the room. Ty's smile immediately changed my mood. He held his arms up and I climbed up next to him in his bed. Being in his arms wasn't hard. It was just as I had always remembered.

"Did you miss me?" Ty asked while holding me tight.

I sat up and looked at him. "I did miss you." I knew the last thing he remembered was me walking in on him with someone else, but he refused to bring it up. It was like his past mistakes had been erased. Now, I wasn't trying to be an insensitive bitch, because he did just wake up from being in a coma, but he couldn't get away with it forever.

I stayed with Ty until visiting hours were over. He was sad to see me leave, and being with him had kept my mind off of Colt, but the long drive home brought everything back.

When I got to my house I couldn't take it anymore. I locked myself in my room and dialed Colt's number. It rang and went to voicemail. I tried again, getting the same result. Finally, I sent a text..

I think we need to talk –S

Ten minutes passed and not a single word. Then finally my phone vibrated.

Nothin to say – C

They were not the three words I wanted to hear. I felt my heart tearing apart.

Colt didn't love me. He had kept his promise that he wouldn't get that attached to me.

Chapter 22

Colt

I didn't need to hear Savanna telling me that we were over. I just assume not to talk to her at all. She had already broken my heart. I didn't need to hear it out of her mouth.

For the next week I did nothing but work during the day. At night, Sam and I would venture out in the woods, or hang out in the barn with the horses. On several occasions, Harvey and I would stay up late drinking and playing poker.

As long as I kept myself busy enough, I was able to avoid thinking about Savanna. With my cousin's return home fast approaching, my aunt and uncle stayed focused on him. They no longer threatened me or even paid attention to what I was doing. Staying out of their way was becoming a habit.

The day before Ty came home, my uncle came over and asked me to help set up the large tents in the yard. Harvey and I got right on it. At first they were a real pain in the ass, but once we figured them out, we got them all up in no time.

After carrying at least one hundred chairs that some person from church had delivered, I was beat. I started to head back to the carriage house when I saw Savanna pulling in the driveway. I stopped walking and just watched her car as it drove past me. In the passenger side was Ty, giving me a friendly wave. Savanna never looked my way, it was one thing that I couldn't help but notice.

Realizing I couldn't be rude, I headed in the direction of the car. Savanna got out and froze when she saw me approaching. I turned my hat forward and gave her a nod. It was all she was going to get without me losing it and telling her my real feelings.

Savanna focused her attention on getting Ty's wheelchair out of the back of the car. I took it out of her hands and got it unfolded, before helping to get my cousin out of the car.

"I thought you weren't coming home until tomorrow," I stated while getting him in the chair.

"The doc said I was fine to leave. Said my body had enough time recuperating," Ty explained.

Pushing Ty across the dirt driveway was difficult even for me, so I insisted Savanna not do it. My aunt met us at the door and once we got him inside, I was shocked by what I saw. Savanna stood in the living room frozen as she looked around noticing all of her pictures had been put back out. It was like my aunt was erasing all of the months she had emotionally damaged the girl.

I don't know which one of us was more pissed, but shockingly, Savanna put on a smile and gave Ty all of her attention, like nothing had happened. Knowing that I couldn't take much more, I saw myself out, without anyone even noticing.

I needed to avoid seeing Savanna, so I took Sam and headed into the woods. We played fetch until my arms felt like jello. When it started to get dark, I headed back to the carriage house and locked the door behind me.

About an hour later I heard a knock at the door. I was surprised to find Savanna standin' there looking at me. "Sorry to bother you. I was wondering if I could just get my bag."

"Stay right there. I will get it for you." I left her standing in the doorway. I was positive my uncle or someone was standing around watchin' us and I didn't want to give them any reason to doubt what I was doing. Savanna was looking down at the ground when I got back to the door.

"Here you go. I packed everything up, even your things in the bathroom," I stated.

She looked up at me. "Colt...I."

I held my hand up. "Don't Savanna. There is nothin' left to say."

I could barely speak. For the first time in my life I wanted to curl up and cry like a damn baby. I couldn't keep seeing her. I needed to leave town.

I closed the door without saying another word, but watched through the window as she got in her car and drove away. After the party, I would tell my uncle that I had to go. Hopefully, he would understand why.

Savanna

How could he be so cold to me after
everything we had been through. He knew how hard
all of this had been. I know he saw those pictures
missing before, he had to notice the difference. I saw
his face when we got in that house.

I didn't understand why he wasn't even being
my friend. Was he just feeling sorry for me the whole
time we had been together? Was it all a lie?

I was really getting tired of crying, but I
couldn't really help it. Once again, my mother sat up
with me, holding me until I finally fell asleep.

Ty had insisted that my parents attend his
welcome home party, so I decided to just ride with
them. We got there a half hour early, but a bunch of
people were already there, including some of the girls
that had been involved in the fight with me. I felt my

anxiety growing as we approached Ty. The girls had already started giving me dirty looks. One of them bent over and whispered in Ty's ear before walking away. I couldn't help but notice where his eyes went as she walked away from him. Some things never change.

As I went to turn to give my attention back to Ty, something caught my attention. Colt stood where the blonde was walking. He was wearing a sleeveless shirt that showed off his muscular arms and that mustang tattoo he had hidden at the top of his arm. I knew that the back of it revealed the large one he had on his back. It wasn't Colts gorgeous body that I really noticed. It was the fact that he saw what Ty was looking at, and he knew that I caught it too. When our eyes met, I got butterflies in my stomach. I wanted to walk toward him, but just as I started to, I heard my name being called. Ty was wheeling toward me as I turned around. He had a fresh smile on his face and pulled me onto his lap.

"When did you get here babe?" He asked.

"Just a few minutes ago," I explained.

"You gonna give me a kiss or what?"

I leaned down and kissed him softly on the lips, not being able to stop myself from thinking about him watching that girl.

"You okay?" He asked.

"Yeah, I just haven't seen all these people in a long time. Guess I am overwhelmed." I tried to sound convincing, but I don't know if he believed me.

To avoid conflict, I stayed by Ty's side. It seemed everyone was nicer when he was around anyway. After a few hours, the tents were full of people. I was pretty sure the whole town had come. I looked around for Colt a couple times, but never was able to find him. I don't know why I kept trying. He obviously was done with our little fling. I guess that was all I was to him.

Ty had a bunch of catching up to do, so as the night went on, I found myself just sitting near him trying to stay out of his spotlight.

Finally, he stood up and whistled so that everyone looked our way. I was shocked to see him actually standing considering he had to be taught to do everything all over again. I could tell it was a struggle, as he leaned on his chair for support.

"I have an announcement to make," he said as he looked all around. "I want to thank everyone for coming out tonight. You don't know how much it means to me. I hope everyone is enjoying themselves tonight." A bunch of whistles and screams came from somewhere in the yard. Ty laughed then continued. "As most of you know, Van and I have been together for a long time. We haven't always seen eye to eye, but through it all, we managed to find our way back to each other. I wanted you all to be here tonight to witness me taking our relationship to the next level."

My heart started beating out of my chest as I watched Ty drop down on one knee. This couldn't be happening. He pulled something out of his pocket and put it out in front of me. "This was my grandmother's ring. I want you to wear it and say yes to being my wife."

In the crowd there were a bunch of noises, mostly people clapping and yelling what my answer should be. I looked around the room. First seeing the shocked look of Ty's parents, then seeing my own.

My mother knew my true feelings, so I saw the anguish in her eyes and knew exactly what she was thinking. Finally, I found the one person I was looking for. Colt stood in the corner of the tent. His arms were crossed but he was looking right at me. Even from a distance I could see disgust in his eyes. He didn't want me. I closed my eyes and tried not to look back.

I could say no and give up the only real relationship I ever had. Or, I could say yes, considering that at least I could have the forever I always wanted. I really needed time. This was all too sudden. Ty was acting as if nothing had happened. But, the truth was, I never wanted to feel that alone again.

"How about an answer beautiful," Ty asked again.

I looked down at him, with tears in my eyes that had nothing to do with his proposal. "Yes. I will marry you." I helped Ty stand up as he wrapped his arms around me and brought his lips to mine. I looked in the direction of where Colt had been, but noticed he was gone.

I didn't get the clapping and celebration that I had always pictured and honestly I wasn't that excited. I mean, I looked down at the ring on my finger, the ring I always knew would be mine someday, and I felt nothing.

I distanced myself from Ty, almost immediately as he continued to mingle with all of his friends. I needed to be alone. There wasn't one person here that could ever understand how confused I was.

Brina finally showed up just as everyone was starting to leave. Ty was not her favorite person and she claimed she had to work. She wasn't too happy with what was sitting on my finger either. My parents had already left, after asking me a thousand times if I was okay. Ty's parents still wouldn't look at me.

His frat buddies had pulled him away and I could hear the rowdy bunch of them somewhere out in the dark field. Brina came over and put her arm around me. "Need to talk?"

I shrugged.

"Van, where have you been this past month? You stopped returning my calls. You were never home and when I saw your mother, she thought you had been with me. You need to tell me what's going on. Did you join a secret cult? What gives?"

"I can't talk about it," I said as I started to head toward the barn. I just wanted to be with Daisy. I didn't care about the party at all. Ty had already ditched me just like always to hang out with his friends. He still had no idea how awful they had all been to me. Didn't he notice that not one of them came up to congratulate me?

Once we got in the barn, Brina spun me around to face her. "Spill! Now!"

"I was seeing someone, okay? It's over now and I just can't talk about it," I admitted.

"Holy shit! Just tell me who it was. Please tell me," she begged.

I started to cry again. "I can't tell you. I can't ever talk about it. It doesn't even matter anymore. It was over the moment Ty woke up."

She grabbed me and wrapped her arms around me. "Jesus Van. Whoever this mystery person was, they did a real number on you. I am so sorry sweetie. You don't deserve to hurt like this."

"It hurts so much," I confessed.

"Give it time. Everything is going to be okay. You have a wedding to look forward to. You can have the life you always wanted now."

That was the problem right there. This wasn't what I wanted anymore.

When Brina finally calmed me down, she stayed until I insisted I was fine. I told her I was going to find Ty and see if he was ready to call it a night. I watched her pull out of the driveway and noticed the light to the carriage house was already out. Maybe Colt had met a cute girl and was giving her a whirl, just like Ty had always said he did.

Thinking about him was like a kick in the gut. I rushed over to the field where people stood around a small fire. Sitting on Ty's lap was the blonde who had beat me to pulp. I stood there just staring, not knowing what to say or do. Before I even knew what was happening, I was running. I ran away from everyone, as fast as my legs could take me.

Ty was never going to change and Colt didn't want me. I just wanted it all to be over with. I couldn't take the pain anymore.

The thunder rolled in the distance and lightening continued to crash, but I continued to run. Nobody would be looking for me. Nobody cared.

Chapter 23

Colt

I couldn't stand around anymore acting like nothing was wrong. I went to the carriage house and grabbed my cell phone. After a twenty minute phone call, I was able to book a flight for tomorrow night. I couldn't wait to get the hell out of this town.

I couldn't believe she said yes to his proposal right in front of me like I meant nothing to her.

Savanna was breaking my heart over and over again. I needed to get away from her so that I wasn't constantly reminded of what I couldn't have.

I grabbed a six pack of beer and headed out to one of the fields. After I finished beer number five, I heard the thunder rolling in. I decided that I didn't want to talk to anyone for the rest of the night, so I climbed up into the combine and got myself comfortable. After the bottle of rum I had finished off and now the beer, I was too drunk to find my way back before the rain came.

When the first drops hit the combine's windshield, I could tell it was a serious storm. The lightening was hitting every couple of minutes and the rain was so heavy it sounded like rocks.

Even through the loud pattering of the rain, I could hear something else. I thought it was an animal, or possibly Sam followed me out here and was scared of the storm.

I was wrong.

As the lightening crashed, I saw a silhouette hunched over about one hundred feet from where I was standing. Assuming it was some drunk person lost, I climbed out and went to check. I got about five feet away and knew it wasn't a stranger.

It was Savanna.

The rain was coming down something fierce, but we both stood there just staring.

I didn't know what to do. She didn't want me. I felt rejected like she had just tossed everything we had away.

When she started yelling I was even more confused.

"How could you? How could you just push me away like I meant nothing to you?" She screamed.

"What are you talkin' about Savanna? That's not what happened and you know it!" I said defensively.

"I poured my heart out to you. I told you that I loved you," she yelled.

The rain was really coming down and lightning was hitting all around us, but neither of us moved. In fact neither of us even paid much attention.

"That's funny because the moment your precious Ty woke up, all your feelin's for me went down the tubes."

Savanna came walking toward me, breaking the gap between us. As the lightening continued to crash around us, I could see the pain in her eyes. "Is that what you think? I tried to call you. I tried so hard, but you kept pushing me away. Why did you continue spending time with me if I meant nothing to you? I let you in. Do you have any idea how much you hurt me?"

"I pushed you away because I couldn't stand to see you with him. I did it so that you could be happy. Isn't that what you want? Don't you want your happy ever after with Ty?" I yelled.

She pushed me again. "Damn you Colt. I hate you for hurting me like this. I hate you. I hate you so much for not wanting me. You made me love you, but you never wanted us to be together," she continued to beat on my chest and I let her.

Finally, when enough was enough, I managed to grab her hands. "Stop fightin' me! I didn't want to hurt you Savanna. I would never hurt you. Stop being so stubborn and listen to me. I love you. I love you so much that it's killin' me inside. I can't stand being without you, not even for a day. Seeing you with him hurts too much."

I let go of her hands and we stood there just standing in the pouring rain. At the same time, we both collided into each other's embrace. I could taste her sweet skin even through the raindrops. Her lips pressed so hard against mine and there was no way I could stop myself from kissing her. I picked her up into my arms, before we slowly made our way to the muddy ground.

I pulled away, but only to look at her. Her hair was stuck to her face, and even though we were getting muddier by the minute, I moved it out of the way.

"You really love me?" She asked.

"Darlin' you have no idea."

I found her mouth again and the water helped me trace my lips easily around every inch of it. Her tongue mingled with mine and I couldn't help but run my hands down her perfect skin. I wasn't surprised when she tugged at my shirt and tossed it somewhere in the field, after she pulled it over my head. Her nipples were so hard and my fingers played with them over her wet shirt. Not wanting to have to feel her through clothes, I pulled her shirt over her head and lay it behind her. She rested her head back down and moaned as I ran my lips around the pink of her nipple. When I finally put it in my mouth and sucked, she screamed out in pleasure.

Her knee came up and rubbed against my erection, and immediately I felt her hand unbuttoning her own pants. She wanted me right here in this field and I was going to give it to her. Nothing was going to stop me tonight. Not the rain and not any one of my family members. She was mine.

As she slid out of her wet pants, I did the same, both of us moving faster than we ever had before. Being away from her for a whole week had made the anticipation of what was happening even more heightened. We weren't being gentle. With one hard thrust I entered her. She cried out. "Yes! Colt. Please.."

I found her lips again and licked them as I thrusted into her harder each time. Her hands grabbed around to my ass and I felt her nails digging deeper with each motion. I pushed inside of her even further by using her shoulder to push off of. Her hands dug even deeper and started pulling me to move even faster. I grabbed one of her legs and pushed it up against my chest so I could get deeper. Savanna called out into the stormy night, but only I could hear her. I could feel her insides tightening as I continued to thrust my hard shaft inside of her. As I heard her crying out my name, I couldn't hold it any longer. I felt my release and let it happen until I finally collapsed over top of her.

Our heavy breathing continued even after minutes had passed. We were lying naked in a freshly planted field. Our bodies were covered in mud and our clothes were scattered all around us. We didn't care. Even with the thunder and lightning crashing above us, nothing mattered.

I put my head over hers to block the rain from hitting her in the face. "You okay Darlin'?"

Her wet hands came up and touched me. "I am now."

I stood up and reached out my hand. "Come on, let's get out of the rain," I said as we started looking around for our clothes. We grabbed the wet pile and made a beeline for the combine.

Once inside we cuddled together. Our clothes were soaked and we didn't bother putting them on. I tried to hang them up to drip dry, but it was unlikely it would happen overnight.

I held Savanna close to me. I couldn't believe she was really here in my arms.

She stood up and started getting her wet clothes on. "What are you doin'?" I asked.

"They can't find us here together. We can't hurt him like that."

"Come home with me Savanna. We can leave tonight," I pleaded.

I didn't want to face my family either. I knew if I wanted to be with her, it had to be done.

She shook her head and continued to get dressed. "I have school. My family is here. I can't just leave."

"What are you sayin'? Are you sayin' that we aint goin' to be together?"

She kept shaking her head, tryin' to get her wet shirt to slide down her stomach. Her teeth chattered and she seemed like she was out of her right mind.

"No. I can't do this right now. I need to get back."

She went to open the door and I grabbed her arm. "No!" I pulled her away from the door. "You wait just a minute. Now I can't read your mind Darlin', but you seem like you are running right back to him. I need to know what you're thinkin' Savanna."

She looked up at me. I pushed my forehead against hers. "Please don't ask me that right now Colt."

"So am I right? Are you running back to him?"

She tried to grab my hand, but I pulled away. "Please. You have to understand. I can't just leave him right now. It has nothing to do with how I feel about you, about how much I love you," she whispered.

I raised my voice. "You love me? You sure have a pretty fucked up way of showin' it Darlin'. Just so you know, I am not goin' to sit around and watch you playing house with my cousin. My heart can't take much more."

"Please don't make me choose right now. Please," she begged.

I shook my head. "Savanna, I think you are amazin'. I should have told you that I loved you before you walked into that hospital, but I really believed that I never had a chance. Seeing you with him, especially tonight when he proposed, it crushed me. I don't regret what we just did. I would do it all over again if I had a choice. But, I can't sit around and wait for the time to be right. It isn't fair to me and it sure aint fair to Ty. If you are truly in love with me, you won't waste anymore time makin' your decision. The storm has passed if you need to go."

Savanna reached up and kissed me with tear filled eyes. "I choose you," she whispered in my ear, before running out into the night.

I slumped down against the combine door. It was too dark to see where she went, and I probably should have tried to walk her back, but my stubborn ass just sat there, letting my future walk away from me again.

Chapter 24

Savanna

I cried the whole walk back to the farmhouse. The rain had put out the fire, but I noticed people still standing around in the tents. The girls weren't around Ty anymore, and he immediately spotted me as I was walking in. "Van are you alright? What happened to you?" He asked.

"I saw you with those girls and I got upset. Before I knew it, it had started raining. I climbed up in a combine and waited out the storm."

"Why don't you go inside and get some of my warm clothes on." He suggested, while avoiding the part about the other girls.

I wrapped my arms around my wet clothes as I made my way into his house.

His mother greeted me at the door. "Where were you?"

"I got caught in the storm," I admitted.

"If I find out that you were sneakin' around with my nephew just moments after my son put that ring on your finger, you will have hell to pay," She threatened.

I kept walking past her. It wasn't worth the fight and she would be able to tell more than anyone that I really had been with Colt. I couldn't stop thinking about him. I left him out there, not willing to give him a straight answer. He told me he loved me and I still walked away.

When I got into Ty's room, I grabbed a hoodie and pair of boxers and changed out of my wet clothes. My heart started racing and I considered running back out there. In fact, I knew it was exactly what I needed to do.

Throwing caution to the wind, I started walking out of the house, only to be stopped in my tracks by Ty. He was wheeling himself toward the couch when he spotted me. "There is my future bride. Don't you look all cute in my clothes. I tell ya, I can't wait to sleep with you in my arms tonight," he confessed.

I just froze. How could I hurt him right now? How could I rip out his heart and not feel bad about it? Did he even deserve that? Wasn't I the one that set all of these events in play?

Ty held out his arms, once he got on the couch. "Come over here and give me some love."

I swallowed my pride and went and sat next to Ty. His strong arms wrapped around me as he started kissing me on my neck. Between the smell of women's perfume and booze, I wanted to gag. How could this not have bothered me before. Was I so blinded by our fairytale life that I never noticed how much of an ass he really was? Did it really take me falling in love with someone else to see the real Ty?

Due to the fact that I was not really into his kissing, Ty pulled away and looked at me. "Something is wrong babe. Can you please tell me what's going on? I know that you waited months for me, but it was only a day in my eyes. You have to excuse me for loving you just as much as before the accident. Just tell me what's going on. Are you still mad about what happened that night?"

I leaned forward and put his face in my hands. "It's just all so much to take," I admitted.

"Van, I hate to ask this, but you haven't been yourself since I woke up. Something is different about you. You used to want to touch me all of the time. You used to kiss me a million times a day. Do you realize that I have had to ask you for affection? I need you to be honest with me. I won't be mad, in fact I won't judge you, but I just need to know. Was there someone else in your life while I was in the hospital? Is this why you are being so distant? Listen, I will forgive you. I will understand if you just needed to let loose. We can get past it babe."

This was my chance to come clean. To tell him I couldn't possibly marry him. This was my opportunity to get him to break up with me. I swallowed my pride and looked into those eyes that I had loved for so long. "Ty, at first there was nobody, not even your friends were nice to me. I was all alone, feeling like everything was my fault. One day someone came into my life. They listened to me and offered good advice about never giving up on you. One night after a few drinks things happened. It had nothing to do with my feelings for you, but I just wanted to feel wanted. Do you understand?" I bit my lip and waited for him to respond. Tears filled his eyes, and I swear it was the first time I had ever seen him cry since we were little kids.

"Wow! I never pegged you as someone that could have a one night stand babe," he just sat there. His fingers moved my still damp hair away from my face. "Van, did you think if you told me I wouldn't want to marry you? I deserved it really, for what I did to you the night of my accident. I knew you would be at that party. I knew you were going to show up looking for me, but I was selfish and thought with my dick instead. Shit, I did it with no regard for anyone else. I am sorry for that babe, but I want you to know that I forgive you."

This was the opposite of what I expected. Now Ty knew I had slept with someone else. He didn't know who or how serious it got, but he knew. This was not good.

"I didn't mean for it to happen," I added.

"So, you going to tell me who the lucky guy was?"

Oh Shit!

"It doesn't matter. He wasn't even from here or from school." I admitted.

"Mysterious. Okay, we don't have to talk about it." He leaned in and kissed my cheek. "Can we talk about our future now? I was thinking we could get married this fall, here at the farm when the leaves change colors."

I tried to be calm. To pretend I wasn't upset that he didn't seem to even care that I had been with someone else. Why wouldn't he care? If I found out he was with someone, I would want to know every damn detail. I couldn't help but wonder if he was hiding something himself and maybe that was why it was so easy for him to forgive and forget.

"Van. Earth to Van?"

"Sorry. A fall wedding? This fall? Don't you want to finish school first?"

"We are both going to be twenty this fall. I figured it would be a fine time to get married. We can still finish school and do everything we always planned. I just want to hear you with the last name Mitchell when we graduate."

I started coughing, gagging really. I did not expect that to come out of his mouth. "Ty, can we please talk about all of this tomorrow. I am exhausted and after being out in the rain, I feel like I am getting sick already." I tried to weasel my way out of the conversation.

He shook his head. "Okay. Well, can I get a little ass before we go to sleep?" He asked in his normal conceited way.

"I don't think that's a good idea. You just got out of the hospital."

Ty stood up and worked hard to balance himself on his two legs. He slid into the wheelchair and started heading for his bedroom. "Nothing is going to stop me from sleeping with my girlfriend tonight."

I couldn't do this. I had just slept with Colt and there was no way in Hell I was going to be with Ty an hour later.

I followed him back to his room, but insisted that I wanted to take a hot shower. Thinking he would fall asleep while I took my time, I headed into the bathroom and started to undress. I could easily sneak out of the house and run back to Colt, but his family would find me and Ty would never forgive him. After our conversation and the fact that being with someone else didn't even faze him, this was no longer about me. It was about Colt and Ty. Whatever decision I made, I needed to keep their relationship intact.

Just when I thought things couldn't get any worse, I heard the bathroom door opening. After a bunch of banging, I saw the curtain opening. Ty stood there looking at me. His main focus was from my chest to my crotch. "Why don't you help me get out of these clothes so I can join you?"

Figuring that he had to use all of his strength to hold himself up, I helped him get undressed thinking he couldn't possibly be able to want sex in this shower. I helped him inside and although the room was tight, we managed to be facing one another. "You are so beautiful Van. I thought I lost you that night. I can't believe you are really here," he said as he leaned in and kissed my lips. He pulled away when I didn't kiss him back, but then he froze. His eyes were fixed on my chest. When I looked down I saw why. On the side of my right breast, there was a mark from where Colt had sucked. "What the fuck is that?" He asked while raising his voice.

I tried to play it off. "Brina pinched me tonight. She said I was being a wallflower."

"For a second I thought it was a hickey. I was ready to beat some dudes ass."

I was guilty of so many things and the lies were just building up. Why did I even come back to this house? I was so stupid.

I played it off and gave him a weird look like he was insane. Finally, he realized that we couldn't be intimate in his weakened state. I helped him get washed, which I noticed he was enjoying way too much. Even as I washed him, I couldn't help but look at every inch of his body. He had lost almost all of his muscle, in fact I heard him saying he lost thirty pounds. His chest was always broad, so he didn't look too skinny even after the weight loss. Ty was a determined person and I knew he would gain back the weight and get right back to where he was before the accident.

With a little maneuvering, I managed to get him out of the bathroom and tucked into bed. It took us a good thirty minutes and once he realized my struggle, he gave up on trying to get into my pants. I pretended to be exhausted when he wrapped his arms around me. My back was facing him and he couldn't see the tears falling down my eyes. He didn't know that I was constantly thinking of Colt. I wanted to run to him, but I couldn't. I was stuck in this situation and I knew that someone would get hurt no matter what direction I went.

When I woke up the next morning, Ty was still sleeping. Knowing that he would have a hangover, I snuck out of the room quietly. The house was empty, so I ventured outside to start picking up from the party. I noticed Harvey and Ty's dad taking down the tents. They saw me and looked all around.

"Where did you come from?" Ty's father asked.

"Inside the house. Ty is still sleeping," I explained.

He turned and shook his head, then got back to taking down the tents. For the next half hour, I walked around with a trash bag, cleaning up beer cans and trash. Out of the corner of my eye I spotted someone coming up the lane. Colt had his head down, his still wet shirt was strung over one of his shoulders. I tried not to look, but I couldn't help wonder what he was thinking. He had to be mad. There was no way around it. I left him lying in that combine while I ran back to his cousin's bed. I had become a common whore.

Ty's mother broke my stare. She got close enough that she didn't have to yell, which was always a bad sign. "Funny how my nephew looks exactly like you did when you came in last night. I warned you about seeing him. I don't know what kind of games you think you are playing, but it won't be on my watch."

Her threats couldn't stop me from looking one more time at Colt. He nodded as he walked by, but his brows were creased and I knew immediately he was pissed.

I wanted to talk to him, to explain that I hadn't changed my mind, but with his aunt watching my back, it was impossible. What made matters even worse was when Ty came hobbling out the door on a set of crutches, the same time Sam came running out of the carriage house and ran right to me.

He caught me off guard standing behind me, grabbing me into a hug. "Looks like you made a friend," he said as he kissed the back of my neck.

"I didn't expect you to get up so early. I tried not to wake you," I explained.

I turned around to face him. He shrugged and smiled. "I wanted to surprise you. I had my dad get these out of the attic last night," he said holding up one of the crutches. "I think I did pretty good getting around. I didn't fall on my ass yet."

We both smiled.

"So I was thinking that since Colt is in town, we could all go out tonight. Let's go talk to him about it," he suggested.

I did not know what to do. The last thing I wanted to do was be in the same room as both of them. Especially not after what happened last night.

I saw Ty's mother giving me a dirty look again as I followed behind him. "Wait. He might not even be awake yet." I tried to divert him by lying.

"I will wake his ass up then. Will you just come on. I need you to get the door for me."

This was such a bad idea.

Chapter 25

Colt

After the wild sex in the storm and sleeping in the combine, I felt like shit. Savanna felt so good being in my arms. My mother always said life throws you tests. Well I wasn't sure if Savanna was one of them, but I was definitely failing.

After she ran away last night, I sat there for the longest time tryin to figure a way out of this mess. She was right. One of us was going to get hurt no matter what choice she made. I had watched her last night with him, and even when he proposed, she never seemed happy. When she found me in that field and told me she loved me, I believed her. I could see it on her face and feel it when she touched me.

There wasn't any other woman that had ever made me feel the way she did. She had turned me into someone who cared about someone other than myself. I just couldn't let her go, even if it meant losing my cousin.

I heard the front door opening just as I was climbing in the shower. I hurried up and did my best to wash the dried mud off my body. After a few minutes I climbed out.

"Knock much?" I said as I kept walking into the bedroom. I saw them both standing there, but I just couldn't look at her, not with him standing there too.

"Fuck you Cuz. We came over to invite you out for a night of food and drinks," Ty yelled while I was grabbing some clothes.

This kid had no idea. He had no clue that last night I told his fiancée that I loved her, and then I bedded her in the field, because I couldn't help myself. I was a piece of shit. I knew it. I felt like Hell when I woke up this morning, but I didn't regret a second of it.

I don't know why I did it, but I came out of the room in just a pair of shorts. When Savanna noticed, I saw her eyes get real big. Good thing she was standing behind my cousin. I had to keep the peace with Ty, at least until Savanna figured out what the hell she wanted. "Yeah, that sounds like it would be fun."

"Sweet! Well make sure you wear something without the word John Deere on it. I think I know a few blondes that would love a piece of you," Ty replied giving me some secret eye signal.

I looked down and tried not to laugh.

"You don't have to set me up. I'm kinda seein' someone already," I admitted. "She aint even a blonde."

Ty came in further and sat down on the couch. I assumed it was still hard for him to stand, but got the impression he was really trying. "You still seeing the one that lives with you?"

I shook my head. "Nah, she's history."

I leaned on the other side of the couch while Savanna stood behind Ty. She did it so she could watch me without him knowing. I wanted to look at her too, but really didn't want to cause more problems than I already was.

"So who is this new girl? She a redhead?" Ty drilled me.

I shook my head again. "She has brown hair actually."

"Damn, why didn't you bring her with you?" Ty asked.

"She spent a couple weekends with me," I confessed.

At this point Savanna was beet red. I glanced up and wanted to laugh out loud. She was giving me these giant eyes mouthing the words "Shut up".

Then, I just couldn't help myself. "You know, I think I will be open minded tonight. It's like you always said about different zip codes. Maybe my future wife will be there tonight." I looked right up at Savanna when I said it.

She tried to play it off. "Zip codes? Really? When did you all discuss something like that?" Her question was directed to Ty.

He turned around toward me. "What the fuck man?" Then turned back around to Savanna. "He used to say that shit, not me. You know how he's with women. Don't listen to him babe. You know you are the only one for me."

I rolled my eyes while he was talkin' to her. I saw him rubbing some girl tits just last night. Being a cheater was just how my cousin lived. It was a damn shame Savanna never figured it out before.

Savanna decided to change the subject. "If we are going out, I am going to need to go home and get clothes. Did you want to take me on the way tonight or get my stuff now?"

I grabbed the crutches and leaned with them under my arms while Savanna and Ty decided what they were doin'. "Well, being that I can't drive, I guess Colt will have to drive you. You think you can run her to town real quick for me?" He stood up and reached for the crutches. "Give me those. I got to piss."

I watched him hobble to the bathroom. "I can take her."

Once he was out of sight, I turned to look at Savanna. "We can't be alone," she whispered as I broke the distance between us and brushed my lips against hers.

"Making love to you in that field was the hottest thing I have ever done," I whispered to her before moving to the kitchen before the bathroom door opened.

Savanna couldn't keep a straight face. She looked down and tried real hard not to smile or blush, but I knew I got under her skin.

"Can't you ride along too?" Savanna asked Ty, while giving me another warning look.

"I guess I can. Did you guys want to head out now? We can get breakfast in town," Ty suggested.

"Let me grab a shirt and we can go," I replied.

I wanted to take Savanna without Ty, but knowing her leg would be pressed against mine on the ride, was good enough for me. I met the two of them outside and after Savanna ran and got Ty's wallet, we headed out.

Savanna told us to wait for her while she got her things together. Ty and I rolled all the windows down and sat there quiet until she was out of sight.

"Something is different with her man. Last night she admitted that she slept with someone else. After all the women I've been with behind her back, I couldn't be mad at her, but I would be lying if I said that it didn't bother me," Ty said.

I looked straight out at the road. After being with me in that field, I felt like she left me, but she really was trying to look for reasons to make him break up with her. "Do you trust her?"

"That's the thing. I always have trusted her, but she was really secretive about this guy. She wouldn't even tell me his name. How do I know it's over if she won't tell me?"

She was going to kill me but I was a grown man and I couldn't wait forever. "How is she bein' different? Didn't she stay with you last night?"

"Dude, I tried everything last night. I tried to sweet talk her, tried to shower with her, hell I even cuddled with her, but she wouldn't show me any affection. Things are different. I really thought after putting that ring on her finger she would be happy."

I wanted to smile, but I felt bad for my cousin. Still, Savanna didn't run into his arms last night like I thought. She was fightin' him instead. "I don't know what to tell ya Ty. How bad was it before the accident?" I pretended not to know.

"We weren't together at all. She said she couldn't focus on school with all my partying. I think she thought I would stop for her, but you only live once, and I want to enjoy my college years. If Van doesn't want to party with me, than there are a lot of other chicks that will," he admitted.

"Besides proposin', have you even talked about your relationship since you woke up?"

He shook his head. "I hate talking about that shit. What do you think is going on? Have you ever been cheated on?" He asked.

"Yeah, it sucks, but I also had never done it back, so it really hit me hard. Maybe Savanna had a hard time when you were in the hospital. Maybe she felt alone and turned to someone for support. I can tell that things are strained with her and your parents. Your mother seems to be really givin' her a hard time."

"My mom just wants me to be happy. She always said Van wasn't right for me. Maybe I am just over thinking everything. Van has never even been with anyone else before. I guess I am just jealous that someone else touched her. I always felt like she only belonged to me. She's so damn pretty now. Hell, I remember her getting all pissed at you for calling her a boy. I can tell you, there aint nothing boyish about that girl," he admitted.

I got ready to say something but he wasn't finished. I was glad too. I knew exactly how hot she was. I could imagine every inch of her body. I had it memorized.

"You should talk to her and see if she will open up to you. Just try to find out who the guy is tonight. Here she comes. Act like we are talking about football."

Savanna got back in the truck. Her hair was wet and she smelled amazing. When I climbed in next to her, I couldn't help but press my leg against hers.

We had to touch in the truck while driving, but being this close to her, when she was smelling so good, was making me crazy.

We stopped to get something to eat, but I could tell from Savanna's body language she was uncomfortable. A bunch of people came up to our table and started talking to Ty. I caught Savanna giving me a couple glances and I tapped on her foot with my own. She gave me a half smile and continued eating her food.

After what turned out to be lunch, we headed back to the farm. I wasn't really looking forward to watching my cousin paw all over Savanna, especially hearing from him that they really never got back together. Technically, she never cheated on him. And, since they weren't sleeping together, I just wanted her more. When this began, I was okay just being her friend, but my idiot cousin was proving more and more that he was the wrong person for her. I knew it because I was the person she should be with. I wanted to protect her, and to cherish her every day.

We parted ways once we got to the farm. Ty had an appointment with a physical therapist, who had arrived minutes after we pulled in. Savanna headed right into the barn to be with Daisy and I made my way toward the corn field. The irrigation system kept turning off, so I promised my uncle I would take a look at it.

I had all my tools sprawled out across the dirt as I tried to put the new part into the motor. I heard the sound of hooves approaching and looked behind me to see Savanna. She jumped down and approached me before I could say anything. In her hand was a bottle of water. She handed it to me and I looked directly into her eyes while I took a big drink. "Thanks!"

"I just wanted to say hi," she said.

I grabbed her chin and leaned into her. My lips touched hers and I kept them there for a few seconds before pulling away. "Hi yourself."

"I have to go before they come looking," she said as she started to walk away.

I grabbed her hand and pulled her back to me. "He wants me to talk to you tonight about the guy you were seein'."

"Really? What are you going to tell him?" She asked.

I kissed her again before responding. "Part of me wants to tell him that you are crazy about the guy and to just give up, but it would look terrible when he finds out I am the guy."

Her arms wrapped around me. "It's the truth. I am crazy about you. It doesn't help that you are so damn sexy."

"Stop talkin' like that or we will have to get muddy again." I kissed her one more time, then smacked her ass. "Get back before they start wonderin'. I will see you later Darlin'."

I watched her ride away from me. I didn't know how we were going to keep doing this. We needed a solution, before I took matters into my own hands.

My uncle wanted me to stay here and help out with the farm. I didn't mind helping or even staying, but my problems with Savanna were definitely a huge conflict. Ty had no idea how awful he was to her. The poor girl had been a victim in it all. I felt sorry for her.

Chapter 26

Savanna

I spent the rest of the afternoon with Daisy. We rode out to the hole and then back to the barn. I gave her a good hose down and then cleaned out her feet. She loved it when I brushed her and I decided to braid her mane too.

When I finally headed back into the house, everyone was heading toward the dining room. Ty's mother had made her famous fried chicken. We all sat at the table and started making our plates. Colt walked in just after me and I saw Ty's mother shaking her head. Good thing Ty wasn't paying attention. Everyone else at the table knew I had been in the barn for the past hour with my horse. Sam came running in the room. She found me immediately. Colt tried not to noticed, but I saw the crooked smile on his face before Ty said something. "She really likes you. That's the second time she ran right to you. Guess I need to get you your own lab."

I smiled and tried to just keep eating and ignoring the obvious time bomb that was ready to blow up in my face.

I insisted on doing the dishes, while all of the men went into the living room. Ty's mother came into the kitchen with more dirty looks. I turned to her with dripping hands. "Can we please talk?" I asked.

"What do you have to say Van?"

"You are wrong about me. I have loved your son since I was a child. I have done everything to make him happy and when he was partying too much I broke up with him to try to make him stop. What happened to him was horrible, but I never cheated on him. I swear to you."

She shook her head and folded her hands across her stomach. "You forget that I caught you more than once," she whispered.

"We didn't plan that. It just happened. I am so sorry. I can't take you hating me like this. Please!"

She shook her head. "Do you know why I am so angry with you now Van? It isn't about the accident. My son explained what happened. I know what he did that night," she leaned over the counter, like it was hard to talk about. "Never in all the years that you have been with my son, have I ever seen you look at him the way you look at my nephew. It's not just you either. He looks at you the same way. Now I love Colt, but my son is the most important thing in my life. He's going to figure it out. How long do you think you can hide it? How long before he catches you together? Do you know what it will do him?"

I put my head down. "I'm trying. I don't know how to tell him. Either way it will crush him."

She got closer to me, but I was no longer afraid she was going to hurt me. "I said things I shouldn't have to you, but I was just so damn angry. I see that this is hard. I wish I could tell you to stop seeing Colt, but you are both adults, and I can tell that it's never going to happen. He's a good man. He's honest. Figure out a way to tell him the truth, before you both rip out his heart. He has been through too much already. He looks up to Colt, idolizes him even. This will crush him."

She scrunched up her face and walked away before I could respond. I refused to cry. Instead I finished the dishes in silence and made my way to the bathroom to get ready to go out. We decided on going straight to the bar since we already had dinner. I grabbed a short jean skirt and a shirt that buttoned up that I could tie around my waist. I was going to wear flip flops, but my boots were better to dance in. I straightened my hair and applied makeup to my face. I hadn't done it in months and my tan was darker than the cover up, so I only did my eyes. When I stood back and looked at myself I realized Colt had never seen my hair like this. I unbuttoned the top three buttons and let my cleavage hang just out of the top.

I looked down at my ring and felt myself getting upset. I should have said no. Things would have been over with. Now they were harder.

When I walked out into the living room, the guys stopped talking. They stared at me with their mouths open. "Do I look bad?" I asked knowing damn well I didn't.

Ty started whistling, while Colt kept his reaction to himself. I watched Ty throw a pillow at his cousin. "Dude, get your own," he said.

They exchanged a laugh, and I couldn't help but feel awful. Colt said nothing after that comment.

We got Ty situated with his crutches and headed out toward the pickup. I climbed in first and felt Ty reaching his hand up my skirt when I crawled in the seat. I could see Colt clinching his jaw when it happened. His knuckles turned white as he gripped the steering wheel. I pushed his leg with mine for him to calm down.

The bar was packed, but we found a table in the corner. We got Ty situated and then went to the bar to get drinks. While waiting for the waitress, Colt didn't waste any time telling me how jealous he was. "I didn't like watching him touch you."

"I know."

"You look beautiful. Meet me tonight. I can't be with you all night like this and not be able to touch you Savanna." He grabbed a beer and took a drink. "I can't stop picturing you naked."

I pushed him before grabbing two more beers and heading back to the table where Ty sat.

"One for you and one for me," I announced, handing him a beer.

Ty didn't waste any time waving down some of his friends. Within minutes of us being there, our table was surrounded by people. After a half hour, I got up to go to the bathroom and when I came back my seat was occupied by no other than that bitch Heather. She smiled as I approached, but Ty knew how pissed I was about it. Heather on the other hand refused to take a hint. I grabbed Colt by the arm and pulled him out to the dance floor.

I never turned around to see if Ty was watching. He had given me enough reason to go out and have a good time. Colt responded right away and we started dancing together, trying to keep a good distance so we wouldn't be too obvious. The truth was that I wanted to grind my ass right into him, until he couldn't take it anymore. After three songs, we walked up to the bar to order two beers. I looked back and watched Ty doing shots with all of his friends, including the blonde bitch. I changed our order to shots and Colt cocked his eyebrow. "Not a good idea Savanna. I can't get drunk around you and you can't get drunk around me. It's fuel to the fire."

Before he could protest anymore I grabbed the shot and downed it. "Fuck it!"

He looked down at the shot and then back at me. I shrugged my shoulders and grabbed his shot, sucking it down before he could respond.

"Savanna," Colt said when I signaled for two more shots.

"Do the shots and then come dance with me. Your cousin is over there groping all over the girl. He isn't even paying attention to us."

"Are you mad about it?" He asked.

"Colt, please shut up and dance with me."

A slow song came on and everyone started gathering up someone to be their partner. I looked toward Ty out of habit and saw him gesturing Colt and I to go ahead. I didn't waste any time reaching up and touching his strong arms. We started swaying to Luke Bryan singing "Do I". I couldn't stop looking into Colt's eyes even when he looked the other way and warned me to stop.

His hands were around me. He did manage to touch the exposed skin on my waist. Slowly he moved his fingers as we swayed around to the song. In my ear I heard him singing the song. I wanted to melt.

His deep southern voice sang… "Do I turn you on at all when I kiss you baby? Does the sight of me wanting you drive you crazy? Do I have your love? Am I still enough?........Baby do I?"

I closed my eyes and listened to him. The alcohol was taking effect and we were probably getting way too close, but I couldn't help it.

When the song ended we broke apart and headed back to the bar. Colt got three beers and we made our way back to the table. I thought Ty would at least be mad, but he never even noticed.

He held up the beer. "Thanks. You guys having a good time? You keeping my girl safe out there Cuz?"

Colt put his hands on my shoulders. "She's safe with me." He nudged me and pulled me back out to the dance floor.

After a few more songs I couldn't help but notice Ty had a serious look on his face. He seemed to be involved in a conversation with quite a few people at once. Every once in a while I caught him looking up at me. "Colt I think he's talking about me."

We kept dancing. "You are worrying. He's just catching up with people. Relax."

We both finished off the beer and I was really starting to feel tipsy. Another slow song came on. Colt didn't waste any time pulling me into the dance. I was really feeling the alcohol. This time the song was Brantley Gilbert, "You don't know her like I do".

I hadn't ever listened to the words to the song much until Colt started singing them. "You don't know her like I do. You'll never understand. You don't know what we've been through. That girl's my best friend......."

He took my hands and pulled them up to his chest. I watched him singing the song to me. Then he pressed his cheek on my forehead and continued singing. I was obviously feeling the effects of the alcohol more and more as I didn't see anything wrong with our embrace, but as the song started coming to an end and Colt continued to sing, something told me to look over at the table.

I could see Ty's breathing from all the way across the room. His fists were clenched and he stared at the two of us. Colt leaned down. "Don't freak out," he said before walking over to the table.

I followed behind him almost scared to look at Ty again. The people he was sitting with started to get up. Ty seemed to relax when we sat down and waited for him to explain.

"What's up? You havin' a good time?" Colt asked him.

"Why didn't either of you tell me about the bonfire?" He asked.

I tried to talk, but Colt held up his hand. "The day I came into town I ran into Brina. She conned me into gettin' Savanna to come out with us. I didn't know that everyone in town treated her like she killed you herself. We no sooner got to the damn party, when she got jumped. I carried her out of there and got her cleaned up."

He turned to look at me and then back to Colt. "Let me talk to my cousin alone, Van."

I could see the fire in his eyes and was reluctant to get up from the table, but Colt nodded and I walked away. I watched them talking and then I could tell they were yelling. I started walking back but neither of them said anything.

"Everything alright here?" I asked.

"It's fine. There is this party I wanted to stop by. If you don't want to go, Colt said he would take you home," Ty announced.

His words were cold and he looked upset. "Are you okay?" I asked.

"I need to go to that party to deal with the little tramps that attacked you. You can come with me or stay here, but either way I am going. Colt seems to think you should stay," he explained.

"If I never saw Heather and her bimbo friends again I would be fine with that," I admitted.

"Can you guys help me out of here?" Ty asked.

I found his actions odd, but he had been drinking so I didn't try to over think it.

We got him out to the parking lot and one of his friends helped get him in their car. He leaned over and kissed me before closing the door and speeding off.

I looked to Colt. "Was that weird?"

"My cousin does a lot of weird things."

He held out his hand and pulled me back inside. It was getting late and the slow songs were becoming more frequent. After all of our drinks and Ty leaving, we weren't worried about how close we were dancing. Colt's hands slid down over my butt and he rocked our bodies together to the rhythm of the music. When the songs got faster he turned me around and let me grind my back into him as his hands played with the skin on my stomach.

We were both sweating. Our eyes were only on each other. We were being too obvious, not thinking anyone would ever find out. When the last song of the night came on, we were so caught up in each other to realize our hands were everywhere they shouldn't have been.

I had forgotten about everyone else in the bar, in fact all I could see was Colt.

He reached down to my ear and whispered in it. "Let's get out of here. I need to be inside of you." His lips drug over my ear. I pulled away and licked my lips. He took my hand and led me out of the building and straight to his truck.

Chapter 27

Savanna

We didn't bother leaving the parking lot. Colt slid over and took my lips into his mouth. Our skin was soaked with sweat and we tasted like salt. The first thing I reached for was his shirt. I had been so close to his chest all night long. I needed to feel it, to see it. I ran my tongue across each of his nipples before he pulled me back to his lips again. His hand slid up my skirt and I felt his fingers enter inside of me forcefully. I let out a loud moan when I felt them penetrating me. Our kisses got rougher and so did the way he thrusted inside of me. I grabbed the dashboard with one hand and the headrest with the other, trying to push his fingers inside of me harder. His other hand untied my shirt and pulled it open revealing my bra. He didn't bother unhooking it, instead he pulled it down and took my nipple into his mouth. I could feel his teeth dragging over it. I cried out in the night as I felt my body start to tremble.

As soon as he removed his fingers, I slid over and unbuttoned his pants. He moved over so that I could straddle him. I leaned up and removed my underwear with one hand, while I stroked his hard shaft with the other. I practically jumped right on him, sliding down perfectly over it. He groaned at my first thrust and held my waist. I leaned back against the dashboard so that he could touch my chest and guide me up and down. In just minutes we were both crying out in ecstasy.

Colt held me tight even though we were both soaked with sweat. "Sorry it was so fast Darlin'. All that grindin' earlier really got to me," he admitted.

"You think it was easy for me? I wanted you when I saw you walking back from the field this morning," I confessed.

"We need to figure out what we are doing Savanna. I can't keep hiding this. I want you in my life. Not temporary either. I want you to come home with me. I will do whatever it takes, just say you will consider it."

I leaned down and kissed him again. When I went to say something I heard something loud hitting the truck. I jumped off of Colt and tied my shirt before opening the door. Ty pulled me out of the truck by my hair and stood there staring at his shirtless cousin.

"You mother fucker! How could you do this to me?" He yelled toward Colt.

Colt jumped out of the truck and threw his shirt back over his head. He didn't back down to Ty though. He kept walking toward him.

I jumped up and tried to get between them. "Please don't fight!" I screamed, but Ty pushed me out of the way.

"Shut up Van!"

Colt pulled me behind him. "Don't you touch her like that."

"You don't tell me how to touch my girl," Ty yelled back.

"Do you think she would have run to me if you were treatin' her good before your accident? Do you think she deserves to be lied to?" Colt yelled. His chest was rising and falling and I really thought he was going to hurt his cousin.

"Oh, is that how you got in her pants? You told her all of my dirty little secrets didn't you? I looked up to you and you used all of my secrets to get into my girlfriend's pants. You fucking asshole. I wish you were dead, you common bastard."

"I didn't tell her shit!" Colt yelled.

"Bullshit! There is no way she would have fucked you if she hadn't found out how many girls I was sleeping with the whole time we were together. She told me a long time ago that it was the only reason she would ever leave me. I know you told her," he screamed back.

This time I jumped in the middle of them. I was so shocked. All of this time Colt knew that Ty had cheated on me. I felt betrayed by both of them. "He never told me. ..... But, you just did," I said as I walked away from both of them and leaned on the truck. I was so hurt and angry that I didn't care if they beat the shit out of each other.

"I don't understand. Van wait!" Ty called out.

I wouldn't look at him.

I heard Colt clear his throat. " Leave her alone! Look Ty, it started out just as friends. We didn't mean for it to turn into more, but I never told her anything. I didn't want her to love me because she hated you. I wanted her to choose me on her own. I am sorry. I know you think I am the worst cousin ever, but, I swear to you, I love her."

I turned to look at them when it got too quiet. Ty took his crutch and threw it at the back of the truck. "All my life I wanted to be you. You could get any girl you wanted. Hell, they always wanted you. Why couldn't you just tell her no? It takes two people, even I know that. Which one of you made the first move?"

When neither of us said anything he asked again. "Tell me who started this," He screamed.

I walked toward them. "I did. Colt told me no, several times."

Colt's face was all scrunched up. Both of them were still breathing like they had just ran for their lives. I stood there looking at the pain on both of their faces. "After the accident everyone blamed me. Your friends and even your parents called me a murderer. Everyone on campus stopped being my friend. I had to see a shrink after I tried to kill myself. I spent every day in the hospital because I believed I put you in there. I felt so guilty that I couldn't let myself live."

I looked up at both of them and then continued my story. "When Colt came to town, he didn't judge me like everyone else. After the party where I got jumped by Heather and her slutty friends, Colt took me back to the carriage house and stitched up my face. He took care of me for days so nobody would see what happened. He listened to me and let me cry over and over about you. He never judged me or asked for anything in return."

Colt had his eyes locked on me. He was clenching his jaw, trying to control his temper. I looked back down to the ground. "He never hit on me. We were just friends Ty. He was just doing it for you. But, as the days passed and I finally was able to be around someone that didn't hate me, things changed. I can't tell you exactly when, but I just wanted to feel wanted." I walked over to Ty and grabbed his hand. I put the ring in his palm and closed it. He closed his eyes shut and when they opened they were full of tears. "I'm sorry Ty. When you woke up we tried to fight our feelings, but I can't stop wanting him. I can't marry you. I hope one day you can forgive me." I started crying and walked away from both of them. Colt looked at me as I walked past him, but I was still angry.

"What am I supposed to say?" I heard him asking Colt. "So, you meant well. At some point you went too far man. Did you think about me when you were fucking her? Did you feel bad at all? Because, you don't have to tell me you couldn't stop yourself. She's hard to deny. I just can't understand how you couldn't stop yourself for me."

Obviously, Colt had just had enough! He moved forward depleting the distance between them. "Just stop with your sob story Tyler! For years I have listened to you go on and on about all the girls you were sleeping with behind her back. As she lay there every night cryin' to me about you, I kept the truth from her. I felt like an asshole lyin' to her. She felt horrible for sleepin' with me, when all the while you had done it to her over and over. Oh and by the way, I really liked how you told her about the women, but made her think they were my conquests and not your own. What the fuck Cuz? How could you make me out to be that guy? For someone that wants to be with her forever, you sure have a shitty way of showin' it."

At this point I had turned all the way around. My mouth hung open. Everything made sense now. My tears dried up and I felt so angry.

"Is it true? All of it?" I turned to face Ty.

He threw his hands up in the air. "You know what. I am tired of lying. Yes! It's all true Van. I fucked them all and they kept coming back for more too. You were always so caught up in yourself and school to notice I had needs. If you would have been there for me, it never would have happened."

I ran toward him throwing my body at him. He fell down to the ground, but I continued to beat on his chest, until I felt strong hands pulling me off. "Get off me!" I screamed.

Colt didn't let go. With one hand he held me back, and with the other he pulled his cousin back up to his feet.

Ty looked so mad.

"I hate you. I went through Hell for you," I screamed.

Colt continued to hold me back. "Ty, you and I are family. I am real sorry for what I did. I just have to ask. Do you love her enough to want her to be happy? Do you want that for her? After everything? I've watched you both grow up. I know you want her to be happy."

"Fuck you Colt." Ty ran his hand through his hair. "Van?"

I turned to look at him but refused to speak. Everything I had ever known was shattered into pieces.

"I'm sorry." His eyes were full of tears. "God I can't believe I am saying this... Is he really what you want? Do you really love him that much?"

I ran my fingers into Colt's and he immediately tightened his grip. I couldn't speak. I was too choked up between the pain and anger and the alcohol. I nodded my head up and down.

He looked to Colt. "If you hurt her I will fucking kill you. This is wrong in so many ways." He held out his hand to his cousin. "We are blood. I might hate you both right this second, but I also love you. This shit hurts, but I guess I deserve it."

"Ty." Colt tried to say something, but Ty stopped him.

He shook his head. "Van, Colts right for you. I was never ready to settle down. Shit, I couldn't even be faithful after I proposed. That's why I was leaving the bar tonight. I got halfway down the road and told them to bring me back. I had this feeling in my gut that something bad was going to happen. I came back in the bar and I watched you."

He pointed from me to Colt. "I saw you looking at him the way you never once looked at me. I saw your hands all over each other. I've danced with my fair share of women, but none of them remotely came close to that show. I don't even think it was the touching. You were both so in sync with each other. As if that wasn't enough, I hid and watched my cousin take you in that truck. I should have stopped you, but I couldn't believe it. For the past week I have tried time and time again to get you to touch me. You just kept pushing me away. I knew there was someone else, but I never realized it was my own family. Someone that I think of as a brother."

He pointed to Colt. "And you….I asked you if you knew who she had been with. You lied right to my face. I should have known though. The signs were there. My God even the fucking dog was a sign. No matter how many people were around, all she wanted to do was be around you. How could I have been so damn blind?"

I put my hand over my mouth. Ty was only about a foot from me and Colt was standing in between us.

Ty held his hands up and just started yelling. "DAMMIT!"

He covered his face in his hands for a few minutes while we just stood there quiet. Everyone in the parking lot had been gone even before Colt and I were done our little bit in the truck. We were all alone.

Finally, Ty looked up. "I just can't believe this!"

"So what happens now?" I asked, trying my hardest to change the subject. I knew Ty was confessing his deepest secrets and even though I was very much over him, I felt so betrayed. The last five years were a lie. I needed to get away from him. He was in pain, but right now more than ever I felt like he deserved it.

"You go home," Ty announced.

"What about you?" To be honest I was afraid to be with them in that truck.

"Van, I just told you I loved you both. You may not want me, but you will always be a part of my family. The best man won right? He knows it's the truth. How long do you really think I could have gotten away with it? With lying to you and cheating on you? Colt may have kept his mouth shut, but Heather threatened to tell you tonight." He grabbed my arm and made me look at him. "Van, I am sorry, for everything. When you almost die you look back at your life and wonder if you are on the right track. I can't keep lying. It hurts so bad right now, I'm not going to lie, but I will get over it."

As angry and confused as I was, I leaned over and kissed him on the cheek. "Me too."

"Now if you all don't mind. I would really like to be dropped off at that party. I need to forget about everything that I saw and heard tonight and I'm done with stealing cars," Ty joked.

Was he really just going to go out and pick up someone after Colt and I broke his heart? How could I have not seen this side of him? I had been so worried about hurting him.

I turned to walk toward the truck, but Ty said something so we turned around. He was on his cell phone. "Just come back and get me. No, that isn't an issue anymore. It doesn't matter if you pick me up. Hurry up please." He looked over at us. "You guys don't have to wait. I have a ride coming."

I looked at Colt and then back to Ty. "We will wait. Right Colt?"

Colt nodded. He started to pull me against him, but Ty held up his hand and started shaking his head. "Guys please. I have seen and heard all I can take tonight. Just wait until I pull away for shit's sake."

I looked at Colt and then walked over to Ty. I reached out my hand and helped him walk with the one crutch he still had against him. "We have been friends since we were little. I need to know that we are going to be okay. I know I hurt you Ty. You have no idea how bad I feel, but you hurt me too. I should have known about the other girls, but I didn't want to believe it. I feel like such a fool."

We were all three too drunk to be discussing any of this.

He turned to face me and moved a piece of hair out of my face. "I am an asshole Van. For what it's worth, I will always love you. You know I told you all those stories about Colt because I wanted you to think he was the asshole. Every girl wants him and he doesn't even care. I figured one day he would come visit and I wanted to make sure he never had a chance."

We both laughed. "Yeah, I wasn't very nice to him at first. He took it really hard too. Asking me who the heck told me such crap."

"At least it worked for a little while," he said.

"Yeah, I guess."

I saw a car pulling into the lot. Ty turned to me as Colt walked over with his other crutch. "I can't believe this is really happening," I said.

Ty took my hand and kissed it. "I always said I will give you your forever." He pointed to Colt. "If it wasn't for my accident you never would have found it. I love you Van. See you tomorrow."

I held my hand up and watched as he climbed into Heather's car. I didn't know what hurt worse. The fact that he had cheated so many times, or that she was the one to come save the day. I turned around and saw Colt holding out his hand. I didn't waste any time. My hand met his and we walked to the truck. I had to laugh when I got to the door and saw my underwear on the seat.

"Well that would have been a riot," Colt joked.

We sat there for a second. "Why didn't you just tell me the truth? Would you really have left knowing I was making the wrong choice?"

He put his head on the steering wheel. "Savanna, at first he was my family. I couldn't betray that. I was trying to protect you both. Once I had told you one thing I couldn't go back and tell you something different. Besides, I didn't want you to choose me because he cheated. I wanted you to love me because of who I was to you."

"I get it. It sucks, but I get it."

"Savanna, I need to know if you will consider comin' home with me next month. I can't stay here. I have a house in Kentucky. My parents are there. I know you are in school here and I can't ask you to quit."

He was right. Ty was actually the smallest problem. I couldn't finish college without my scholarship. This wasn't something I could decide after everything that happened tonight. "Take me home. We can talk tomorrow."

Chapter 28

Colt

Savanna and I didn't talk much on the way home from the bar. It was only about a ten minute ride and I knew she had a lot on her mind. Mix that with a bunch of alcohol and she was all messed up with emotions. We got out of the truck and noticed that the lights were off in the main house. I put my arm around her and walked her straight into the carriage house. Sam greeted us then went flying outside to relieve herself.

Savanna walked inside like a zombie and plopped down on the couch. She stared at the television, even with it turned off. I kneeled down in front of her. "Darlin' you okay?"

She nodded her head, but wouldn't speak. I stood up and picked her up in my arms. She wrapped her arms around me as I carried her to the bed. I sat her down and started taking off her shirt. Once I had it off, I grabbed a t-shirt. She let me unhook her bra and put the t-shirt on. She even stood up and let me take off her skirt and replace it with a pair of boxers.

I reached over and pulled down the covers so she could climb into bed.

After letting Sam back in and checking on Savanna, I decided to get a shower. I wanted this whole charade to be over, but I had no idea it was going to go down the way it did. Savanna was in shock. I hated her hearing that I had kept Tyler's secret life from her. He was my blood and at first I had no idea that she and I would become involved.

Once I got in the shower, I stood there letting the water fall down on me. I knew I still had to deal with the repercussions of getting involved with Savanna. Ty wasn't going to wake up tomorrow and be as calm as he appeared to be tonight. He was drunk and although a bunch of truths came out, the effects of the alcohol kept either of them from rationalizing.

When I turned off the water and opened the curtain, I found Savanna with her head in the toilet. The sound of her throwing up filled the room. She must have just come into the bathroom, because her vomiting was pretty loud.

I grabbed a towel before sliding down on the floor behind her. I held her hair and even held my nose while she continued to throw up all of the liquor she had consumed,

When she finally seemed like she got it all out, I grabbed a wet rag and rubbed it all over her face. She smiled and stood up. I reached in the cabinet and found what she was looking for. Her toothbrush was one thing I hadn't packed.

She stood there watching me as she cleaned her teeth. After her final spit, she turned to me, wrapping her arms around me. "You always take care of me."

"It's because I am crazy about you."

We walked back into the bedroom and lay down side by side. After a few minutes Savanna came closer and put half of her body over mine. I liked having her so close, especially after everything tonight.

I stroked her back with my fingers. "Where do you see yourself in five years?"

She shrugged. "I always pictured being married to Ty. I figured we would start a family and live close to our families. He was always a part of my plans so I never considered I had other choices."

"When I graduated college, I didn't know what I wanted to do with my life. I wanted to run a company and live in the city for as long as I could remember, but when the time came to do it, I wanted to make my family proud. I do the books for my father and a few other farms back home. I have my own house and my own parcel of property off my parent's farm. I will never be rich, but I do well for myself considering I don't have a mortgage. Savanna, whatever you decide, I want you to know that I never thought I was missin' anything in my life until I got to know you."

"I turn twenty five next month. I see you and I know I am ready to settle down and start a family, but I also know that you are only turnin' twenty and askin' you to make a decision like this aint very fair. If you need to stay here and finish school, I will understand. It will be hard, but we can get through it."

Savanna finally smiled. "I believe you."

"Does that mean you would consider having that future with me?" I asked.

She smiled and looked up at me. "Are you offering?"

"I think I am."

"Then maybe I will consider it," she said as she leaned up and kissed me.

A few more minutes passed. I started to let myself fall asleep, but Savanna startled me. "Will he be okay?"

"Who? Ty?"

"Yeah."

I kissed the top of her head. "He will be fine Darlin'. He just needs some time. I think you both need time to assess everything that happened last night or this morning for that matter."

"I can't believe he caught us, or the fact that we walked out to that parking lot and got it on. God, it doesn't matter if he didn't love me. Seeing that with your own eyes has to hurt."

"Yeah, it does. I feel real bad about it too. I mean, it had to be a real kick in the balls for him. When it happened to me, well at first I wanted to kill my friend, but then I realized it wasn't just him in that bed. For the longest time I felt like I wasn't good enough, like I wasn't doin' somethin' right. I ended up havin' a girlfriend and treatin' her real bad, because I didn't want to get hurt again. You need to understand that you are worth fightin' for Savanna. I'm not gonna sugar coat things. When we first started messin' around, sure I wanted to take care of you, but we were just friends. I promised myself that I wouldn't ever have feelin's for you. But, somewhere down the road, I got to know all of the little things about you. Your favorite foods. Your favorite color. The way my touch tickles you. The way you blush when I take off my shirt. How your hair looks when you first wake up."

I stroked my hand through her hair and she giggled. "How you are the most carin' person I have ever met. Most of all, how you made me want to love again." I squeezed her tightly with my arms. "I fell in love with you Savanna. With all of your quirks and habits and everything else you had to offer. I just wanted you."

"You always say the right things," Savanna said as she giggled and looked up at me.

I got ready to say something else and I heard the door opening. Now since I knew I had locked it when we got back, it could only be one of three people. Without moving an inch from the spot I was in, I watched Ty walk into the bedroom.

"You have a lot of nerve Cuz," he said standing over the bed.

I gently pushed Savanna to her side of the bed and stood up. Although, I think being in just boxers wasn't how my cousin wanted to approach me. He stopped and gave me a once over before heading in my direction. "You need to check yourself Ty."

He came at me and threw the first swing while leaning on a crutch to keep his balance. I took the hit in my shoulder, but only to be able to grab him and throw him down on the bed. Savanna stood up and started yelling.

"Stop it! Ty you can't fight him. You aren't strong enough. Just please stop!"

We ignored the little lady. I grabbed him by the collar of his shirt and pulled him up to my face. "She aint yours."

Ty tried to shove my hand away. "Wrong! She will always be mine."

I knew this was going to happen. My cousin got all calm and lovin' when he drank, but when he was sober he was a hellfire. "We went over this already last night. Don't you remember? It was right before you got picked up by the little blonde," I added.

Ty smacked my hand away and I backed away. "She picked me up because I caught my fiancée red handed banging my cousin in my own father's truck. What the fuck? This shit isn't happening," Ty said as he started rocking back and forth on the bed, holding his hands over his head.

Savanna didn't shock me at all when she climbed up behind him and hugged him. Her eyes were fixed on mine the entire time.

"Ty, you can't keep doing this to me. It isn't fair to either of us."

I clenched my fists, knowing that with having Savanna's arms wrapped around him, Ty felt like he somehow had the upper hand in all of this. He forgot he used to tell me all about his schemes, I guess to somehow try to impress me. He wanted Savanna to feel sorry for him, so that she would think about giving him another chance.

"Don't Ty. It isn't going to work. She already made her choice," I announced.

Savanna smiled at me. "Colt. Give us a minute please?"

Reluctantly, I made my way out of the room. I stood outside the door listening. There was no way in Hell I was going to let him take advantage of her kindness.

"Ty, do you remember everything we talked about last night?" Savanna asked.

"I remember everything actually. Especially the visual parts."

I rolled my eyes. Of course he would rub that in.

"I am sorry that you had to see that."

"What part?" He asked.

"All of it," She confessed.

I wanted to be in the room. I wanted to answer, instead of Savanna. This had to be horrible.

"Can I ask you something?"

"Anything," Savanna replied.

"How did you know you loved him? When did you know it was real?"

I couldn't see Savanna's face or watch her body language as she answered. I just listened. "I suppose at first it was lust. I just wanted attention. I felt so alone for all those months. I yearned for affection. There just came this point where, when I wasn't with him, he was all I thought about. I tried to picture my life without him and it hurt deep down inside of me. He was always doing things and saying the right things, even when he wasn't trying to impress me at all. He wanted to know me, in every way."

"You can keep going. I need to hear it all. Even the parts I don't want to hear." Ty announced.

"From the first time he touched me, it was different. He made me feel like I was the only female on the planet. I can't resist him. He makes me happy, like I could never want for anything else, ever. Ty, I thought I knew what the deepest love felt like. I loved you for so long, and I am so sorry if this hurts you, but I have never felt this way before."

I was shocked she said all those things. Not shocked she felt that way. I felt the same. I was however, shocked she told him. Her honest confession kept my cousin from speaking. After a long period of silence, I walked back into the room.

"I get it," Ty said as he saw me walkin' in.

"You get what?" I said as I sat beside him.

"You two. Honestly, it makes sense. You are so much alike that I don't think you even realize it.

Not that this changes anything, but after what happened last night, I told Heather I didn't want to see her anymore. I think seeing what I did, what I caused, made me see what a fool I have been. I need to change. Honestly, I need to admit that I was never happy being with Van. If I was then I never would have cheated, not once. I let the best girl I have ever known get away."

I put my arm around my cousin. "You hungry?"

"Nah, I need to get out of here for a while. My parents are going to wonder why Van is in here with you. I need to get this all out in the open." Ty replied.

Savanna cut in. "They already know. They caught us together....the night you woke up."

"What the fuck? Is there anything else I need to know?" He asked.

Savanna stood in front of Ty. "They forbid us to see each other. Your mother threatened me and your dad told Colt he had to leave. He only stayed for you."

Ty shook his head. "You let me propose, hell they let me propose, knowing all along you were in love with Colt?"

"There were so many people there. You had just got home. I couldn't hurt you like that," Savanna admitted.

"I appreciate that. If it's any consolation, I told everyone at the party that I ended it with you."

Ty's confession actually made Savanna laugh. "I need to ask you a favor. Your parents are not going to understand things. Please don't tell them about the parking lot. They think I am such a whore already. I just can't live with that."

"How about my cousin and I go have a family talk. You stay here and get cleaned up. I think If I distance myself from the two of you right now, I will turn around and get all pissed again. I need to just be around you guys for a while. I know it sounds convoluted, but it's just how I deal."

I stood up and helped Ty get into a standing position. I didn't lean over and kiss Savanna. Things were super awkward. I was still expecting Ty to rip out a pistol and shoot me to death. We walked out of the carriage house, once I got a shirt on, and headed toward the main house.

"If I could stand up long enough I would have kicked your ass by now," Ty stated as we approached the porch.

"You could try," I teased.

"I don't fucking forgive you."

"I know." I pulled the porch screen door open as he hobbled his way inside.

Ty turned around before going in the house. "I was a shitty boyfriend. I lied about the one person I looked up to in life. Honestly, I figured this would hurt a lot more than it does. I think she was more like a piece of property and not a person. Sounds shitty right?"

"She's never been that to me," I admitted.

"Yeah. Thing is....seeing you with her last night. I want to feel that. When I walked back in that bar and saw the way you two were, well first it was a kick in the gut, but after that I was so jealous that I never felt like that myself. The way she looked at you....it was fucking insane."

I couldn't help but smile. I knew what he saw. Savanna and I had been too drunk to care, but the truth was written all over our actions. I remembered feeling like it was just us there on that dance floor.

I also knew that Ty never really respected Savanna. For years he had cheated on her and disrespected her. As much as I wanted to feel bad about what I had done, I couldn't. It may not have been right, but I didn't do it alone.

"I'm not sorry for lovin' her. You also know that technically she wasn't yours when we were together. She never cheated on you, except for the past two nights when she was wearin' that ring." I realized what I said too late. Ty's fist came up and got me right between the eyes. He fell back against the wall, while I wiped away the gushing blood coming out of my nose.

"You deserved that, you dickhead."

I smiled and held my nose up, pinching it. "Yeah, maybe I did."

"You going to hit me back?" Ty asked.

"No, you can have that one for free. I deserved it."

"Did you do her before or after the proposal?" He asked.

"You seriously want to know?"

"Yes! Dammit just spill. All the shit I have done. I need to know she aint that perfect," he spat out.

I was trying to keep the blood off the floor, so I grabbed my shirt and pulled it over my head. I held it up to my face as I talked. "It was during the storm. After you put that ring on her finger, I needed to get the hell away from the both of you. I went out to the combine with a six pack of beer. When it started storming I was already half lit. I heard someone crying and found Savanna standing out in the storm alone." There was no need to give details. I was sure he didn't want them.

"So what was she crying about? How did it turn out with sex? Because, she slept in my fucking bed that night. Now I get why she rejected me so much. She was all filled up already."

I stuck my finger in his face. "Don't talk about her like that Ty. She was upset because of you, because of everything. You were so caught up in your friends that you never even came lookin' for her. Your own fiancée."

"So you had sex in a combine. You one upped me there," he laughed.

"Actually....," I held my hand up. "Never mind!"

"Well, now I want to know," he ordered.

"It doesn't matter. Just drop it."

"You know I am really trying to be understanding. I wish everyone could realize that it still feels like last year to me. Even back then I didn't really have Van. She was already slipping away. I was stupid to think I could go around behind her back forever. She deserved better," Ty admitted.

"Well, I am tryin' to do right by her Ty. It hasn't been easy for us so far. Between trying to deny our feelin's and me livin' so far away. Hell, I don't even know what she's goin' to decide. I can't very well ask her to give up her life here," I explained.

"Well I have to warn you. She puts school before everything. It's really important to her."

We were interrupted when my aunt came walking to the door. She opened it up and looked from Ty to me. "What's going on here?" She asked.

"Just let us come inside and we will explain," Ty said.

We walked in the house and I sat down at the kitchen table. My aunt brought over the paper towels and a wet rag. "Which one of you is going to start explaining?" She asked.

I looked from Ty and then back to my aunt. "I think you should tell her."

Ty laughed. "You would." He looked down and for a second before he started talking. "Mom, there is a bunch I need to tell you."

My aunt cut him off. "Son, after seeing you dropped off by some girl this morning, I am going to assume that I already know what's going on. From the look of Colt's nose, I have to ask. Where does this leave the two of you?"

She was referring to Ty and I. That was a question for him, more than me.

"We are blood. Nothing is going to come between that," Ty explained.

"I am guessing the broken nose helped with the hard feelings?" She said in a sarcastic way.

"You could say that."

She gave my nose a good look. "I don't think it needs to be reset. It may not even be broken." She was sticking an icepack on it before turning around. "So where is the reason for all this fighting?"

Ty chimed in. "We left her in the carriage house for protection."

I chuckled and shook my head. Even Ty seemed to laugh at himself.

"I am not even going to ask. I am just glad you boys are okay with all of this," she said.

I stood up and excused myself from the conversation. Ty held out his hand before I left. "Will I see you guys later?"

"I reckon if you want to. We can have a serious game of Rummy if you're up for it," I explained.

"Yeah, Sounds good. I will knock before I come in," Ty said.

At that moment I caught my aunt shaking her head. I kept walking. She could baby her son all she wanted but I was a grown man.

Chapter 29

Savanna

Colt came back from the main house with two black eyes and a very swollen nose. He insisted that he and Ty were on good terms and he deserved the punch that Ty had given him. I didn't feel very comfortable with them making plans to spend time together, but Colt insisted that it was important to him. I thought they were crazy, in fact insane. Who makes up that fast?

I wasn't about to argue with them. Their family handled things differently than normal society. Blood always came first no matter what the issue was. I could tell that Ty was more tore up about things than he was admitting, but as long as he seemed calm around me, I wasn't going to worry about it.

After getting Colt a new icepack, we laid down on the couch watching movies. Neither one of us said much. I knew Colt wanted me to give him answers about what I wanted to do, but I honestly didn't know. I loved him, I was sure about that, but I was determined to finished school before I made any decisions regarding my future.

Colt would be here for at least another month, I had time to make my decision, and make sure it was the right one. He had everything figured out in his head, but I just wasn't ready to give up everything.

After the first movie. Colt fell asleep. His face looked terrible and I had to laugh at how similar it was to when I got jumped by those girls. He was sitting up with his arms draped over me. I grabbed them and scooted myself to the side. I loved watching him sleep, even sometimes when he snored. I sat back against the other end of the couch and really looked at him. His brown hair was starting to curl up a little on the ends, especially when he had his hat on. He didn't bother shaving this morning so there was a shadow of stubble all over his face. His full lips were parted just enough for him to breathe out of his mouth. I loved the small freckles that traced over his nose from the sun. I also couldn't help but love the fact that he was more than sexy when he didn't have a shirt on.

He was the whole package, the kind of guy that every girl says doesn't exist. Sure, he was rough around the edges when it came to talking about feelings. He had refused to talk about our relationship, even though he and I both knew it had been turning into more.

Still, I knew the real Colton Mitchell, the one who risked his own family's approval to be with me. I still hadn't discussed Ty's mother, but she clearly wasn't freaking out, otherwise I wouldn't still be on her property. I didn't know how Ty had come to terms with me and Colt so quickly. One minute he was flipping out and the next he was calm and understanding. Was it that easy to just walk away? Ever since I got involved with Colt, the fact that we were hurting Ty tore me up inside. He made me feel like such a blind idiot for not seeing all the signs. All of the times I caught him with girls numbers, or talking to them in private. I was so stupid. Ty was gorgeous himself. Of course maybe I was partial, but Colt had a more adult look to him, while Ty was just an average college football guy. Colt's chest was broad, from years of working on the farm and playing sports. Ty was getting there, but he was shorter, at least by four or five inches. His arms weren't as defined, and now they were pretty small considering he hadn't been out of a bed in months.

Still, I knew that Ty would be back to himself in no time. I wasn't worried that he would be alone for long. He may have rejected Heather, but she wasn't the only skeleton in his closet. There obviously were plenty more to choose from, not to mention any ones that he hadn't given a turn yet.

Thinking about it made me feel like I got kicked in the stomach. I had invested my whole teenage years into our relationship, and never once was he that serious. No wonder we fought all of the time.

I stood up and decided to go out to see Daisy. I just wanted some time alone to think about things.

I no sooner got into the barn when I saw Ty standing with Daisy. He was petting her, talking to her. I approached them and he smiled. "Hey."

"Hey yourself," I answered. "What are you doing out here?"

"I was waiting for you actually," he confessed.

I smiled, but felt really weird about that. He couldn't have known Colt would fall asleep. "Did you want to talk?"

I stood on the other side of Daisy and ran my hands down her braided mane. Ty looked over at me. "Yeah. I wanted to talk to you without Colt. You see I may have stepped back to give you guys a chance, but I know for fact that you won't leave. I know you Van. You won't leave school for him. I also know that somewhere in that head of yours, you still love me. You may think Colt is great now, but what happens when it's just you and I again? What happens when you get so lonely and I am here waiting for you? This new romance with him might be great right now, but it can't last and you know it."

"Screw you Ty. I can't believe I never noticed how much of an asshole you are. You have no idea what I am going to decide and frankly it's none of your business anymore. You lost that when you couldn't keep your dick in your pants."

He hopped over to face me and grabbed my arm. "That's where you are wrong. You are always my business. I don't give a shit who you are dating. My cousin included. If you didn't love me, you wouldn't have stayed in that hospital room for all those months."

"I felt terrible for what happened to you. Your right, I stood by you because I thought you were my future. Things changed Ty. I am not proud of how they happened, but they did. I fell in love with Colt. I love him because he's everything you never were!" I argued.

I'd never felt scared of Ty. We had our share of throwing things at each other, and screaming until we lost our voices, but he never hit me. When his hand came over and grabbed my throat, I didn't react fast enough. He pushed me against a beam in the horse stall. "You little bitch! I gave you five years. I asked you out when nobody else would. I let you be my girlfriend even before you had tits. Do you know how many other girls wanted to have the title of my girlfriend?"

I grabbed his hand, and at the same time he realized exactly how he had reacted. He pulled his hand down and I could tell he was sorry for it. I backed away, enough that he couldn't reach me. Then I went into detail, because he deserved it. "I can't tell you when I started loving him, but I wanted him from the first moment. His touch did things to me. He didn't fight me very long. All I had to do was get him tipsy and he gave into me. That night was the best sex I ever had. He became my addiction. I wanted him all of the time. I needed him to touch me."

Ty put his head down. I could tell I was getting to him. "Stop Van. Please don't say anymore."

"After a while, I felt like I couldn't be away from him. I missed him so much when we weren't together. After your parents finally caught us, and we were forced apart, I felt empty inside. He shut down and wouldn't talk to me once you woke up. At first I didn't know he felt the same about me. He wouldn't ever talk about it, but after your proposal, he confessed his feelings when he found me crying in the rain. He took me into his arms and made love to me in the middle of that field. He did things to me that you could never do."

"ENOUGH! God Dammit Van! Shut up!"

A small smile formed on my face. "You asked for it. Don't you ever touch me like that again! I can't believe I ever loved you."

I should have left right then, but I didn't. Ty slowly slid down until he was sitting on the ground. He put his hands over his head, and his head between his legs. "Go! Get out of here Van," he said with his head still down.

I turned to leave, but I heard sniffling. Ty never got upset. He never cried. I had seen him tear up, but he never cried. Not since we were kids. I couldn't be heartless to him, even after he went off on me like he did. I couldn't be as low as him. My words had intentionally crushed him. I had stooped to his level.

I knelt down beside him and reached out to touch his shoulder. "Ty, I am so sorry. I shouldn't have said that stuff. You just made me so mad."

He pulled away from my touch. When he looked up at me, I saw the tears. "I never thought I would lose you. I know I cheated. I know I lied. I just never thought you would ever leave me."

I kept kneeling next to him, but kept my hands over my knees. I was thinking of what I could say, but nothing came. I had left him. I wasn't ever giving him another chance.

He wiped his eyes and his nose then looked up at me again. "I don't blame you for wanting Colt. I could tell you he's a piece of shit, but we all know it's a lie. He's a fucking awesome person. I actually felt bad for hitting him today. Do you believe that? He took you away from me and I felt bad for hitting him."

"Ty." It was all I could get out.

He reached over and touched my arm. I let him, this time not feeling threatened. "We were drunk last night, otherwise I would have denied everything. I don't know how long you would have even believed me anyway. It seems like me being in that hospital for months has caused everyone I know to get their feelings out. At any rate, I want you to know something Van. I want you to know that I don't blame you for moving on. I can't believe you stuck around for as long as you did. I love you, but it isn't the way you want to be loved. You already know that."

"Yeah, I get it."

"I want to hate you so much, but I just can't. I shouldn't even be mad at either of you. It's just too new. I am really trying here," he explained.

"I meant what I said about being friends Ty. I know that's such a cliché, but it's true. I need to know we will always be close. Maybe someday you can tell me all about your secret life." I said trying to break the mood.

He looked up and showed his dimples. Those deep brown eyes looked up into mine. Suddenly, all of his indiscretions were put aside. I wrapped my arms around him and hugged him so tight. "I will love you forever," I whispered, trying to put aside the fact that he had grabbed me and called me a bitch.

He put his arms around me too. "I love you too Van."

Before I knew what was happening, he put his lips over mine and held me so that I couldn't pull away. When he finally let go, due to the fact that I was smacking him, he had a smile on his face.

I heard the barn door slamming shut behind us and my heart dropped. I stood up and smacked Ty. "You asshole. What have you done?" I asked while running out of the barn.

Ty was actually laughing behind me. What a dick!

I found Colt walking away from the barn. I know he heard me running toward him, but he didn't turn around. I grabbed the back of his shirt, forcing him to stop. He turned around with a grin on his face.

"That was not what it looked like."

His hand came up and brushed against my cheek. I saw him taking a deep breath as he looked into my eyes. "I can't blame him for tryin'. I don't know how long I could have stood back and let you be with him."

I wrapped my arms around his waist. "You believe me?"

He kissed the top of my head. "Savanna, I trust you, besides, my cousin would never give up that easy. We have the same blood, remember?"

I pulled away and reached up to touch his face. His beautiful eyes looked directly into mine. "You really are the perfect man."

He started laughing. "Who says that?"

"Ty."

Colt grabbed my hand as we started walking toward the carriage house. "He would say that."

Chapter 30

Colt

When I woke up and Savanna wasn't anywhere around, I knew exactly where she would be. After walking into the bathroom and taking a look at my face, it was worse than I first expected. Both of my eyes had turned purple and the bridge of my nose was swollen. I was lucky it was still pretty straight.

After assessing the damage, I headed out toward the barn. I wasn't prepared for walking in and hearing the two of them confessing their love for each other, and when I saw my cousin closing in on Savanna's lips, I had to turn and walk away. I wanted to kill him, but before I could turn around and head in there to do it, I saw Savanna. All I had to do was see the look on her face to know she was telling me the truth.

We got within inches of the house before I decided I had enough with Ty's shit. I turned back around to head in the direction and when I did, I saw him standing there, leaning on one crutch just waiting for me to come at him.

Savanna was already running after me, but I continued moving. In the distance, I saw my uncle walking up the lane. If I wanted to get a punch in, I needed to take it right away. Ty was ready for me. He dropped his crutch and used all he had to jump on me as I approached him. I had to give it to him, it was his only chance of getting the upper hand. Even before his accident, he had never been as strong or big as I was. As we started tumbling to the ground, Savanna was screaming and trying to yank us apart. Ty attempted to head butt me, but I managed to move out of the way. I gave him a good fist to his side and heard him gasp when I did it. His arm came up and tried to hit me on my head, but I grabbed it and used my legs to flip us over. Once I had him pinned, I punched him right between his upper cheek and nose. It felt good, there was no denying it. He had it coming.

After that first punch, I felt someone dragging us apart. "God Dammit! I am not havin' this shit between you two. Break it up!" My uncle yelled.

Savanna was standing back. She had her hand over her mouth and tears in her eyes. My uncle looked like he was going to kick my ass himself. After helping up his son, he cornered both of us. He took one look at my face and shook his head. "You guys been at it all day?"

Ty got all serious. "Pretty much."

"I ain't havin' this on my watch. All this over a damn girl? You both know better," my uncle said. He shook his head and waited for me to say somethin'.

"She made her choice," I stated while looking to my cousin the whole time.

"Fuck you Colt. You stole her while I was down and out, you pussy bitch," Ty yelled.

"You weren't even together. Stop your damn cryin' and get over it. She picked the better man. Move the hell on with one of the little sluts you bedded while you were with your girlfriend." He deserved everything I said. I just didn't care about saving our relationship. I knew this was goin' to happen. Everyone else might have been fooled by his calm reaction last night, but I wasn't. He was still pissed and lashing out. That was what he did best.

"I said cut it out!" My uncle yelled. He shook his head and started pacing between us. "You two are the closest thing to brothers that you are ever goin' to get." He turned to look at me directly. "Colt, did you know your aunt used to be obsessed with your father?"

"He mentioned it before," I admitted.

"We were thirteen. She would hang out with me to watch my brother. She told me she would never be with me. Finally, he got an older girl pregnant and crushed all of her dreams about them getting together. The rest is history. I know your situation is more involved, but I know what it's like to want something that you can't have and have your heart broken while you wait." He stood between us and looked at Ty. "I don't know everything that you've done, but I saw you the other night with that blonde. Then I saw Van here soakin' wet runnin' back to the farm later that night. At first I thought she saw you and ran away upset, but yesterday mornin' I watched Colt here, walkin' home with wet clothes. I tried to wake him that mornin' and he wasn't asleep in his bed. So, I am just assumin' you two were together. I don't want to know what happened. It doesn't even matter. I tried to keep you apart and obviously, you didn't listen. Now if I didn't need the help, I would send you packin', but I do need it. This shit needs to be worked out. I can't have this goin' on."

Ty and I just kept giving each other dirty looks. I tried to be nice to him and consider his feelings, but it just wasn't going to do a bit of good. Ty was as stubborn as they come. "I will do whatever it takes, except let her go. I just can't do that."

Ty crossed his arms across his chest, while Savanna sighed and shook her head. Finally, she threw her hands in the air and started walking away from all of us. I should have been ashamed for fighting like I was a teenager, but I was sick of his ass.

"I'm done here!" I said to my uncle before running after Savanna.

Neither of them said anything as I walked away.

I found Savanna on the couch. I could tell she was pissed from the look on her face. Ironically, she looked sexier than I had ever seen. I sat down next to her, but she wouldn't look at me. Like a little kid, I danced my face in front of her and made silly faces. She tried to hold in her laugh, but finally she broke.

"Stop doing that. I am trying to be mad at you," she said as she pushed me away.

I didn't know why, but I felt determined. My night's agenda was to make Savanna smile and forget about the crappy day. I stood up and pulled off my shirt. She tried to ignore me by turning on the television, but I got up and started dancing in front of it. I flexed my chest like some wrestler would do. She kept attempting to look past me, even closing her eyes, as I got closer. When I could clearly see that she wasn't giving in, I knelt down in front of her and kissed her hand.

"How are you doin' Darlin?"

She moved her shoulders. "I actually think I should go home. I mean, I am just causing too much stress for your family right now. If I took myself out of the equation, maybe you and Ty could work things out."

"Savanna, I will only be here for another month or so. I really don't want to lose any time together, especially when you haven't decided what you want to do yet."

She stood up and walked away from me. "Would you just stop talking about it. I can't take it anymore! I can't take the yelling and the fighting. I feel awful inside about everything."

I sat down on the couch and looked at her, really looked at her. "Savanna, I don't understand. What are you sayin'?"

"Please just take me home Colt. I need time to think about everything. This is all just getting to be too much for me. I just need to breathe."

Women can be impossible, every man will say that, but Savanna was makin' absolutely no sense. One minute she was all about being with me no matter what, and the next she just wanted her space. I shook my head, got up, and grabbed my keys. "Let's go then."

She didn't say a word as we walked out to the truck. I looked over and saw her focused on the ground. She never looked my way. She never shed a tear. She was just quiet.

We got a mile down the road and I just couldn't take the silence. "Savanna, please talk to me Darlin'. I know things happened fast for us, but you make me feel better than anyone else ever has. I just want to take care of you."

I noticed how far away she sat from me. The distance was killin' me because usually she sat with her legs up against me. She looked out the window and refused to answer at first. When she finally did. It wasn't what I expected.

She waited until we pulled up at her house. I got out to walk her to the door, but she stopped me halfway up the sidewalk. "I never expected to feel the way that you make me feel. I never even thought it was possible to love someone the way that I love you." She paused for a moment. "Colt....Ty was right. I can't leave with you. I am so sorry."

I reached out for her, but she had already turned and ran into her house. I stood there just waitin' for her to run back into my arms. To tell me that she was just joking. But, she never did.

I waited a good ten minutes, flabbergasted about what just happened. Whatever Ty said to her in that barn got her thinkin'. I wasn't even sure, at this point, where we stood. I was sure about one thing. I had a little over a month to convince her to change her mind. I was not about to give up on her that easy. It would be a cold day in Hell before I walked away from Savanna Tate.

After tryin' to call her three times, I finally gave up and drove straight to the liquor store. I didn't have anyone to talk to, so a bottle would be my best friend tonight. I headed straight into the carriage house only to find my cousin sitting in front of the television playing a video game.

"What the hell are you doin' here?" I asked.

"I saw you both leave. I figured you wouldn't be back for a while, and honestly I was sick of the fucking third degree I am getting inside the house."

I shook my head and walked into the kitchen to grab a glass. While I was pourin' one for myself, I decided to grab one for Ty. "What are they sayin' about me?"

"You don't want to know. They pretty much hate you as much as they hate Van right now," he said while laughing.

"Fantastic."

"Lighten up! They really don't give a shit. They are trying to appease me. I even told them how I was hittin' a new piece of ass whenever it was available. They know the truth."

I sat down next to Ty and slid a glass in his direction. "Guess it's just you and me then."

Ty hit pause on the game and leaned back, taking the first sip of his drink. "You got hard shit. What's up Cuz? She leave you already?"

I cocked an eyebrow. "She wanted to go home."

"I know her man. She will be back."

I shook my head. "Nah, I don't think so. She said she couldn't leave with me. I guess I never should have gotten involved with her. I feel like shit now."

My cousin held up his cup. "I hear ya Cuz. Trust me when I say, she will drive you insane. She's so Goddamn driven. All she cares about right now is getting that degree. It means everything to her." He played around with his glass. "I've seen how she looks at you. Even when you aren't looking, she is. That girl has it bad. Never in all the years we were together, did I ever get that look."

"Maybe it's just the sex," I said sarcastically.

"Fuck you man. I'm trying to be nice here."

"Sorry."

"Whatever! What I was going to say is that I know she really does love you. I don't know what she went through, but you came into her life when she didn't even want to live anymore. You gave her something to live for. You saved her Colt. Van isn't someone to let that just go. I may have been a shitty boyfriend, but I do know her. Maybe not the way you do, hell you probably know her favorite color and what music she likes. It doesn't matter. I know she won't just let you go. Give her time. Being around both of us has to be fucking confusing. Especially considering our love hate relationship right now."

I finished my drink and got up for a second one. Ty managed to get himself standin' "This fucking metal in my leg is giving me Hell."

I grabbed his glass and filled them both. "I hope you are right about Savanna." After taking a few big gulps, I looked over at my cousin. "Her favorite color is blue. Not light blue. Not dark blue. Just a medium blue."

Ty shook his head. "You do realize you sound like a teenager?"

"I aint never felt this way Ty. I know in the pit of my stomach that she is it. Maybe the timing is bad, but she's the girl for me."

"Want me to call her?" Ty asked.

"Hell no! You did enough. She wanted to leave because of some shit you told her. Thanks for that, you little prick."

He started laughing, "You deserved as much. If we are being honest here, you were a shitty cousin."

"I tried to resist Cuz. I swear I did."

He picked up his paddle and started playing his game again. "I bet you did. How long did it take her to get to you?"

"About twenty four hours."

"Are you fucking kidding me? Do you know how long she made me wait to have sex with her? You lucky son of a bitch."

I shook my head and laughed. Finally, I picked up a paddle and played football with my cousin, as if nothing had happened between us.

Chapter 31

Savanna

Walking away from Colt was not what I pictured myself doing. I wanted to come home for a few reasons. The first being that Colt and Ty needed to work things out. If I told them that is why I left it never would have worked, but I had a feeling that by tomorrow, they would at least be on speaking terms. The second reason I left was because I wanted some time alone to think about everything. Colt and I had spent pretty much the past seven weeks together. The first month we were hot and heavy as much as we could be, but the past two weeks were focused on Ty. When I thought that Colt didn't want me, it was the hardest for me to deal with. I felt empty inside and I knew that no matter how much I tried, Ty could never fill the void. By some miracle, Colt was just as in love with me as I was him.

After Ty found out, well everything had been crazy since. I just wanted some me time. I need to talk to my mother. My parents weren't the richest people. They barely made ends meet and I knew that their one wish for me was that I would graduate college. My mom also knew how I felt about Colt. After the shortest engagement in history, I figured I should sit down and tell her what all was going on.

When I got into the house, I broke down and started crying in the foyer. My mother came running out of the kitchen and managed to sit me on the steps. "What's wrong Van?"

"Oh Mom, everything is a mess," I cried. "Ty and I are over. He has been cheating on me since we were first going out. I gave him back the ring and everything."

My mother sat beside me. She stroked my hair and held me close to her. "I am so sorry he hurt you honey."

I shook my head. "That isn't the worst part Mom. It isn't the worst by a long shot."

She pushed the hair out of my face. "What's wrong honey? What happened?"

"It's Colt. He loves me. Ty knows. They won't stop fighting. I just can't take it anymore," I admitted.

"Well, after Ty confessed to cheating, I would imagine you made your mind up who you want to be with?" She asked.

"Actually, I made my mind up right after I said yes to Ty. I saw him with a bunch of girls and got upset. I went running during the storm and ran into Colt. He told me the truth about how he felt. I had been so stupid to not know."

"Oh honey. Forgive me, but I am really confused. Are you upset because of Ty? Did Colt say he couldn't be with you?"

"No Mom. Colt wants me to be with him. He wants me to move home with him this fall," I explained.

My mother stopped rubbing my back. When I looked up, she was looking straight and rubbing her face, something she did when she was thinking.

"Mom, I told him I can't go. I have to finish school. This is my only chance. I have to stay."

She shook her head and started to tear up. "Van, the past year has been horrible for you. I can't imagine everything that you have gone through. We didn't even know if Ty was going to make it. Now, it turns out he wasn't the guy we all thought he was. I just want you to know that when you first told me about Colt, I saw a sparkle in your eye that I had never seen before. He does something to you. I never thought I would ever say this, but you are my daughter and you being happy is more important to me than any kind of diploma. If you want to be with Colt, then give him a chance. If you don't then I know you will regret it."

"How did you know that Dad was *the one*?"

She shrugged. "He gave me you."

I pushed her shoulder. "That isn't funny."

"Okay. I guess imagining my life without him makes me feel like I can't breathe. We have had tough times, but always managed to stay together. Relationships are hard work honey, I doesn't matter how old you are."

"Even though I met Colt when I was around ten, we have only been together for a little over a month. I just don't want to rush into something that I am unsure of."

My mother put her hand on my knee. "This past year has been the worst of your life. I am just wondering if you wouldn't be better going to another school. Nobody is telling you that you have to quit. Half of your tuition is through federal grants. Most are transferrable. I am not saying you should or shouldn't leave, but sometimes starting somewhere fresh can make life a while lot easier."

I leaned my head on her shoulder. "Sometimes, I feel like you are trying to get rid of me."

"Savanna, you act like it's far away. Kentucky is only a car ride away. It can't be more then a five hours drive to that farm."

"It's just all happening so fast. I mean, I want to hate Ty for all the years he lied to me, but I just can't. I want to tell Colt that I want to be with him, but I am so afraid of change. I just don't know."

I got up and walked up the steps to my room. I just wanted to be alone for a little while and think about everything.

My bedroom was just how I left it. The bed was always made. Posters of scholars filled my walls and books covered the shelves. I sat down on my bed and looked around. I had dedicated every moment of my life to one certain goal and after just the small amount of time I had spent with Colt, none of this seemed right anymore.

My phone continued to ring and vibrate until it finally died. I didn't bother charging it, because there wasn't anyone I wanted to talk to right now. Ty and Colt were probably still beating each other to a pulp. I didn't blame either of them for having hard feelings. Colt and I had jumped into something with no regard for what it would do to anyone else, mostly because we never thought it would become something so serious.

Ty really did a number on me. When I sat back and thought about it, I hated myself for not realizing what a cheater he was. He always seemed to love me, but now I wondered if he even knew what the word meant. He clearly used his other head to do his thinking. Colt on the other hand, was almost too perfect. I didn't deserve him, in fact, I had no idea why he loved me. Even the fact that he took the risk and slept with me that first time seemed strange.

At any rate, I couldn't deny the way that man made me feel. Everything made sense when we were together. He brought me out of the darkest part of my life. Maybe my mother was right? Maybe I did need to just start a new future? Doesn't everything happen for a reason? Maybe all along I was supposed to be with Colt?"

I woke up the next morning still laying on top of my covers and in my clothes. After a good stretch, I reached over to check my phone and remembered I let it die. I plugged it in and waited for it to power up. I had a bunch of missed calls. I started to feel bad as I dialed into my voicemail. Hearing Colt's deep voice sent chills down my body. He didn't say much in his first messages, but the last one was different.

"Darlin, I have to go home. My father got hurt yesterday and is in the hospital. I tried to call you on the way to the airport. Please call me when you get this. I love you."

With shaky hands, I dialed Colt's number. It went straight to voicemail.

I tried three more times.

Reluctantly, as I contemplated calling Ty, my phone started ringing. Thinking it was Colt, I picked it up before looking. "Hello?"

"Hey babe, it's me Ty. Listen Colt had to leave and you wouldn't answer your phone."

"When is he coming back?"

"I don't know if he can. If my uncle is bad off, I imagine he won't leave."

Tears started running down my face. The last thing I said to Colt was how I wasn't going to go home with him.

"Ty, he thinks I don't want him. You have to help me."

I heard him laughing. "Seriously? Do you know how fucked up that request is?"

"Please."

"He will call you when he lands."

"How do I get to his parents farm?"

"Are you serious right now?"

"Ty please! I need the address."

"You can't drive all that way yourself. Come pick me up. I will go with you."

I didn't even question it. "I will be there in fifteen minutes."

I kissed my mother before running out of the house. She saw my bag packed and just shook her head smiling. She had no idea I was about to drive out of state to prove to my boyfriend that I was ready to let go of my past and have a future with him.

When I got to the farm, Ty was standing outside waiting for me. He was now using some crazy looking cane. He hobbled in the car and leaned over to kiss my cheek. When he pulled away, he giggled. "Sorry, it's habit."

"Whatever! You are here to navigate."

"Just to be clear. I am doing this because I owe you for being a shitty boyfriend. I want you to remember that when you are in my cousin's arms tonight."

I looked over at him just before pulling off the dirt road. I couldn't help but smile thinking about being there with Colt.

After driving four hours, I was starving and had to stop to eat. Ty was keeping me good company. He never once attempted to change my mind about Colt. He did however ask if we could be secret fuck buddies. That was Ty though. He finally stopped when I started talking about the size of Colt's package. He made gagging sounds for at least five miles of travel.

When we made it to the Kentucky border, I felt something wrong as I was driving. Ty noticed it too and told me to pull over. "Looks like you got a flat babe," he announced.

I smacked him on the arm. "Stop calling me that! You lost that privilege, remember?"

"Yeah, whatever. You going to get out and help me, or pout more?"

I shook my head and got out of the car. I wasn't even sure if I had a spare tire. We made it to the back of the car and had to remove a year's worth of crap from the trunk to get to the spare. Ty bitched and shook his head the whole time. There was a bunch of our stuff in there. I still had some of his clothes in bags from when we would sleep out at the barn.

"For someone that wants to move on, you sure have a bunch of my shit."

"Cleaning out my car was the last of my priorities you jerk!" I flipped him the finger, while he continued to dig the remaining items from the trunk. I was getting nervous as he lifted up the carpet covering where a spare tire would be.

Thankfully, there was a tire in there. It was a donut, but it would work. "So does it need air?" I asked.

"Probably. Did you even know you had it?" He asked.

"Not really. I never looked for it before."

He shook his head. "I remember when you got this car. I went with your dad to check it out."

I smiled and helped him get all set up before I started putting all of the crap back in the trunk. Ty got right to work changing the tire. He even started to sing while he worked. I couldn't help but giggle and give him funny looks. He was taunting me, trying to get me to laugh at him.

By the time the tire was replaced, we climbed back in the car and started heading for the closest gas station to get some air in it. Due to the fact that Ty moved slower than a slug, I jumped out and insisted on doing it myself. He hopped out and said I didn't know anything about tire pressure and would do more damage than good. Because he pissed me off, calling me incapable, I stormed into the store to get us some snacks.

When I came back out, I handed him a root beer and a bag of his favorite chips. He smiled and opened them up right away. "Thanks babe. You always did know me best."

I shoved him again. "Seriously Ty, stop with the babes. Obviously, I didn't know you enough, otherwise, I wouldn't have been repeatedly cheated on."

He turned to face me while I started driving. "Van that was always my dick making those decisions. My heart always belonged to you." His hand brushed my knee and I pulled over the car as fast as I could.

"Don't touch me Ty! Did you really just say that your dick made the decisions? Do you know how ridiculous you sound? You made the decisions. I was never enough for you. More than anything in this world, I hate liars and cheaters. Now, I am really trying hard not to hate you, but dammit, you deserve where you are at. How could you be so self centered. If I found out all of that stuff and didn't have Colt, I might have just offed myself. Don't you know how much you hurt me? How much you are still hurting me?"

He slowly set the bag of chips down and lowered his head. I had raised my voice and even though he had secrets, he did know me. He knew I'd had enough of his games. "Van, I'm so sorry. You're right. I never thought about what it would do to you. I can spend my while life trying to get your forgiveness, but it will never happen will it?"

"I loved you so much Ty. God, when you were in that hospital it was Hell. I wanted to take everything back and have the future that we always talked about. I wanted to love you forever. There was never anyone else for me. When we broke up, I never even talked to another guy. I just wanted to focus on school, I never really left our commitment." I turned off the car and faced him. My eyes started filling with tears and I hated that he was seeing me cry over him. "If Colt hadn't come into my life, I don't know what I would have done if Heather or someone else told me the truth. I tried to consider learning it any other way than I did that night when we were all drinking, but none would have been any easier. You shattered me. Even though I already knew my relationship with Colt was what I wanted, hearing the truth about you, well it hurt just the same. All those years, you lied to me. I was never enough. Why couldn't you just let me go? Why did you keep me if you needed more?"

He hesitated before answering. I felt his hands reach up and touch my cheek. For that moment, I didn't make him stop. He brushed away my tears. "Because I couldn't imagine you being with anyone else. I didn't want anyone else to have you."

"It's not fair Ty. What you did was wrong."

"I know it. I just couldn't share you. I wanted to only want you Van. I swear I tried to be good. I just can't do it." He reached over and pulled me across the seat, into his chest. "I swear to you that I love you. I have only ever loved you Van. I never would have divorced you. I would have given you all the kids you wanted. I would have given you everything."

I shook my head and pulled away. "I believe you would have, but what I really wanted was to be the only one for you. That's all I ever wanted."

He looked away. "I know babe. I know."

I didn't correct him. I felt his pain in his voice. He knew he screwed up. He knew I was never going to be his again. It was enough punishment. Me being with Colt was the constant reminder that would haunt him forever.

I reached over and played with his hair. "I forgive you Ty, but only because I know you seeing me with Colt is torture. I feel bad for that, as stupid as it's. Every other woman would want revenge, but I can't be like that. I just want to move forward."

Before I could speak or move out of the way, Ty leaned over and kissed me. He grabbed the back of my head and held me there against his lips. There was no tongue or some kind of romantic attempts, it was just a kiss. When he pulled away, he looked right into my eyes. "Saying good bye to you hurts me so much. I try to be tough, but you make me want to never cheat again. I am such a fucking idiot. I had to lose you to realize that you are all I want. I don't want to see you with him." He turned to look out the window and hit the side of my car with his fist. "Dammit!"

As much as I wanted to see Colt, I needed to be here for Ty. I couldn't just ignore his feelings, even if he was a total asshole. "Are you okay?"

I reached over and grabbed his shoulder. He immediately pulled away. "Just don't. My life is ruined. I can't play football. I lost my license. I am being sued and I lost you. What the fuck do I have to live for?"

He started crying.

After I tried to grab him again, he got out of the car and leaned against it as he just let go. I gave him a couple minutes before I climbed out. He tried to wipe away the tears as I approached. I didn't hesitate as I reached both of my arms around his and put my head against his chest. I didn't say a word. There was nothing I could say. I couldn't change anything for him and I wasn't going to lie and give him false hope. We were over. He lost his ability and was in trouble with the law. He made those choices himself. I couldn't fix him.

When he finally put his arms around me, I knew he was at least calming down. He kissed the top of my head. "I am never going to find someone as good as you. I fucked up so bad."

I looked up at him. "There is someone out there for you Ty. When you find her, you will know. You won't want to imagine your life without her and you won't ever want to be with anyone else."

"I already felt that way, but I let her go," he said sadly.

Our faces were about six inches apart. I could feel him breathing. His hands cupped the side of my face. I couldn't look at him so I closed my eyes.

As I felt our noses come in contact, I refused to open my eyes and see him crying. "Ty please don't do this," I whispered.

His lips brushed against mine. "One last kiss. Say good bye to me Van."

I felt his hands running though my hair and knew at any moment he would pull my lips against his. "I love him. I can't kiss you."

He didn't let go. He pressed his forehead on mine. "It was worth a try."

When I opened my eyes, I saw the tears on his cheek. I took my fingers and wiped them off. His beautiful brown eyes and long eyelashes stared at me. "You have to let go of me."

"I don't want to let go." He answered by pulling me closer to him.

"I mean you have to let go of me in general. I need to know you are going to be fine if I decide to move here."

He rested his head on my shoulder. "What if I can't let go? What if I refuse to?"

"Please Ty. I need the chance to be happy. It isn't like you will never see me again. The distance may repair our friendship."

He pulled away from me, finally letting me take a step back. "Do you really want to still be my friend? I think I have proved that I am a piece of crap liar on several occasions."

"I couldn't bare not being your friend Ty. We have been friends since elementary school. I can't just let you go like that." I grabbed his hand and got him to look at me again. "A part of me will always love you, it just isn't how you want to be loved. I'm not trying to punish you. I just want you to know how I feel honestly."

"I know." Finally, his demeanor changed. "We better get back on the road if we want to make it by dinner time."

Without saying another word about our conversation or embrace, we both got back in the car and started driving again.

I trusted that Ty knew exactly where we were driving, but as we pulled up to an extremely large ranch, I was a bit confused.

"Are we stopping here for directions or something?" I asked.

Ty just laughed and shook his head. "You don't know do you?"

"Don't know what?"

"Van, this is Colt's parents place. From the look on your face I would say you had no idea."

I looked around as I was driving up the paved lane. White fencing surrounded both sides that led up to a huge two story white house. Behind the house were four giant silos, and five tremendous buildings. Cattle were in every pasture. In all the time that Ty and I had been together, he never mentioned this place or how much money they had.

"They own all of this?" I asked while driving up the long lane.

Just as I said it, I noticed the large sign stating it was the "Mitchell Ranch".

"Before you get your panties in a bunch, you need to realize that Colt doesn't care about the money. He went to college and got his business degree. I think he does the finances for quite a few farms if I'm not mistaken. This is all his dad's. Colt had always been independent. I don't think he was deliberately keeping it from you, I just think he doesn't want to be known for it."

"He said he built a cabin on the property somewhere. Can we see it from here?" I asked.

Ty started laughing. "Van they own like five thousand acres. You have to drive to his place."

I felt like I didn't know Colt. It probably wasn't the big deal I was making it out to be, but I felt like this was something he should have told me. Obviously, asking me to move here, I would have found out.

After telling me where to go, we pulled up at the front of the house. Ty hobbled out of the car and I followed behind him.

Chapter 32

Colt

When I got the call about my father, I knew I had to get the first flight out. Through the years, my father and I had grown closer. As a kid, I didn't have a lot of respect for the man. He let the money and his success dictate our lives.

I never cared about the money. I never wanted new cars from him, or to be sent to some elite schools. I hated that my friends knew me as the rich guy, so when I went to college, I tried to reinvent myself and be independent. My father had a fit. He said I was ashamed of the dynasty he had created for our family. He didn't understand I wanted different things for my future.

It never occurred to me that something could happen to him. We had such animosity between us that I couldn't stay away and not let him know how much he meant to me. Money or not, he was my father and I loved him. He may be hard around the edges, but he was the only one I had.

Savanna and I hadn't left things on good terms. I wanted to keep calling her, but she wasn't returning my calls as it was. I needed to talk to her, to tell her that I would wait for her as long as it took. Being at the hospital didn't make it any easier. I couldn't have my phone in the room and it killed me not to go outside and check for my messages.

My dad wasn't doing well. I didn't get the exact details of the fall, but apparently he was on a ladder out in one of the barns when something caused the ladder to fall. He had ruptured his spleen. Now, I didn't know too much about that part of the body, but my mother said it was serious and that he could die.

He had been in surgery since I arrived and all I could do was stay by my mother's side and support her. She had loved my father since she was a teenager. I had been an accidental pregnancy that created a twenty five year marriage. I don't think either of my parents regretted being together. They still held hands and wanted to always be around each other. My mother was a wreck. Finally, I contacted their primary care doctor and he prescribed something to help with her nerves. She was reluctant to take it, but he assured her she would still feel normal with no crazy side effects.

Being that he was being labeled as critical, we weren't able to be in the room with him. I asked my mother if she wanted to go home and rest, but she insisted that she wouldn't leave. After being up with Ty the night before and rushing around trying to get here, I was exhausted. I couldn't leave the hospital, especially not knowing if I would ever see my father again.

My father could afford the best doctors and for one of the first times, I was glad he had the money. A specialist was already on their way, but time was of the essence. He obviously had internal bleeding and they were doing their best to get it contained and stopped.

I took a short bathroom break and when I came back the doctor was standing over my mother. She was shaking her head and crunching up her face as it filled with tears.

I sat back down next to her and reached my arm around her, as the doctor nodded and walked away. "What is it?"

"It's not good Colton. It's not good at all," she said as she put her head into my chest.

My father always told me men don't cry. I could feel the wetness filling my eyes and tried to fight them. My mother needed me to be strong. I wasn't sure if I was hurting for myself as much as I was hurting for her. The idea of her being without him was unbearable. He was in his early forties, not some old man. They had so much life left to live. How fair was it that it could be cut short.

"What did they say?" I finally asked.

She shook her head. "They are having trouble getting the bleeding to stop."

"How long did it take for someone to find him in that barn?" I asked.

"I don't know honey. He was in the office on the phone and came rushing out saying that he had to go help Conner since Earl is out with his wife. She's having a baby you know. Anyway, Conner came in yelling that your father had fallen. We called for an ambulance, but when they asked Conner about it, he said he hadn't seen your father for at least an hour. He found him just lying there."

"Hell, that aint good," I admitted. I squeezed her hand. "He's a stubborn man. He will fight."

She looked over to me and tried to smile, but it wasn't necessary. "I hope you are right. I can't imagine losing him."

I had to look away from my mother. She was trying her damndest to be positive, but right now we had no guarantee. My father could die any second and there was nothing that either of us could do.

"I am so glad you are here Colton."

"Mom, there is no other place I would be. He and I may not see eye to eye, but I do love him. I just wish I could have told him that," I confessed.

"He knows. You are both so much alike. You may not see it, but I do," she said as she stroked my cheek.

I tried to give her a smile. "Yeah, maybe."

"Did Conner go back to the ranch after he dropped you here?" She asked.

Conner was my cousin and since his father died four years ago, my mother had taken in her sister and her kids. Conner was the oldest and he worked his ass off for my father. He may not have the Mitchell last name, but my father treated him as if he was a son.

"I brought Sam home. I didn't know what was goin' to happen. He took her back to the ranch and said he would be back to get us whenever we needed him to. Is Aunt Karen coming?"

She shook her head. "She said she would be here after she was done with a prayer tree for your father. I need all the prayers I can get." She immediately changed the subject. "How is Tyler? I feel so bad that we didn't come out for his party. You know things are so hectic this time of year. We were sponsoring that festival in town this past weekend and had to be there, otherwise you know we would have come."

"It's fine. They understand. Ty is back to his normal self, minus the fact that he's out of shape and has a bum leg. He walks with a gimp for now."

"Is that pretty girlfriend of his taking good care of him?"

I pulled my arm back from around her neck and looked down. For the first time I felt like I was going to be a disappointment for the news I was about to give her. "They aren't together anymore."

That wasn't enough for my mom. "What do you mean? They have been together forever?"

"They broke up before the accident. She was just being a good person sticking by his side until he woke up."

"I had no idea. I mean, your aunt seemed to have issues with her, but she's funny about her son. So do you think they will get back together?"

I chuckled and looked to my feet. "I doubt it. She has someone new in her life now." I couldn't look her in the eye. Beads of sweat were forming on my head.

"That town is so small. Does Tyler know the new guy?"

I couldn't take it anymore. "Mom, he has known the guy since he was born."

She gave me a weird look.

"It's me."

She put her hands on her face as if it would wipe away what I just said. When she looked at me with her new face, her eyes were huge with shock. "How could you do that Colton? You know better."

"Mom, it's so complicated. Ty had been cheating on the girl for years. He used to call me and brag about it. She never had a clue. After the accident, the whole town disowned her. Some people even jumped her and beat her up, calling her a murderer. I happened to be there to witness it. She was alone and injured and I just wanted to take care of her. I wanted to keep her safe for Ty."

I rubbed my hands into my head. "We couldn't help it. I couldn't stop myself. I tried at first. It just happened."

"Does your cousin know? You have to excuse me for being confused. I heard they got engaged at his party."

I let out an air filled laugh. "Yeah well, we had trouble telling Ty our secret. He cornered her into that proposal and she couldn't embarrass him in front of everyone in town. It doesn't really matter because he caught us the next night together."

"I am guessing that's where the black eyes came from?"

I had forgotten all about them. She hadn't even mentioned them. With everything going on with my father, she probably hadn't even noticed. "Yep! It was the first of a few fights between us."

"What does your aunt and uncle think of this? They must be furious?"

"Not really. They wanted Ty away from Savanna. I guess I did them a favor," I replied.

"You are talking like you are serious about this girl. Forgive me for saying this, but do you think she's after the money?"

I turned and looked at my mother. She could see in my eyes that she really hit a nerve. "She doesn't know about the money. It's the only lie I ever told her. That money isn't mine, it's yours. I took

Dad's offer when I built the house, but I don't need his money. I do fine on my own. As far as Savanna goes, she's the best person I have ever known. She deserves to be happy."

She rubbed my arm. "Are you in love with this girl Colton? This is all so sudden. Forgive me for being cautious."

"Yes, I love her. I've never felt this way about anyone. She's the one. I know it every time I look at her."

"If you are sure about this than you are going to have to bring her home for us to get to know her. I can't have my son marrying someone I don't know," she claimed.

"That might be hard. She just told me she couldn't come home with me. I asked her to move here with me this fall. She won't leave school. She's on a scholarship and can't afford school herself. In fact, right now she can't afford anything, since she quit her job to be with me more."

She turned her body toward me. "Listen here. You are worth it. If she loves you the way you love her, it will work out. Maybe you could wait for her to finish school. I know it will be hard, but it isn't long when you are talking about forever."

As soon as the words came out of my mother's mouth she realized what she was implying. She and my father may not have that forever anymore. Life was short and you never know when your time was up.

"Thanks Mom. I promise that you will love her as much as I do." I grabbed her hand again. "Let's get Dad home and I will figure out how to drag her here." I gave my mom a wink. She needed to smile even if it were for a second.

Before my mother could reply, my Aunt Karen came walkin' in. "Colt," she said as she bent over and hugged me. Conner stood behind his mother and gave me a nod.

"I am so glad you made it home safe." She looked over to my mother. "Any news?"

I watched my mother telling my aunt everything she knew.

Finally a doctor came out from behind the double doors of the waiting room. "Right now he's stable. He isn't out of the woods yet, but we got the bleeding to stop."

I felt Conner's arm grab my shoulder and we all seemed relieved.

Once the doctor explained everything to my mother, he suggested we go home and get some rest. My mother refused to go home.

"You should go home and rest Colt. Karen and I will stay here in case he wakes up. I will call you," she said.

I couldn't argue. I was exhausted. After hugging them both, Conner and I headed out. I needed to get home and charge my phone so that I could call Savanna.

When I finally made it home, I got the surprise of my life.

Chapter 33

Walking into Colt's parent's house was surreal. The house was huge on the outside and even bigger on the inside. Some old lady gave Ty a hug and me a quick smile as she led us into the kitchen. "They are all still at the hospital. Conner headed out about an hour ago to go back. It's such a shame about your uncle. I hope he pulls through. He's a good man. He's always taken such good care of my family."

Ty thanked the lady he called Lucy. When we got back into the car he explained that she had worked for them for many years. Her husband had died in some war and she was left alone to raise her daughter. Ty said they had lived here on the ranch ever since he was a kid himself.

Ty navigated through an old dirt road. There were a few parts where I wondered if he was taking me back into the woods to take advantage of me. After driving for at least ten minutes, we came to a clearing. There was a large lake on one side and a pasture on the other. The road ended in front of a house. Colt said he lived in a cabin, but this was much more. I wouldn't have ever called the two story home a cabin. There was a wraparound porch on the lower level and a deck with two chairs on the second level. It was made from logs, but this was no cabin. To the side was a two car garage. One of the doors were open and I could see a new Mustang parked inside. We were in the right place.

"Van? You alright? You look like you saw a ghost," Ty was saying as he waved his hand in front of my face.

"It's not little."

"Colt's dad insisted on it. Come on, let's go inside. I have to piss," he replied.

I was instantly nervous. I had driven all the way here and never even considered what I would say to Colt. It had been an impulsive decision completely. I watched Ty hop out of the car and head toward the house. At the last minute he turned and walked toward the woods.

"Where are you going?" I should have never asked. He just started peeing against some bushes. I gave him a dirty look as he turned and winked at me. "Stupid!"

I took a few deep breaths and started walking toward the steps. After the first two, my heart was starting to beat out of my chest. I got to the porch and noticed the porch swing on one of the ends. It looked out at the pasture and lake. It was beautiful. I could see myself sitting there with Colt, having morning coffee while laying my head against his shoulder.

My fists started knocking immediately following my vision. After three knocks, I heard the door creaking open. I heard Ty whistling as he made his way to the porch. I turned to smile and then focused on the door opening. All I wanted to do was jump into Colt's arms. Everything would fall into place once I had my arms around him.

Except, Colt wasn't who opened the door.

A blonde who appeared to be at least eight months pregnant opened the door. Her hair was wet and she had a towel around her neck. I gasped, unable to say a single word.

"Can I help you?" She asked.

I felt Ty wrapping his hands onto my waist. "Where is Colt?" He asked over my shoulder.

"Probably still in the shower," she said with a smile.

I could feel my body shaking. I actually felt like I was going to pass out. "Who.....who are you?"

"Why? Who are you?" She asked defensively.

"I'm Ty," he announced, trying to hop in between us. I knew he was trying to protect me from whatever I was about to do or say.

"Oh his cousin? This must be Van. I have heard so much about you," she claimed.

"Who are you?" I said again, before I even realized the words came out of my mouth.

She started rubbing her stomach. Then she said what I feared. " My name is Miranda. I am Colt's........"

She was interrupted by Colt, who was coming down the stairs in only a towel. Beads of water covered his wet body. "Savanna? What are you doin' here?" He said as he walked toward the front door.

I only knew of two exes'. I couldn't remember if he mentioned their names, but obviously she was back for one reason. She was pregnant with his baby and he never told me about it.

Miranda backed away as he headed in my direction. Tears filled my eyes and I turned myself into Ty's welcoming arms. "Please get me out of here," I said against his chest.

"Wait! What the hell is going on?" Colt said as he came walking out of the house. I don't know how Ty got off the porch so fast, but he got me almost to the car before Colt got to me.

His hand grabbed my arm. "You drove all the way here for me?" He asked.

"I guess I should have warned you first. Maybe you could have got your company to stay somewhere else while you played the seduction card on me some more. You think because you grew up with money you can go around fucking girls in different places, telling them they are the only one for you? You are nothing but a liar!" I said as I tried my best to open my car door.

Colt's still wet leg caught the door. I couldn't help but notice Ty laughing and shot him a dirty look. This was obviously his dream outcome. Me discovering Colt as a cheater......I was such a fool.

"Savanna dammit, will you calm down?" He tried to grab my arm, but I was crying so bad that I pulled away from him and started walking away from my car. I had no place to run. I just couldn't handle the pain I was feeling. "Tell me what's goin' on? Is it because I didn't tell you about the money? It isn't important to me. I don't care about any of it. You are all that matters to me."

"How can you say that with that pregnant woman standing at your door? Oh my God what kind of person are you? How can you not care about her? Look at her!"

He shook his head again and scrunched his eyebrows like he had no clue what I was talking about. "Of course I care about her, but she has nothin' to do with us. Savanna please stop walkin' away. I am in a damn towel here."

He caught my waist and pulled me around. "Leave me alone. There is nothing left to say. I am going home. Forget you ever knew me. I will not be some home wrecker or be with a cheater. You should know that already."

He wouldn't let me go. "What has gotten into you? I am neither of those things and you should know that!"

His green eyes stared holes in me. "I just caught you. Please just stop with the lies. I can't take anymore." I tried to calm down but finally broke down and began to sob. "Please get off of me."

"No! Not until you stop fightin' me. You obviously drove all this way for me. What the fuck Savanna?"

Finally I heard Ty walking behind us. "I think I can clear this up Cuz."

We both turned to face him. Colt never let go of my arms.

"She thinks Miranda is a girlfriend. She thinks that's your kid," Ty said smiling. He could hardly contain the smirk on his face. I felt so betrayed like he had set me up.

Colt relaxed his hold on me and shook his head. Then he even started laughing. "She's my cousin Savanna. My mother's sister Karen's daughter. She was here watchin' the place while I was gone. She lives in a house on the ranch too."

I put my hands over my face. "But I thought…"

His arms wrapped tightly around me. "Darlin' I would never do that to you." With his hands, he grabbed both sides of my face. "You are the only woman that I want." He brought his lips to my forehead.

My hands reached around his still wet waist. "I am so sorry. I just saw her and then I saw you. You were both wet from a shower. I just assumed you were together and everything about us was a lie."

"Nothing about us is a lie. I swear it." He looked directly at me when he said it.

"Get a room!" We heard Ty saying behind us.

Colt grabbed my hand. He looked over to Ty and he pulled us past him. "You could have told her, you asshole!"

"It was more fun watching her get all pissed at you. I just wanted her to feel the same about you for a few seconds. Miranda went along with it too," Ty said while laughing behind us.

I shot him a dirty look as we hit the porch steps.

Miranda greeted us at the door. "Sorry for the confusion. I was tryin' to explain before everything got all crazy."

"Nice to meet you. Sorry I overreacted," I replied.

"I can see how this would look. I assure you that the father of this child is a piece of shit! He's nothing like my cousin Colt."

I didn't know if she meant it to be a joke, so I just smiled and followed behind Colt. Ty and Miranda headed into the kitchen, while Colt pulled me up the stairs. "Aren't you going to show me around the house?" I asked.

When we got into a large bedroom and he shut the door behind us. My body immediately pressed against the door as Colt's lips met mine. Our tongues mingled and my hands found his chest. Only moments ago, I thought it had all been a lie, but now I was back in his arms where I wanted to be. His clean skin smelled so good, maybe better than I remembered.

"I can't believe you are here," he said as his lips parted from mine. He stared into my eyes. "I tried to call you and then I got the news about my father. I couldn't stop thinkin' about you."

"I didn't know if you would come back for me. I said things I didn't mean. I was wrong Colt. I had to come. I needed you to know I would do anything to be with you," I admitted.

My hands reached inside the towel and I let it drop to his feet. I leaned against the door and bit down on my lip. I heard a groan coming from somewhere deep inside of Colt's chest. His hands grabbed the bottom of my shirt and ripped it off my head, while I started unbuttoning my shorts.

"God, when you started walkin' away I didn't know what to think. I can't imagine not being able to touch you" Colt said as his tongue drug across my ear.

"I should have trusted you. I let what Ty did get to me. I know you aren't him."

His lips found mine again. I felt his tongue brushing against my bottom lip. His erection pressed against my stomach. He was doing it on purpose, so I could feel how much he wanted me. He picked me up and I wrapped my legs around his waist. The heat between my legs set me in a frenzy. Colt got to the bed and tossed me down on my back. I didn't have time to sit up. His body came down over top of mine.

He leaned up balancing himself on one arm to look at my body. With one snap, my hook in the front bra opened up. His large hands slid down between my breasts. I licked my lips as I watched him looking at me. When his eyes reached my panties, he licked his own lips, which in turn made me even hotter. His hands slid down and reached the fabric of my panties. He ran his hand underneath just at the base from hip to hip. I arched my body because I wanted to take them off, but he kept teasing me. Instead of taking them off, he licked his lips and pulled his hand out from under them. His palm cupped me and I knew my panties were wet with anticipation of being with him. I couldn't resist his touch. He was the sexiest thing ever.

"I want you so bad," I whispered.

"I am in my house with the woman I love. I am planning on takin' my time," he admitted.

He leaned down and kissed the inside of my thigh. It sent chills all over my body. I saw him smiling as he kissed my belly button and ran his tongue in a circle around it. He left a trail of wet skin as he leaned down and kissed my other thigh. His teeth grabbed the elastic to my panties and he pulled them back, dragging his nose against the base of my tender spot.

"Oh my God Colt!" I moaned loudly.

"Mmm, you like that don't you?" He teased. He slowly pulled down my panties, licking his lips the entire time.

His finger slid inside of me as he leaned up and took one of my nipples into his mouth. I watched his lips pull away and his tongue came out to dance around my nipple. He took it back into his mouth and sucked hard. "Don't' stop!" I begged.

He removed his lips from my breast and blew cold air on it, making it even harder than it was. His finger moved faster inside of me while his thumb played with my swollen sex. He teased my lips with just his tongue, while his thumb pressed harder. I felt waves of pleasure come crashing through my body. As Colt watched me starting to orgasm, he finally let me kiss him, never letting my tongue get away from his. When I finally collapsed under his strong hands, he climbed on top of me.

"Do you want me Savanna?" He asked.

I bit my lip. "Yes."

"Tell me. Say it," he ordered.

I tried to grab his shaft, but he wouldn't let me. His teasing was making me want him more than I ever had, which I didn't even think was possible. "I want you. Please make love to me Colt. I want you inside of me. Please...."

With one single thrust, I felt him fill me with his hard shaft. As wet and ready as I was, it was still a tight fit. Colt moaned and got into an immediate groove. I grabbed his ass cheeks and dug my nails into them, pulling him into me harder. He grabbed my breasts with both hands and kissed them together. I loved watching him lick my nipples. I could feel friction building up for another wave of pleasure, so I flipped myself on top of him. Colt grabbed my waist as I started rocking back and forth. I ran my hands all around my breasts without touching my own nipples. I knew he wanted to see it. His moans became frequent, and I continued to tease him like he had me. I took two fingers into my mouth and got them wet then slowly ran them over one nipple while watching his reaction.

"Oh God Savanna I can't hold it." He cried out just as I felt himself tightening up. He held me by my hips preventing me from moving, but I had become so turned on from watching him watch me that I had my own bout of pleasure.

When I finally collapsed over his now sweaty body, he wrapped his arms around me. "I think I am going to need a few minutes before we take a tour of the house," I whispered against his chest.

We both started laughing.

Chapter 34

Having Savanna here in my bed was better than I imagined. I was half tempted to spend the rest of the day with her wrapped in my arms, but what kind of gentleman would I be if I didn't give her an official tour?

After we laid together for at least thirty more minutes, we managed to get up and make our way out of the bedroom. Savanna jumped in the shower while I managed to get myself dressed. I was thinking about jumping in the shower with her, but my cousins were downstairs and it was rude staying up here all day.

She finally climbed out and I dried her off. I handed her a pair of loose shorts and a t-shirt she could wear until she grabbed her clothes out of her bag.

"As much as I hate that you are putting clothes on, I have to admit you look pretty damn sexy in mine."

"You can take them off later," she said as she walked by me.

I smacked her on her ass, causing her to jump. She had no idea how happy I was that she was here.

I decided to start my tour upstairs. After she walked all around my bedroom and looked through my closets, we checked out the other three bedrooms. Besides my master bedroom, the other three were just a bit smaller. When we got into the last room that was full of boxes she stood in the middle with her arms folded. "A lot of extra rooms."

"I'm sorry that I didn't tell you about my family's money. I didn't see it as lying to you. I just wanted you to want me because of who I was, not what I had," I admitted.

"At first it hurt. I felt like you didn't trust me, but Ty kind of explained it to me. I don't want you to ever think of me as some charity case. I would never take your money."

I rubbed her cheeks with my thumb. "Savanna, I mean it when I say that you are the only woman I want in my life. I want to marry you. When you are ready of course. You will never want for anything, I can promise you that."

"What if all I want is to be with you?" She asked.

I shrugged. "I guess I would say I was the luckiest guy in the world."

"Look, it doesn't matter to me how we got together. You saved me from myself. I love everything about you, but I am also forever grateful for the friendship that we have. From the moment I climbed in that car this morning, I knew what I wanted."

I wrapped my arms around her. "How many kids do you want?"

She gave me a weird look. I hadn't thought that she might be scared by that question. She pulled out of my arms and faced me. "How many do you want?"

"I asked you first."

She shrugged her shoulders.

"I always wanted two, but ever since I met you I knew I couldn't keep my hands off of you. If we had more, I would be totally fine with that. I will give you whatever you want. If you want ten kids than we will have ten kids," I joked.

"Actually." She reached her arms back around me. "I wanted eleven."

I knew she was joking. "As long as they all look like you," I said before kissing her.

Our kiss was interrupted by Ty's big mouth downstairs. "Get your asses down here!"

"We better go downstairs," I suggested.

We got to the bottom of the steps and my cell phone started ringing. I rushed over to the table by the front door and noticed it was my aunt's number. "Hello?"

"Colt it's me. You need to get to the hospital right away."

I didn't have to ask questions to know something bad had happened. "I am leavin' now."

When I hung up the phone, everyone was standing there waiting for me. We all ran out to my Mustang and started driving. I'd never driven fast with Savanna in the car, and I got the impression I scared the shit out of her. My father's life was hanging on the line. I needed to get to that hospital before it was too late. I had to tell him I loved him, at least once before it was too late.

When I got onto the main highway, Savanna reached over and grabbed my hand. I squeezed it tight inside of mine. I had no idea what was going to happen with my father and she had never met my mother. As much as I wanted them to meet, I hated that it was under this circumstance. Savanna being here was like a godsend. No matter how long it would take my father to recover, I was so glad that she was here with me. It was funny how months ago I didn't even know someone could ever have this effect on me, but now, I felt like I needed her.

My heart started pounding as we made it into the parking lot at the hospital. If I was too late to say goodbye to my father, I didn't know if I could forgive myself.

Savanna took my hand while Miranda stayed back and waited for Ty. He knew I was in a hurry and couldn't waste time waiting for him. We made it to the third floor and saw my aunt standing outside of the room. Over the loud speaker we heard Code Blue and I just got this horrible feeling it was for my father. Savanna kept up the pace as we made our way to the door of his hospital room. My mother was backed into the corner with her hand over her mouth. The doctors and nurses were working on my father. I heard one of them yell "Clear" and saw them using the crash cart. My father's body took one hard jolt and the monitor started beeping again. I could hear the medical staff calling off his stats. My body bent over and I held onto my knees. I could feel Savanna rubbing my back, and I appreciated her support more than she knew.

We waited at least an hour before the medical staff left the room, after running numerous tests. Unfortunately, the doctor pulled my mother out with him and asked us if we could all come and meet with him privately. He sat us down in a more private waiting room, probably designed for this such situation. I sat next to my mother and held her hand.

She was still crying and held a handful of tissues in her opposite hand.

"Your husband has suffered a severe stroke from the stress of the injuries he sustained in his accident, and the surgery that was performed to stop the internal bleeding. As of right now he's showing signs of damage to his brain. In most cases patients suffering from this kind of trauma do not wake back up."

My mother started wailing. That's how I would have to describe it. I held onto her body as she rocked back and forth. I didn't have time to express my own feelings when she was there, suffering from the greatest loss of her life. My father probably wouldn't wake up. She could never hear his voice again. He would never kiss her goodbye, or sit with her at dinner. They wouldn't go to local events or share dreams of when they were older and took care of their grandchildren. He would never see his grandchildren. My children.

The doctor walked out of the room and left us to deal with the aftermath of his bad news. My aunt crouched down in front of my mother and held her the best she could as she cried. I put my elbows on my knees and covered my face with my hands. Savanna's hand rubbed my back, but I never acknowledged her presence behind me. I couldn't look at anyone. My eyes burned with the tears I was fighting back.

After a few minutes I noticed Savanna wasn't behind me. I got up and looked around the room, but it was only my mother and my aunt here with me. Savanna, Ty and Miranda must have left. I was sure that they didn't go far, probably just far enough to give us some space.

I was standing in the doorway, unable to walk out of that room. I couldn't leave my mother, not now, not like this. I turned around again and looked at my mother. Her face was covered, but her sobs were just getting louder. I swear that being in the room hearing her cry was just as bad as hearing the news about my father.

We ended up spending the night at the hospital. At some point Savanna came in and got my keys. She needed to take Ty and my very pregnant cousin Miranda back to the ranch. Savanna tried to get me to come home to rest, but I refused to leave my mother. We were devastated. This is where I had to be.

The next two days were the same. My mother stayed by my father's side. The nurses even found a place within the hospital where she could shower and remain close in case something were to happen. Savanna came in the mornings and stayed with me until visiting hours were over. My mother slept in the chair in my father's room, while I stayed in the small waiting room where we got the news.

I should have gone home, but just imagining her being here alone was unbearable.

Savanna and I barely spoke. I knew that if I talked about my father and all of the things I worried I wouldn't get to tell him, that it would just make me get upset. She never pushed me to talk about him. The more time went by, the less I said to her. She sat around playing on her phone or listening to her IPOD, while I sat with my mother and my father. It was hard for me to open up, but it must have looked to

Savanna like I was pushing her away. It wasn't on purpose. I had never experienced this type of situation and I had no idea how to deal with it, or how to let her into my house of emotions.

My father died on the morning of the third day. I had still been asleep in the chair in the other room while my mother was sleeping in my father's room. The loud beeping woke me with the Code Blue warning and a feelin' in my gut told me that I needed to get to that room. I jumped up and ran in. I don't remember looking at my mother, but as I watched the medical team doing everything they could, I noticed her hand was in mine.

Everyone has heard the sound of a flatline on movies and television shows, but to hear it live, while all you have left is hope, well it's the worst sound you will ever hear in your life. That sound filled the room, and while my mother cried out, and the doctors and nurses did everything they could, it was all I could hear. My eyes burned, but I refused to blink. They were fixed on my father's lifeless body, just hoping that the sound would stop being a constant and turn back to the reoccurring beep. It didn't happen. While my mother and I stood there in the corner of that dark room, we heard the doctor calling the time of death. I cradled my distraught mother into my arms while the room started to clear out, leaving us alone in there to say our final goodbyes.

I would assume it was the next couple of hours, but I couldn't be sure as time seemed so unimportant. My mother and I managed to move to my father's bedside. She cried over his body. It hurt to watch her touch him, rub his arms and kiss his lips. I watched her kiss them and hold her mouth on them knowing it would be the last time she felt his warmth. I should have been the one callin' my family and letting' them know the news of my father's passing, but I just stood there like it was a nightmare I would eventually wake up from.

Soon after, my aunt and Savanna arrived together. My aunt Karen immediately was at my mother's side with comfort and support. Savanna wrapped her arms around me and told me she was sorry, but I couldn't say anything back to her.

Sorry? Why did people even say that? Did she kill him? None of this had anything to do with her, or anyone else for that matter. My father was gone. My mother was alone. Everything was now in my hands. I couldn't worry about helping my uncle with his crops or fighting with my cousin over a girl, or even if that girl was really going to be my future. The only thing that was pressing to me was my mother. I had to make sure that she was taken care of. I had to keep the ranch running and not worry about anything else. I couldn't afford to anymore. My father tried to make me see what was important and I had fought him tooth and nail. He had never approved of my life. I had to do this for him.

Chapter 35

Savanna

When Colt's father passed away none of us knew what to expect. I tried to be there for him, but there were no words that could ease the pain. His father was gone and that left more than Colt could imagine on his plate. When I decided to come here to be with him, I hadn't expected this turn of events and I clearly wasn't prepared for the way Colt would handle things.

I didn't blame him for being distant, or even shutting down. I knew what it was like to think that the person you loved the most was going to die, but I never had to deal with the death. Ty was going to recover and probably live a long healthy life. In thinking back, I don't remember Colt ever talking about losing anyone that he loved to death. That could only mean that this was all new.

When Colt and his mother finally came home to the ranch, everyone had done all that they could to be there for them. Many women from their church had brought over casseroles and the refrigerator was filled to capacity. I still hadn't officially met his mother. It wasn't my place to throw myself at her at the worst point in her life. Instead, I stayed in the background along side of Ty and did whatever I could to help out.

The first night home, Colt headed to the cabin late. I was just heading upstairs to bed, when he came walking in the door. I got a half smile as he continued walking up the steps into his room. By the time I got there, he had already went into the bathroom and closed the door behind him. I sat on the bed and contemplated waiting for him to come back out, but I heard the shower turning on. I missed Colt, but being around him made me nervous. I was so afraid of saying something that would upset him. He wasn't exactly the kind of guy that wanted to hear people say they were sorry for his loss. Obviously, since he hadn't said much to me since I told him that.

Reluctantly, I headed into the bathroom. Through the glass shower door, I could see Colt's arms pressed against the tile as he let the water beat down over his head. He looked so tired and worn down. From days of not shaving his face was covered in large patches of stubble. He had whiskers before, but this was becoming a full beard. He hadn't noticed me coming into the bathroom, or the fact that I was standing outside of the shower taking off my clothes. I opened the door and stepped in without him even stepping to the side to give me room.

I didn't say anything to him. Instead, I wrapped my arms around him from the back. Finally he stood up and turned himself around to face me. His eyes were bloodshot and for the first time in all of the years I had known him, he looked terrible. I felt his arms touching my waist, but he wasn't holding on tight or even pulling me closer like he normally would do. Those big green eyes stared back at me with no expression crossing his face.

I kept looking into his eyes. "I love you," I whispered, hoping those words were better than saying I was sorry.

Colt closed his eyes and let his head fall against mine. His body started making sudden movements even before I heard the sounds coming from deep within him. He was crying. My hero, the toughest man I knew, couldn't hold in the painful feelings any longer. He was letting go of it all, while my arms held onto him for dear life.

There was nothing I could say to sooth him. He needed to get it out. He didn't need to feel ashamed or embarrassed around me. I wanted to be here for this and for anything else that would come our way. Being here for him and seeing what he was going through, made my decision to be with him even easier. This was the life I wanted. This man, who was falling apart as a result of loving someone so much, was who I wanted to be with.

I held Colt and comforted him even as the hot water began to turn cold. I guided him out of the shower and leaned against him as he sat down on the bed. I stroked his hair and waited until the tears stopped coming. He was looking to the floor between his legs, so I positioned myself on my knees between them. "Colt, are you okay baby?"

He brought his hand up and touched my cheek. "I never got to tell him. He didn't know. It's too late."

I pulled myself up into his arms and squeezed him tight. I wasn't exactly sure what he needed to tell his dad, but he was pretty hurt about it. "I am sure he loved you."

"Savanna please don't tell me how my own father felt about me. You didn't even know him. You have no idea what our relationship was like," he said rudely.

I felt like I wanted to puke. I was being so supportive. How could he turn around and have such an unkind reaction to me? Had I said something that was so horrible to him?

"Excuse me for trying to support you!" I pulled away from him even more.

"I can't do this right now," he said as he stood up from the bed, almost knocking me back on my butt. He grabbed some clothes and put them on as he was walking out of the bedroom door.

I felt hurt, but understood he was just upset. I couldn't blame him for putting a wall up. He was only human. While I waited for him to come back up to the bedroom, I grabbed one of his t-shirts and put it on over my head. After another five minutes of waiting, I heard the front door slamming shut.

My feet hit the floor and started running down the stairs before I even realized what I was going to say to him. When I got down the steps all I saw was Ty. He was heading toward the front door.

"Where are you going? Where is Colt?"

"He went flying out of here. What happened Van?"

I held my hand over my mouth. "I don't understand. I must have made him angry. I was just trying to be supportive," I confessed.

"What did you say?"

"All I said was that his father loved him. I wanted him to be okay."

Ty shook his head. "They didn't exactly see eye to eye." He came over and touched my shoulder. "Listen, this is going to take him time to deal with it. It was all so sudden. I guess he figured he would have plenty of opportunities to settle things with his father. The accident just screwed things all up and now he won't ever have the chance again. Just give him time babe."

The sound of a car motor caught our attention. I went straight for the window, looking out to see what my heart already told me. Colt's mustang was pulling out of the garage and headed away from the cabin.

I shook my head in disbelief and started to cry. Within seconds, Ty was at my side pulling me into his strong arms. "Just give him time," he whispered in my hair.

I didn't hug Ty back, it wasn't meant to be a romantic gesture at all. He was being the friend that I needed him to be. I appreciated it so much, considering we were so far from home and he was all I had.

Ty stayed up with me for hours while I sat on the couch waiting for Colt to return. I was so worried he went to a bar or was driving around upset. I wanted to think that he was somewhere on the ranch, but I didn't even know where to start looking.

Without much to go on, and Colt not answering his phone, I decided to go upstairs to sleep. Ty had been sleeping in the guest room that had an actual bed in it and Miranda had the other room, so my only choice was to sleep in Colt's room or the couch. Either way I would hear him coming inside and be able to talk to him when he did.

I climbed into Colt's bed, the same one I had been sleeping in for the last few days. It smelled of him and I couldn't help but climb into the middle and surround myself with his pillows and blankets. I was so worried about him, but part of me was upset with him too. He really hurt me by walking away. I wasn't here to hurt him, in fact I just wanted to help him get through this terrible tragedy.

It took me a few more hours to finally fall asleep. For a long while I stared at the ceiling and listened to all of the outside critters making weird sounds from the woods behind the cabin. After several more crying fits I eventually succumbed to sleep.

The bright sunlight coming in the window woke me up early. I got up and went to the bathroom, but while I was brushing my teeth, I heard the front door opening and closing. My heart started beating faster as I made my way to the bedroom door, but once I got the door open, I could hear Ty and Colt talking. I didn't intend to eavesdrop, until I heard Ty defending me. While I listened, I sat myself on the first step and leaned against the railing. They were actually in the kitchen and the sound of their voices amplified from the tile floor.

"I don't give a shit Colt. You can't treat her like that," Ty argued.

"Don't come into my house and tell me what to do," Colt defended.

"I have every right to do that when you are acting like this. Look, I am sorry about your dad. He was my uncle and I will miss him."

"Don't talk about my father Ty."

"Are you willing to lose her Colt? Because as far as I am concerned, it's only a matter of time."

"She ain't goin' to leave me."

"You stubborn son of a bitch! I hurt her, but you are killing her. Do you really think it's easy for me to stand here rooting for the two you? Do you have any idea how much easier it would be to take her home and do whatever I could to get her back myself?"

"I need time. I can't deal with her right now. I can't deal with anyone," Colt admitted.

"She dropped everything to come here to be with you. Grow a set of balls and take care of your girlfriend before she changes her mind."

"If she can't give me my space then maybe she should just go home. I told you that I can't deal with it right now."

I stood up on the steps and started walking downstairs toward the kitchen. I didn't know what I was going to say, but I couldn't just listen to them. Every word out of his mouth was hurtful to me.

"I talked to my parents last night. They are on their way here. After the funeral, I am leaving with them. If you don't want Savanna than you need to let her go. She deserves someone that would do anything for her. I think she thought you were that guy."

"For Christ sakes Ty. I can't deal with this shit anymore. My father just died. I need to be there for my mother. If y'all can't understand that then get the hell out of my house!"

Colt's last words cut through me just as I walked into the entryway of the kitchen. Ty was leaning against the counter, while Colt was sitting at the table with his hands in his hair. He heard my footsteps and looked up at me. I couldn't hide the pain in my eyes, but the person that looked back at me was broken. His eyes were sunken in from not sleeping. The hair on his face was thick and disheveled. His hair was a giant mess. Colt looked so awful.

"Savanna?" He asked when he saw me standing there.

I went to say something, but nothing would come out. Instead I turned and headed out the front door. When I got to the porch, I just kept running. I was bare footed and in a t-shirt that came down to my knees, but it was a warm summer morning and I wasn't worried about someone seeing me. After running for at least ten minutes, I ended up halfway between the cabin and the ranch. A field of soy beans was to my right. I stepped off the dirt road and sat down on the ground between the beans and the road.

I felt like coming here was a mistake. Colt was different and this side of him scared me. Losing his father was making him be someone that I didn't know. I was so sure that Colt was my future, but as of this moment, he wanted nothing to do with me. It hurt me so much. I didn't regret choosing him. I loved the man he was, even in this horrible time in his life. However, if he couldn't let me in then why should I bother trying? I needed to know without a doubt that he was going to be there for me. He also needed to know that I would never give up on him, well unless that's what he really wanted me to do.

I heard someone calling my name in the distance and got myself walking back to the cabin. It was disappointing when I discovered that it had been Ty worried about me and not Colt. When I reached the porch, I looked around to see if he was even outside, but never spotted him.

"Hey! Are you okay?" He pulled me into his arms. "I am sorry he's being such an ass. If you want to go home after the funeral, we can ride together."

I pulled away from him and went over to sit on the porch swing. Once Ty joined me, he waited for a reply.

"What if I didn't stay for the funeral?" I asked.

"Van, I know you are hurt, but he doesn't want you to leave," Ty reassured me.

I shook my head. "I know what happened was a terrible tragedy, but I can't help him if he can't stand being around me. He's pushing me away Ty and I don't know what else to do to help him."

"I am so pissed at him for being like this," Ty announced.

I grabbed his arm and stopped swinging. "I don't blame him. This is exactly how I acted when I thought I lost you. By keeping everyone out, he doesn't have to feel. He's preventing himself from getting through this. I just don't want my being here to be an added stress for him. If it would make things easier, I can just go home. "

"You really love him don't you?" He asked.

I started tearing up just thinking about leaving Colt. I couldn't say the words, so I just moved my head up and down, while the tears started falling again.

"Do you want to be alone Van?"

I shook my head and leaned it on Ty's shoulder. He used his legs to swing us slowly, but never said another word. Instead, he just sat there being my support, my rock through all of this.

Chapter 36

Colt

I spent the night in the damn guest room at my mother's after Savanna tried to get me to open up. I knew damn well what I was doin' to her and for the life of me, I couldn't stop myself. I wanted to be alone; to just deal with things on my own.

Ty's little intervention ended up in Savanna bolting out of the house. I looked out the window and watched as she disappeared down the road. Everything that came out of my mouth was wrong. I had been so overwhelmed with guilt and regret regarding my father, that I hadn't seen what I was doin' to my own relationship. I was pushing away the person that I wanted a future with. I was doing it because I didn't want to ever feel the pain of losing the person that I loved after so many years of being together. I didn't want to feel the way that my mother was feeling. There was a part of me that wondered if being alone permanently was a good solution to my issues.

Once I heard them talking on the porch, I headed into my office and closed the door. I hadn't really been in here in months. Good thing that my cousin was pregnant and stayin' here to hide out from her scumbag of a boyfriend. He had several bench warrants out for miscellaneous small crimes he committed in our county. This was the second criminal boyfriend that Miranda had managed to get hooked up with. We all tried to set her up with more suitable guys, but this one went and got her knocked up. Now she wasn't even sure if she could keep the baby and be able to raise it herself.

When my ex finally moved out and I got word that my uncle needed help at his farm for the summer, it seemed logical to let Miranda stay here. She took care of the house, filed all of the incoming bills and statements and kept me from getting too far behind on my duties here at the ranch. People didn't understand how much paperwork was involved in running a business like our ranch.

After sifting through a massive pile of invoices, I opened my laptop and started surfing around the internet. This morning I was supposed to go to the funeral home to make arrangements with my mother. There was no way in Hell that I was going to let her go there alone. Last night I could hear her crying from clear across her six thousand square foot house. I hated hearing her cry, but there was nothing but a bunch of time that was going to fix her broken heart, if that would even work.

My cell phone vibrated and I pulled it out to view the message.

Mom wants to leave in twenty. ~ A. Karen

After responding back to them that I would be there, I closed the computer and went up to get changed. My bed had been made and all of my clothes were picked up off the bathroom floor. I noticed Savanna's things on the vanity top and smiled thinking that I liked the idea of her being here. I wish she could have understood that I just wasn't ready to let her in. It wasn't because I didn't love her, she had to know how much I did, but it was because I just couldn't handle talking about it yet. Savanna kept pushing me to open about it. I didn't know how to do that.

After a quick shower, I looked in the mirror and didn't even recognize the person staring back at me. I was in need of a shave and I looked like I hadn't slept in months. Dark circles were under each of my eyes. I felt exactly how I looked too.

I shook out my hair and just left it to dry on top of my head. I didn't think anyone at that funeral parlor was going to judge me for my appearance. Within a few minutes I was out the door. Savanna was sitting on the porch swing alone. She was looking right at me and I could tell that she was upset. The problem was that I didn't want to get into it with her right now. I didn't have time to talk things out even if I was ready to.

I looked down on the porch deck. "I have to take my mother to make arrangements."

"Okay," she said quietly.

"I'll be back when we're done." I started walkin' down the steps.

"Colt?"

When I turned around I saw Savanna leaning over the porch railing. "Yeah?"

"I love you."

"Me too Darlin'," I said as I headed to my car.

I knew she wanted more, but I had more important things that I had to tend to. My mother needed to be my first priority. I wouldn't leave her by herself to do this.

The smell of a funeral home is something that you never forget. My mother was no longer crying. Instead, she seemed incoherent. She made her selections and signed over the check, but her actions were like a robot. She answered the questions as if they were rehearsed. I helped her make the basic selections when she asked, but mostly I just sat there next to her. Luckily, she didn't have to buy a plot. My family had their own already.

I was glad to finally get back in the car. My mother was quiet at first and when she finally started talking she caught me off guard. "It was nice of your girlfriend to be here for you."

"Yeah, it was."

"Did you ask her to come?"

"No. She wanted to surprise me. I had no idea," I shook my head. "I don't even know if it was a good idea for her to come here. Not now."

"I know what you are doing, Son."

"What do you mean, Mom?"

"You are shutting down, probably even pushing her away. Please don't do that to yourself Colt. You are a good man."

"This isn't how life was supposed to be. This wasn't supposed to happen."

"God has a plan for everyone. Your father lived a happy life Colt. I don't regret a single moment with him," she explained.

I felt myself getting choked up. I wasn't ready to discuss this.

"You have to talk about it," she reiterated.

"I can't."

"Colt, I love your father. I will love him until I breathe my last breath, but he wouldn't want us to waste our future away. He would want us to continue to live. He worked hard to give us the life we have."

I felt her hand touch my knee. Thankfully, I had reached the ranch. I pulled in front of the house and turned off the car. "I fought him on everything. I can't take it back."

"Come inside with me Colt. I want to give you something," she said as she climbed out of the car.

I walked into the house and watched my mother run up the stairs. She came down just minutes later with a box in her hands. It was a shoe box that had been decorated in Star Wars stickers. I remembered the box from when I was a small child. "He kept this. I think you should take it. He would want you to know he had this stuff."

I grabbed the box, not really understanding what it contained. It was cool my dad saved the box, but it made me feel worse inside.

"Thanks. I will look at it when I get home."

"Colt. Do you love this girl? If she left and never came back how would it make you feel?" My mother placed her hand on my chest. "I am asking you this because I don't want you to give up on something that's so important to you. I can tell she loves you. Don't let her be the one that got away. You will regret it forever."

I leaned over and kissed my mother on the cheek. "I'll see you later, Mom."

I headed out of the house with the shoebox in my hand. The drive to the cabin seemed like it took forever. When I got there I noticed I was all alone. I called out and got no answer. Sam was clawing at the back door, so I let her in and headed up to my room. I tossed the box on the bed and sat down beside it. My hand traced the outside as I reminisced on applying the stickers to the box. Back then it was supposed to hold my most special treasures. Of course that meant it had been filled with baseball cards and matchbox cars.

I flipped the lid and found that it was full of a bunch of things. A pair of shoes from when I was a baby sat on top. I gently took them out, inspecting how small they were, before setting them to the side. The next item I pulled out was a Ziploc bag full of all of my baby teeth. I had to laugh remembering how my parents would prepare me for the tooth fairy's visit. Underneath the bag sat my father's Willie Mays rookie card. It was in a plastic sleeve that kept it from being damaged. He always told me it would be mine one day. I turned the card over and looked at the stats. The box had a few of my most favorite matchbox cars, some Star Wars figurines and a giant stack of pictures. I picked up the stack and started looking through them.

They seemed to be in sequential order. The first picture was my parents holding me as a newborn. Next were me taking my first steps, followed by my first couple birthday parties. Whenever I was unsure when a picture was taken, I looked to the back of the picture where my mother always labeled them. I came across one of me and my dad playing catch with a football, and another where we were wrestling around in the dirt. There were a bunch of Christmas pictures and even more pictures of me going hunting with my father. One of them I was missing my two front teeth.

The last few pictures were when I was older. Some junior high photos and pictures of games from high school finished off the stack. The very last picture was my college graduation. Under that last picture was a small card the same size as the photos. I hesitated before I lifted it open to read it.

Colt

Your mother is making me write you this letter. She thinks there are some things that we never got to talk about.

Today was your graduation from college. I know we haven't always seen eye to eye, but I want you to know that I am so proud of you. I've been hard on you because I wanted you to be strong and independent. I didn't want you to ever have to depend on anyone. You may think that I am disappointed in you, but you are wrong.

I kept everything in this box because they were some of my favorite times with you. Do you remember all of our hunting trips? Remember getting stuck in that storm and coming home freezing and soaked. Your mother wanted to ring my neck for getting you so sick.

I still remember the day I took you to buy your first shotgun. The look on your face was priceless.

When you became a teenager, things got even harder for you. You wanted to do your own things, but it was important for me to lay down the law. I couldn't have any son of mine making foolish mistakes that could ruin his future. You had every girl in town offering herself to you. I wasn't ready to be a grandfather. I hope you get that now. You hated me for a while, but your mother and I always felt like the more you hated us, the better parents we were being.

Son, I am writing you this because I think we need to clear the air. If you want to leave and live your life in the city, I won't fight you. I want you to be happy. The ranch will still be here if you ever want it.

I struggled for us to have the life we have now. I don't want you to forget where you came from.

When you find a woman, love her like she's the only woman on this planet. Treat her right and she will never leave your side. Don't ever take her for granted. Be the man that we taught you to be.

Love,

One Proud Dad

I read the letter at least ten times. I knew why he never gave it to me. After my graduation dinner, I announced that I wanted to build my cabin on their property and be in the family business. My father got his dream. He probably told my mother to throw this stuff away and she just never had.

I left everything on the bed while I paced around my room. I was filled with anger and pain. I wanted to run, to disappear. I couldn't deal with any of this. I felt like everything was closing in on me. I just wanted to wake up from the nightmare.

When an hour had passed and I still hadn't heard from Savanna, I headed downstairs. Her car was still not outside. I needed to call her, to tell her I was sorry. I couldn't let her slip away. Being without her wasn't an option for me. I needed her more than ever. I called her phone at least ten times and got no answer. I called Ty's phone with the same result. I left both of them messages and even tried Miranda, but none of them would call me back.

Maybe I was too late? Maybe Savanna had already gone back to North Carolina. Maybe she changed her mind after the way I treated her?

I found a bottle of whiskey and started taking drinks straight from the bottle. I wanted to feel nothing. Just for a while, I wanted it to all go away. I lost my father and now possibly my future.

Chapter 37

Savanna

While waiting for Colt to get back, Ty and I took a walk not too far in the woods. When we heard someone screaming we found Miranda holding her stomach in the driveway. A puddle of wetness covered the ground between her legs.

While Ty hobbled, I ran toward her. She was screaming in pain. "Something is wrong. It hurts too bad."

"We need to get you to the hospital," I said as I took her by the arm and led her to my car.

"My mother had to go out of town this morning. She won't be off her plane for two more hours. You have to call Colt and my aunt," she announced.

Ty was already trying to dial both of them, but we knew they didn't have their phones on while they were planning a funeral. We got Miranda in the car and started speeding our way to the hospital. Ty was sitting up front with me, but Miranda was in the back screaming.

"How long have you been having contractions?" I asked.

"I don't know. A few hours," she replied.

"How far are they apart?"

"Every couple of minutes," she cried.

"Oh shit!" I looked in the rearview mirror and noticed she was laying down across the backseat. "Ty you need to check her."

"You have got to be fucking kidding me right now. There is no way I am doing something like that," he said frantically.

"No! I have to keep driving. Lean your ass back there and look between her legs," I announced as I tried to keep driving while watching Miranda. Beads of sweat covered her face and chest.

"I can't do this!" Ty announced when he attempted and then backed up back into the front seat.

"Stop being a little bitch and do it Ty. This is important!" I screamed.

"Ah damn, this aint right!" He said as he started climbing over the seat. "You need to pull over. I can't see anything," he said as Miranda screamed out in pain again.

I pulled the car over to the shoulder of the road and both of us got out of the front seat. When I got behind Ty, he opened the back door and moved aside. "Oh God I can feel it coming out!" Miranda yelled.

I looked back at Ty. He looked like he was going to puke. Can you make it to the hospital? We are like fifteen minutes away," he said.

"Miranda, I need to take off your shorts and look. Is it okay?" I asked.

She was trying to do her breathing and just nodded at my request. With one swift yank I pulled her shorts down to her knees. I was not prepared for what I saw.

"Oh God! The head is crowning. The baby is coming now!" I said in a panic. "Ty call for an ambulance. Try to figure out where the hell we are."

"I can't have my baby in a car!" Miranda said.

"Keep breathing. Your baby is coming right now. I need you to push when I say. I have no idea if I am doing this right, but I will do everything I can do, I promise."

I took both of Miranda's knees and spread them as far apart as the back seat would allow. The baby's head was almost all the way out. Miranda continued screaming. "It hurts. I'm dying! Please just get it out of me! Help me!"

"Miranda you need to focus. I need you to try to push."

"I can't. It'll hurt worse. Please help me," She yelled.

I don't know what made him do it, but Ty opened the door to where her head laid. He scooted himself in and rested her head on his lap. Ty reached over and grabbed her hand. "You can do it. Squeeze my hand and just try Miranda."

She kept shaking her head, saying she couldn't, but her natural urge to push must have taken over. I gave her a nod and watched as she bore down and pushed with everything she had. The baby's head came out further, but went back in. "Push again. Hold it this time," I called out.

This time she pushed harder. Ty held her tight and screamed with her as his eyes watched the little head coming out from between the girl's legs. When the head was out, the little body started following. It was so slippery that I had to grab her shorts and use them to secure my hold on the infant. Miranda managed one last push before the hips and legs came out. I wrapped the baby in the shorts and heard the sirens of the ambulance in the distance. Miranda still needed to deliver an afterbirth and someone had to cut the cord, but the baby was wailing and Miranda was alert.

"It's a girl!" I said as I held the newborn in my hands. She was so small. My hands were shaking like crazy and I couldn't believe that I had just done something like that. I could only thank God that I had taken a Child Development class this past semester.

One of the requirements was to watch a live birth at the hospital.

Within minutes, Miranda and her daughter were being carted into the ambulance and taken to the hospital. I was covered in blood and other bodily fluids that I didn't even want to know what they were.

Just as the ambulance was starting to pull away, I saw Ty running, well halfway hobbling, toward it. He gave me a quick wave before jumping in the back to go with Miranda.

That left me alone on the side of the road, in the middle of nowhere.

It was getting dark out and I knew I needed to get back to the ranch. I jumped in the car, covered in blood and the smell of everything else that came out with the baby. When I pulled up to the cabin, I noticed Colt's car was back. I looked like Hell and just needed a shower. He had been so distant that he probably wouldn't even care what I needed to do. After his father's funeral we were going to have to talk about our future. As it stood right now, I was considering going home and finishing school. Colt acted like I was in the way here. I couldn't give up everything and be resented.

I climbed the porch steps and walked into the house. Colt met me at the door. He took one look at my clothes and his green eyes got huge. "What happened? Are you okay?"

I shook my head but said nothing. Honestly, I was afraid to say anything to him. I couldn't deal with being rejected anymore. It hurt me so much.

He kept looking me over. "Miranda went into labor. We couldn't get in touch with any of you. How long were you at the funeral place? Where is your phone?" I shook my head. "Ty and I helped deliver the baby in the back of my car. The ambulance came afterwards. Your mom and aunt are on the way there. I need to get cleaned up before I head back there," I said as I started making my way up the stairs.

I was amazed when Colt followed behind me. When he turned on the water for me and stood in the bathroom while I stripped out of my clothes, I was shocked.

"Are you going to be alright?" He asked.

The water was running down my head. I closed my eyes and just tried to get myself to calm down. I must have been running on pure adrenaline. "I don't know."

The hot water felt good and I started scrubbing the dried blood from my fingers and arms. I looked through the glass and saw Colt just leaning against the sink. He wasn't saying anything, but he wasn't leaving.

When I finished washing myself, I turned off the water. Colt approached me with a clean towel and wrapped it around my body. He stood behind me and kept his arms around the towel. The stubbles on his face slid across the back of my neck giving me chills all the way down my legs. "I am so sorry you had to do that today Darlin'. I wish I could have been there to help out."

I smiled. "It was actually amazing. Unbelievable, but really cool."

"How was Ty? Did he pass out?" He laughed.

"No, he was a big help. I was shocked he wanted to go with Miranda."

"Yeah, that was nice of him. They have always considered each other family since they were little kids."

"Are you feeling better?" I asked as I reached up and touched his cheek.

He moved his cheek closer to my hand and closed his eyes. "I had a few drinks earlier. I even talked to my mother about some things."

"Do you want to tell me about it?"

"Will you come into the bedroom with me real quick? I want to show you somethin'," he asked.

I looked at him. He smelled like alcohol, but this was the most relaxed I had seen him in days. He took my hand and led me into the bedroom. Spread all across the blanket were items and a decorated box.

"What's all this?" I asked.

He reached over and pat a spot next to him on the bed. Once I sat down he handed me a small card. "Read this," he said.

I opened that card and couldn't believe what I was reading. My eyes filled with tears as I continued to read the kind words of Colt's father. When I finished, I reached over and grabbed his hand without responding. When I got the courage to look into his eyes they were full of tears.

"I must have read this a hundred times tonight," he said as he touched the card. "I thought he didn't know how much I appreciate him. I thought I would never have the chance to tell him he was my hero. He already knew though. He knew all along. All of the times I thought he didn't care about me. I was so wrong."

I squeezed Colt's hand. I was considering what I should say. The last time I tried to be positive Colt had gotten his feelings hurt. Before I could respond he stood up and kneeled between my legs.

"Savanna, I never listened to my father much. In fact, I made it a point to always do the opposite from what he told me." He reached up and stroked my cheek. "It's time I started listening. You see, my father told me to find a woman and love her like she was the only woman on the planet. He said to treat her right and never take her for granted. Well Darlin', I already found that girl and I will be damned if I am goin' to let her go."

His words went straight to my broken heart. Through the rough whiskers and tired eyes was my Colt. I never got to meet his father, but I think I would be thanking him every day for writing that letter.

"I love you, Colt."

Colt grabbed the towel and slowly pulled it away from my body. "I need to be close to you Savanna. Let me make love to you?"

I didn't have to answer as I sat there naked on his bed. His hands ran up my legs before he stood up and cleared the memorabilia from his bedspread. I backed myself on it as Colt stood there and removed his shirt. His shirt dropped on the floor and he kicked them away from his feet. His boxers came down next and I bit down on my lip just thinking about his perfect body on top of me.

He took his time climbing back on the bed and sliding beside me. I yearned for his sweet lips to touch mine. I felt like it had been forever since I felt them. I knew it had only been a day, but all of the emotions of the past few days were just too much stress.

Colt took his finger and ran it over my lips while he licked his. I let the tip of my tongue touch his course finger. He took the wet saliva and slid it over my lips again. His head came down and kissed me under my chin. His rough whiskers tickled and sent chills down my body again.

I watched as Colt took his tongue and circled it around my breasts before taking my nipple into his mouth. He used his other hand to massage the other one while he teased my nipple with his wandering tongue. I shuddered at the feeling it gave me to have his mouth touching such a sensitive spot on my body. His soft lips trailed down between my breasts until they reached my stomach. He drug his tongue over my belly button and continued kissing down until he reached the tender spot between my legs. I gasped as his tongue entered me and continued sliding inside of me. When it came up and flicked my swollen sex, my feet buckled, I grabbed his hair and cried out. "Oh yes!"

Colt placed gentle kisses up my thigh before placing his lips over my mouth. I could taste myself as he kissed me. I drug my tongue over his bottom lips and groaned as the taste of myself set me on fire. I took my teeth and drug them over Colt's chin. I bit down on his ear lobe and pulled it as I moved down to run my tongue over his neck. I could hear him moaning and it was turning me on more. He flipped my body over top of him. I straddled him and took in the sight of his perfect chest. He reached up to move my hair away from my face and I couldn't help but traced the mustang tattoo on the inside of his arm.

His strong hands pulled my face down to his. I teased him by draggin my tongue across his open lips. He tried to pull me closer but I teased him again. When our lips finally met, our kisses intensified quickly. My hands reached around his waist and squeezed his butt. I could feel his erection pressing against my sex and I wanted to feel him inside of me. I could feel his hand reaching down to position himself where he needed to be, but instead of entering me, he kept it there, teasing me as I panted for more of him.

"Tell me Savanna. Tell me what you want."

I could barely breathe. "I want you."

"What do you want me to do?"

"I want you forever. Please Colt."

"Say it again."

I tried to thrust myself against him, but he liked the game of it and pulled back. "I want you forever. Please make love to me."

Slowly, I felt him sliding inside of me. He groaned against my neck. He slowed his pace down as he continued to mingle our tongues together. I ran my hands up and down his chest and pinched his tiny nipples. He squinted his eyes. My hands traveled to his back and I held him tight, making him lean his body into mine.

After some time, his thrusts became more powerful. He grabbed my waist and pushed for more friction between us. Little moans kept escaping me as I felt his hardness sliding in and out of me. When Colt finally started to come, he used his strong arms to hold me still. He buried his face into my neck and let out a gasp before collapsing on the bed next to me.

He stroked my hair. "I'm sorry for how I acted. I shouldn't have shut you out. It was all just too much for me to talk about. I promise I will tell you my feelin' from now on Savanna. I won't take you for granted again Darlin'."

I touched his arm that was still in my hair. "I missed you."

"I don't want you to leave," he confessed.

"I'm not."

"No, I don't want you to ever leave," he reiterated.

I smiled and leaned in to kiss him. "I know what you meant Colt. I'm not leaving. I don't know what I am doing about school, but I don't want to be without you. If I went home I wouldn't be able to focus on school or anything else. Maybe one day I can go back, but for now I feel like I am right where I need to be."

"What if you didn't have to give up anything to be with me?" He asked.

"I don't understand. It isn't really possible."

"Darlin', it's possible. Next week, when the funeral is over and all of the family has gone home, I say we jump in one of the ranch trucks and drive to North Carolina. We can pick up all of your things and stop by the farm to get Daisy. When we get back you can pick your courses for fall classes. You can decided if you want to take them online or to drive to Louisville every day." Colt's said confidently.

"I can't afford college. I don't have a job," I explained.

"I am going to need a office assistant. You are going to need that business degree. All perks of your new job of course," he joked.

"I can't let you do that. I will save up and finish."

He took his hands and put them on both sides of my face. "One day you will be my wife. Let me do this for you. You are moving here for me, so let me pay for you to finish school. I have all kinds of information printed on my desk. In fact, I spent the better part of the afternoon researchin' it all." He confessed.

"Was that before or after you got drunk?" I joked.

"Before. Smart ass. So are you going to give me an answer?" He asked.

"What was the question? I forgot!"

"Do you want to be the wife of a rancher? Can you handle this life I live? We have plenty of room for the eleven children you want to have."

"After seeing a birth today, I think I may draw the line at two children," I laughed.

"I promise to give you everything," Colt added.

"I might hold you to that."

"I hope you do, Darlin'."

Epilogue

Colt

It had been two weeks since we buried my father. My mother was doing better, but only time would heal the emptiness she felt without him. The night after the funeral she hugged me and told me that one day they would be together again. She meant those words and they even made me feel better.

Losing my father was unexpected, but I guess everything in life is that way. When you find something special, you should never take it for granted, even when you have to fight for it. Every time I look at Savanna, I see his words.

We had a long ride back to North Carolina. Ty insisted on driving back with us. We took the big ranch truck with a back seat. He sprawled all out and talked for the entire trip. I couldn't complain much, because ever since he helped deliver Miranda's baby, he hadn't been trying so hard to get in between Savanna and I. In fact, since he'd chewed my ass out about me being an idiot, he had left us alone.

Ty helped us load the truck up with everything from Savanna's house. He wasn't supposed to be lifting heavy things, but you couldn't stop that kid from doing anything. I was surprised how supportive her parents were being about her move. Her mother made us a huge lunch to eat before we got back on the road. She gave me a big hug and thanked me for saving her daughter. I never felt like I saved her from anything. I think she saved me.

If she hadn't been there for me the past two weeks, I don't know what would have happened. Before finding Savanna, I cared about myself and never worried about anyone else. She changed me. She made me want more.

My father's death was another eye opener. I had new responsibilities on top of the old ones. The ranch was my responsibility and I promised my mother that I would keep it going.

When we got to Ty's farm, my aunt and uncle came out to greet us. While shaking my uncle's hand I slipped him an envelope. He didn't know that inside of it was a quarter of my father's life insurance policy.

We didn't need the money, but my mother insisted on splitting it up among the family, including starting a trust account for my unborn children. She told us about it one night at dinner. I wasn't sure who was more shocked, me or Savanna.

I guess she needed things to look forward to. Savanna was becoming her new favorite person. She had drug her all over town and spent most of her days showing her off. Before we left, she told me I needed to go ring shopping soon. She said Savanna was too pretty to walk around town without a ring on her finger. I would have gotten her a ring eventually. We were practically engaged anyway. I knew we would be married one day, and so did she, but it was important to appease my mom.

Daisy wasn't that happy to be leaving Thunder. Both of them were steady yelling and bucking all around. My aunt wanted us to stay for dinner, but Daisy was too wound up to attempt moving her later. We got her loaded in the horse trailer and said our goodbyes.

Ty wasn't too happy about this being the real goodbye. His head was down and avoided sayin' much. Savanna walked over and put her arms around him. She kissed him on the cheek and he pulled her back into a hug.

"Are you sure you want to move in with this douche bag? We can still get married," he joked loud enough for me to hear.

She gave him a playful smack on his chest. "Very funny."

"Seriously though. I love you Van. I always will."

I couldn't be mad or jealous. He didn't mean it in a way like he was going to wait for her. He meant it's a caring friend, or soon to be cousin.

She touched his cheek and told him to be good before saying her goodbyes to his parents. They were lucky they got that after being so mean to her for all those months.

When we pulled out of the farm, I saw my uncle opening the envelope. The check was enough for him to pay off all of his loans and be debt free. My father would have wanted that for his brother and his family.

Savanna reached over and grabbed my hand. I squeezed it back. "You sure about this?"

"Drive fast so we can get home tonight. I want pancakes tomorrow," She teased.

"Darlin' you can have pancakes everyday for the rest of your life."

To be continued…..

Thank you for reading Letting Go, Part One in the Mitchell Family Series…….

Look for Part Two Folding Hearts on sale Now.

Part Three coming Nov. 2012

If you enjoyed this book, please share a comment or review.

Let me know what you think of this book by contacting me at the following:

Somnianseries@gmail.com

http://twitter.com/jennyfoor

http://www.facebook.com/#!/JenniferFoorAuthor

http://www.jennyfoor.wordpress.com

http://www.goodreads.com/jennyfoor

www.thesomnianseries.webs.com

Jennifer Foor lives on the Eastern Shore of
Maryland with her husband and two children.
She enjoys shooting pool, camping and catching
up on cliché movies that were made in the
eighties.

6453R00270

Printed in Great Britain
by Amazon.co.uk, Ltd.,
Marston Gate.